PERFECT STORM 4

BOBBY AKART

WELCOME

Welcome to PERFECT STORM 4, the final installment in the Perfect Storm survival thriller series by Author Bobby Akart. Join Bobby Akart's mailing list to learn about upcoming releases, deals, contests, and appearances. Follow this link to: BobbyAkart.com

PRAISE FOR BOBBY AKART AND PERFECT STORM

"Author Bobby Akart has done it again. I have read every book and series that he has written. It never ceases to amaze me how he comes up with new and creative ways to introduce characters and concepts that are fresh and engaging."

"How long could you survive a collapse of society? The families in this new series are put to the test in this thrilling, nail biter."

"You will fall in love with the characters immediately!"

"Bobby Akart continues to deliver the top thrillers of the year. Year after year after year!"

"Well written with characters that are so real, you are right there with them urging them on."

"Once again this author has crafted a believable end of days scenario with compelling characters that I can't seem to put down."

"Author Bobby Akart has put together another scorcher of a story in Perfect Storm."

PERFECT STORM 4

by
Bobby Akart

OTHER WORKS BY AMAZON CHARTS TOP 25 AUTHOR BOBBY AKART

The Perfect Storm Series
Perfect Storm 1
Perfect Storm 2
Perfect Storm 3
Perfect Storm 4

Black Gold (a standalone terrorism thriller)

Nuclear Winter
First Strike
Armageddon
Whiteout
Devil Storm
Desolation

New Madrid (a standalone, disaster thriller)

Odessa (a Gunner Fox trilogy)

The Lone Star Series
Axis of Evil
Beyond Borders
Lines in the Sand
Texas Strong
Fifth Column
Suicide Six

The Pandemic Series
Beginnings
The Innocents
Level 6
Quietus

The Blackout Series
36 Hours
Zero Hour
Turning Point
Shiloh Ranch
Hornet's Nest
Devil's Homecoming

The Boston Brahmin Series
The Loyal Nine
Cyber Attack
Martial Law
False Flag
The Mechanics
Choose Freedom
Patriot's Farewell (standalone novel)
Black Friday (standalone novel)
Seeds of Liberty (Companion Guide)

The Prepping for Tomorrow Series

Cyber Warfare
EMP: Electromagnetic Pulse
Economic Collapse

Copyright Information

ACKNOWLEDGMENTS

Creating a novel that is both informative and entertaining requires a tremendous team effort. Writing is the easy part.

For their efforts in making the Perfect Storm series a reality, I would like to thank Hristo Argirov Kovatliev for his incredible artistic talents in creating my cover art. He and Dani collaborate (and conspire) to create the most incredible cover art in the publishing business. A huge hug of appreciation goes out to Pauline Nolet, the *Professor*, for her editorial prowess and patience in correcting this writer's brain farts that happen more frequently with age. Thank you, Drew Avera, a United States Navy veteran, who has brought his talented formatting skills from a writer's perspective to create multiple formats for reading my novels. A round of applause for Kevin Pierce, the beloved voice of the apocalypse, who brought my words to life in audio format.

Now, for the serious stuff. While the Perfect Storm series is based on scientifically plausible events, certain parts of the story have been fictionalized for dramatic purposes, and they're not intended to reflect on any actual person or entity.

Accurately portraying the aftermath of a devastating perfect solar storm required countless hours of never-ending research and interviews with some of the brightest minds in the world of planetary science.

Once again, as I immersed myself in the science and history, source material and research flooded my inbox from around the globe. Without the assistance of many individuals and organizations, this story could not be told. Please allow me a moment to acknowledge a few of those institutions that without their tireless efforts and patience, the Perfect Storm series could not have been written.

Many thanks to the preeminent researchers and engineers who provided me assistance, tutelage, and scientific background at the following:

The Space Weather Prediction Center in Boulder, Colorado
    The Aerospace Corporation in El Segundo, California
    The Haleakala Observatory, home to the Daniel K. Inouye Solar Telescope, in Maui
    NASA's Jet Propulsion Laboratory in Pasadena, California
    The Geophysical Institute at the University of Alaska, Fairbanks

A special note of thanks to Joel Smith, a certified personal trainer and good friend who, in the course of casual conversation one day, provided me the inspiration for Fred Stewart. Fred was a man who'd been observed sleeping in his car by Joel and some of his friends. They often wondered about his life.

Well, within seconds, I created a character bio for Fred, including a full name, his career, and how he would fit into the Perfect Storm series. You see, every character has a story to tell, both real and imaginary.

Of course, a special thank you to the Team, my loyal friends who've always supported my work and provided me valuable insight from a reader's perspective—Denise Keef, Joe Carey, Shirley Nicholson, Bennita Barnett, and Colt Payne.

Thanks, y'all, and Choose Freedom!

ABOUT THE AUTHOR, BOBBY AKART

Author Bobby Akart delivers up-all-night thrillers to readers in 245 countries and territories worldwide. He has been ranked by Amazon as #25 on the Amazon Charts list of most popular, bestselling authors. He has achieved recognition as the #1 bestselling Horror Author, #1 bestselling Science Fiction Author, #5 bestselling Action & Adventure Author, #7 bestselling Historical Fiction Author and #10 on Amazon's bestselling Thriller Author list.

His novel *Yellowstone: Hellfire* reached the Top 25 on the Amazon bestsellers list and earned him multiple Kindle All-Star awards for most pages read in a month and most pages read as an author. The Yellowstone series vaulted him to the #25 bestselling author on Amazon Charts, and the #1 bestselling science fiction author.

Since its release in November 2020, his standalone novel *New Madrid Earthquake* has been ranked #1 on Amazon Charts in multiple countries as a natural disaster thriller.

Mr. Akart is a graduate of the University of Tennessee after pursuing a dual major in economics and political science. He went on to obtain his master's degree in business administration and his doctorate degree in law at Tennessee.

With over a million copies of his novels sold in all formats, Bobby Akart has provided his readers a diverse range of topics that are both informative and entertaining. His attention to detail and impeccable research has allowed him to capture the imagination of his readers through his fictional works and bring them valuable knowledge through his nonfiction books.

SIGN UP for Bobby Akart's mailing list to learn of special offers, view bonus content, and be the first to receive news about new releases.

Visit www.BobbyAkart.com for details.

DEDICATIONS

With the love and support of my wife, Dani, together with the unconditional love of Bullie and Boom, the princesses of the palace, I'm able to tell you these stories. It would be impossible for me to write without them in my heart.

This story was written during a difficult time in our lives. For my long-time readers, you know that our English Bulldogs, Bullie and Boom, affectionately known in my stories as the princesses of the palace, are the center of our universe. At Christmas in 2021, Boom Chukka suffered a significant tear in her gastrointestinal tract caused by chewing a pressed rawhide bone.

Because of Dani's watchful eye, she noticed Boom-Boom's gums turn more and more pale. I also noticed that her poop became black and tarry. Both of these were symptoms of internal bleeding. I relay this to you because, one day, you might experience this with your beloved pups.

Internal bleeding is nothing to be trifled with. Without urgent care, your fur babies can die within days, if not sooner.

We rushed Boom Chukka to our vets in Georgia. The entire team, led by Drs. Rambo and McNair, came to her rescue. By the early evening of New Year's Eve, her packed cell volume (PCV) and hematocrit (HCT) fell below twenty percent where thirty-five percent is normal. Thanks to a dog-to-dog blood transfusion from Dr. McNair's dog, Liza, Boom-Boom was able to survive long enough to transport her to the University of Georgia Veterinary Hospital in Athens.

Just before publication of Perfect Storm 3, Boom Chukka required surgery. An epulis, a stalk of pinkish tissue, had formed on her jaw and the mass had begun to grow over her back teeth. Five years ago, Woolie Bullie was required to undergo surgery that removed half of her lower jaw to prevent the spread of an epulis to prevent her from undergoing radiation treatment. Placing an English Bulldog under anesthesia at this late stage in their lives was a risky proposition. However, we trusted Dr. Rambo to perform the surgery and closely monitor our beloved Chubby. (Doomsday series readers might recall the introduction of Chubby and the Roo in book two, Haven.) Boom Chukka pulled through like a champ and the tissue was declared benign.

In between books three and four, our girls endured more medical excitement. Boom Chukka developed a cough. At first, in an effort to suppress our fears, we made light of it by referring to her cough as a *funny, squeaky sound* (a line in the Christmas Vacation movie). After some blood work and x-rays, the veterinarians were equally divided as to whether the multiple spots on her lungs were the result of scarring caused by pneumonia earlier in the year of the c-word—cancer. We were nervous wrecks during those ten days as we awaited the radiologist's assessment.

To say their conclusions were inconclusive would not do the report justice. There were four possibilities. Three involved the word pneumonia and one was possibly cancer. As Dr. Thomas McNair put it, *this is a bullshit report.* Translation—worthless. So, we continue to love Boom Boom and hope that she doesn't have cancer. Further tests would require minor surgery and anesthesia, not an option for an English Bulldog approaching fourteen years of age.

Meanwhile, Woolie Bullie has developed a sleep pattern that nobody is able to explain. She wakes up every night at midnight and three a.m. Like clockwork, as in you can set your watch by it. She begins to squall and bark and demands yummies. The entire household is called to action to reduce our pup's anxiety which is all we have as an explanation.

Despite the sleep deprivation that's beset us since October, we have to monitor her closely for a condition known as gastric dilation-volvulus (GDV), also known as bloat. Her squalling and barking caused excess air into her stomach allowing gas and fluid to accumulate. As her bloated stomach continues to stretch, it's prone to twisting or flipping. It's a death sentence unless immediately surgically repaired.

So, there you have it. Another year of telling stories has come to an end amidst a perfect storm of medical ailments besetting the pups who've given us so much joy and comfort over the years.

It's now Christmas, 2022, a year since Boom Chukka almost died in our arms. With the help of God watching over our entire family during this difficult time, Boom Chukka fought to live another day, and then another. As of this writing, Bullie and Boom are the ripe age of thirteen years, five months. However, they firmly believe they're one-year-old pups.

I urge you to love those who are closest to you, including your four-legged, bestest pals.

AUTHOR'S NOTE

March, 2022

For years, I've tackled the disaster thriller genre. As an author, the hardest part might be choosing how to destroy the Earth, therefore imperiling all of mankind. Look at all the options I've written about: asteroids, nuclear electromagnetic pulse attacks, pandemics, earthquakes, volcanoes, bioterrorism, cyber warfare, pole shifts, etc.

However, in a class by itself, is severe space weather. If its ominous name didn't clue you in, severe space weather can cause some serious complications to life on our planet. Much like earth-based weather, it's uncontrollable. It also has the potential for massive destruction and disruption of modern technology. Imagine the collapse of power grids; radio blackouts; satellite interference or even destruction; and airline operations ceasing, all in less than a minute. Without electricity, how would you communicate with your family, call 9-1-1, get clean water or keep food from spoiling? With a radio blackout, how would airplanes land safely? Massive solar flares have the potential to change life as we know it.

Now, if I haven't gotten your attention, let's take a look at the science and a little history, shall we?

Severe space weather is the result of large-scale eruptions of plasma and magnetic fields from the Sun's corona. Known as coronal mass ejections (CMEs), these eruptions can create magnetic storms in the magnetosphere and Earth's upper atmosphere, which can damage power lines, cause blackouts, and even dislocate Earth's radiation belts, damaging satellites.

Thankfully, such magnetic storms are classified as low frequency, but high impact. To be an impactful magnetic storm, CMEs from the solar disk must be fast and massive, launched from near the center of the Sun and directed toward Earth's magnetic field. CMEs also need to have a strong magnetic field with the opposite orientation of Earth's own magnetic field. Although classified as low frequency, when these conditions are met, CMEs are high-consequence occurrences. Here are some examples.

In recent history, the collapse of the Hydro-Quebec grid occurred in March 1989 leaving the province of Quebec without electricity for 9 hours. The outage closed schools, businesses, public transportation and grounded flights at Dorval Airport. Citizens found themselves stuck in traffic on darkened roads without street signals and many workers were stranded in office buildings, elevators and stairwells. The storm was felt in other parts of North America as well, with approximately two-hundred solar storm-related events reported including the failure of a transformer at a New Jersey nuclear power plant.

Amazingly, the 1989 magnetic storm that struck Quebec pales in comparison to other magnetic storms in our history.

The strongest storm in recorded history to directly impact our planet came in September of 1859. The CME behind the Carrington Event, as it became known, was first seen by Richard Carrington, a British amateur astronomer. Nearly eighteen hours after it was observed, the powerful CME impacted the Earth's magnetosphere, triggering a severe geomagnetic storm that disrupted telegraph networks around the world. The rare, fast-moving (CMEs normally impact Earth around 36 hours after being observed) CME hit the planet with highly charged particles enveloped the Northern Hemisphere. Telegraph operators were electrocuted, and fires were ignited as flames traveled along the telegraph lines.

The 1921 Geomagnetic Storm, also known as the New York Railway Storm, included geomagnetically induced currents that would have been 10 times more intense than those responsible for the 1989 Quebec solar storm. Taking place over several days in May 1921, the New York Railway Storm is widely considered the largest recorded in the twentieth century. It is this perfect solar storm event that forms the scientific basis for my book series.

WHAT IF FICTION BECOMES REALITY?

A word of caution when thinking about history and the timeline of events. It's easy to dismiss any discussion of past catastrophes when one considers events like super volcano eruptions taking place every seven-hundred-thousand-years as in the case of Yellowstone. Massive solar storms occur far more frequently. Let's look at a recent event from just ten years ago.

On July 23, 2012, two CMEs erupted from an active patch of sunspots on the far side of the sun which is monitored by the Parker Solar Probe that circles the sun ahead of Earth in the same orbit. Emerging about fifteen minutes apart, the CMEs quickly merged into one massive shock wave of charged particles that washed over the probe's sensors.

Behind the shock wave, this energy raced along at about 2250 kilometers per second—five times their normal speed at Earth's distance from the sun—and the magnetic field strength there was more than ten times that normally seen at Earth's orbit.

If pointed in our direction, such a combination would have produced the strongest geomagnetic storm to have struck Earth in history. It could have knocked out satellites and earthbound power grids, researchers say. Fortunately, the event, a prime example of a *Perfect Storm*, was directed into a region of space where the solar wind and the magnetic field had been weakened by a solar flare 4 days earlier.

While the flare occurred in Earth's orbital plane, the solar matter missed us by the equivalent of nine days. Similar to the Carrington event, the particles traveled from the sun to the Earth in just seventeen hours. Had Earth been in the way at the time, the global damage toll would have crested the $10 trillion mark: the first fourteen-figure natural disaster in history. It was only luck that caused this perfect storm to miss us.

I add this example as a word of caution to us all. These severe solar storms happen with regular frequency. We dodged a powerful catastrophic solar flare in 2012. Next time, we might not be so lucky.

REAL-WORLD NEWS EXCERPTS

THE SUN JUST PRODUCED AN EXPLOSION SO BIG IT WILL BE STUDIED FOR YEARS

~ *Newsweek.com, September 7, 2022*

The September 5 explosion was so big that "science papers will be studying this for years to come".

An enormous explosion erupted from behind the sun on Monday, and scientists think its source could be rotating toward the Earth in the coming days.

On September 5, NASA's STEREO-A spacecraft recorded a significant coronal mass ejection (CME)—an eruption of plasma and magnetic activity from the sun's atmosphere—that occurred on the far side of the sun.

Since the CME did not occur in the direction of Earth, scientists spotted it by its "halo," a giant shockwave that could be seen from Earth's position on the other side of the sun.

"I can safely say the Sept. 5th event is one of the largest, if not THE largest, Solar Energetic Particle storms that we have seen so far since Solar Orbiter launched in 2020," said George Ho, a space physicist at Johns Hopkins University's Applied Physics Lab who works with the European Space Agency's Solar Orbiter satellite.

THE SUN HAS A WEAPON TO DESTROY EARTH AND IT IS CALLED THE CME STORM

~ *Hi Tech Journal, September 20, 2022*

Earth has a nemesis from the Sun and it's called a coronal mass ejection.

The Sun has been increasingly blasting powerful solar storms towards the Earth ever since the beginning of 2022. And, this will continue through 2023 when it reaches the peak of its solar maximum phase.

BOMBSHELL DHS OVERSIGHT REPORT: BIDEN ADMINISTRATION RESETTLED 'NOT FULLY VETTED' AFGHANS IN U.S. WHO MAY POSE RISK TO AMERICANS

~ *Associate Press DHS staff reporting, September 9, 2022*

The Department of Homeland Security (DHS) Inspector General (IG) has issued a bombshell report that accuses President Joe Biden's administration of

resettling Afghan nationals "who were not fully vetted"
across the United States.

Following the U.S. Armed Forces' withdrawal from Afghanistan
in August 2021, Biden opened a "humanitarian parole" pipeline that
has resettled more than 86,000 Afghans in American communities,
many of whom were not screened or interviewed in person.

The DHS IG report reveals that the Biden administration
"admitted or paroled" thousands of Afghans "who were not fully
vetted" before their arrival in the United States and may "pose a risk
to national security" as a result.

The report states, in part:

"We determined some information used to vet evacuees through
U.S. Government databases, such as name, date of birth, identification number, and travel document data, was inaccurate, incomplete,
or missing. We also determined CBP admitted or paroled evacuees
who were not fully vetted into the United States.

"We attribute DHS' challenges to not having: (1) a list of Afghan
evacuees who were unable to provide sufficient identification documents; (2) a contingency plan to support similar emergency situa-
tions; and (3) standardized policies. As a result, DHS may have
admitted or paroled individuals into the United States who pose a
risk to national security and the safety of local communities.

"In January 2022, we issued DHS a Notice of Findings and Recom-
mendations document notifying the Department of the urgent need to
take action to address security risks of evacuees from Afghanistan who
were admitted or paroled into the United States without sufficient
identification documents to ensure proper screening and vetting."

EPIGRAPH

He is the happiest, be he king or peasant, who finds peace in his own home.
~ Johan Wolfgang von Goethe, German Poet and Statesman

Nothing can stop the man with the right mental attitude from achieving his goal.
Nothing on Earth can help the man with the wrong mental attitude.
~ Thomas Jefferson, Founding Father

The opportunity of defeating the enemy is provided by the enemy himself.
~ Sun Tzu, Ancient Chinese military general and strategist

Be content with what you have. Rejoice in the way things are. When you realize there is nothing lacking, the whole world belongs to you.
~ Lao Tzu, Ancient Chinese philosopher

The future starts today, not tomorrow.
~ Pope John Paul II

PROLOGUE

Hogs & Hens Farm
Gibson, Pennsylvania

Joe Sunderland was a long way from home by any standard of measurement in a post-apocalyptic world. To be sure, the two-hundred-mile drive from his farm in the small Central Pennsylvania community of McVeytown might ordinarily take three hours or so. However, once the mighty sun turned anything electronic into scrap metal, his only means of transportation other than a horse became his old International Harvester tractor. The Model 946, built in the early nineteen seventies, sported a six-cylinder water-cooled diesel engine. He'd bought it when his father suddenly passed away over fifty years ago with the proceeds of a Gerber life insurance policy. The policy hadn't been enough to pay the bills; however, it had allowed the family to expand its farming operations.

The Sunderland family had been dairy farmers dating back to the early eighteen hundreds when settlers crossed the Appalachian Mountains to explore the western frontier. While many continued west in search of adventure and rumors of gold, some settled in the fertile valleys of Pennsylvania.

Farmer Joe, as he was affectionately referred to around McVeytown, had several sons, one of whom married his high school sweetheart and moved to Gibson in Susquehanna County, a mile or so east of Cubbison's Farm.

After the perfect storm brought the power grid down, Joe immediately became concerned about the well-being of his son and family. The rest of the Sunderland boys had stayed closed to home in Mifflin County, which was located between Harrisburg and State College, where Penn State University was located. The family, like so many other Pennsylvanians in rural communities, vowed to survive the unexpected trials and tribulations a powerless world had thrust upon them.

However, his youngest son was far from home, and Farmer Joe couldn't rest until he had an opportunity to check on him.

His daughter-in-law's family had operated a small pig farm and poultry operation for many years. She was an only child and had inherited the business when they died. Farmer Joe's son was excited about the prospect of finding his own way with his new wife and soon-to-be-born children.

Farmer Joe remained close to his son, and they talked frequently. However, both of their farms required constant attention, so their visits together were few and far between.

It was with trepidation that the elderly patriarch took off on the IH tractor toward Gibson following the perfect storm. His concern grew as he turned on the highway toward Gibson and noticed the bikers who'd taken up residency at the interstate exit. He quickly adjusted his route to avoid any conflict, opting instead to slowly traverse the fields to the south of the exit.

He was exhausted by the time he approached his son's homestead. He'd slept very little on the way, and when he did, he'd laid his head down in an abandoned barn or in a field under the stars.

Farmer Joe had crested a hill when he first noticed a faint

orangish glow on the night horizon. A breeze caught his nostrils as he drew closer, causing him to cover his face to avoid inhaling the foul odor of smoke.

As he approached, he began to suspect the blazing fire was coming from his son's farm. He urged the tractor on, well surpassing its ten mile-per-hour top speed. It wasn't fast enough for Farmer Joe. He abandoned the machine and began running toward the house, his chest heaving as he gasped for air.

He rushed down the gravel driveway until he saw the shadows of two men administering a beatdown to a third person in front of the burning house. Farmer Joe bellowed at the men, telling them to stop. He called out his son's name. Nobody responded, and the beating continued until he reached the front lawn.

The men lost interest in the beating when their victim became unresponsive. With a maniacal laugh, they turned to lock eyes with Farmer Joe before grabbing up two duffel bags and racing into the darkness. The evil in their eyes was embedded in Farmer Joe's brain as he turned his attention to the lifeless body bleeding profusely on the ground before him.

It was his son.

Overcome with grief, Farmer Joe sobbed at the side of his youngest son's lifeless body, rocking his corpse back and forth as if he were calming a newborn. He closed his eyes and prayed for a miracle. He begged God to take his life and not that of his boy. As grief poured out of him, the roof structure of the farmhouse succumbed to the flames and crashed to the ground, killing his daughter-in-law and grandchildren if they weren't dead already.

For hours until the sun rose, Farmer Joe held his son, alternating between wailing in sorrow and shaking his head in disbelief. By the time the heat of the sun replaced the slowly dying embers of the fire, Farmer Joe's fate had been determined.

He vowed to find the men who murdered his family. Justice would be done.

PART 1

Monday

We all have our burdens to bear.

CHAPTER ONE

Monday
Haleakala Observatory
Island of Maui, Hawaii

Professor Neal Burgoyne stared into the night sky as he sat atop one of the many volcanic rocks forming a barrier around the parking areas of the Haleakala Observatory in Maui. The rocks were strategically placed to prevent an awestruck driver from inadvertently driving themselves off the top of the ten-thousand-foot dormant volcano. The view was mesmerizing as well as distracting.

He was philosophical that evening, contemplating life and the predicament he'd found himself in. While it was hard to imagine focusing on anything other than his small part of the world, his mind wandered to the universe he'd spent a lifetime studying.

There are two possibilities, he thought to himself, waxing poetic, as the hoity-toity might say. *Either we're alone in this vast universe, or we're not. Regardless, both possibilities are equally terrifying.*

Then he chuckled and closed his eyes for a moment, his mind racing back to that fateful day the perfect storm washed over much of North America. Its beautiful hues of greens and blues had brought destruction to man's modern way of living. Fortunately for Burgoyne, he'd escaped New York and arrived back in Hawaii as the proverbial shit hit the fan elsewhere.

Upon returning to the observatory to the chattering students and young scientists who manned it, his survival instincts kicked in. Not only did he need to rapidly make preparations to protect himself, he also needed to provide guidance and leadership to those within his charge.

Every member of the Haleakala Observatory team was up to the task. First, they worked together to analyze the impact of the massive solar storm and the potential destructive power of the electromagnetic pulse it had generated. Then, working together, they hustled around Maui to secure food and other supplies to help them withstand a potential power outage on the island. Hawaii imported many food products and essential supplies from the U.S. mainland. Gasoline immediately came to mind as a precious commodity as well as the mundane, such as personal hygiene and sanitary supplies.

None of the students were particularly interested in weapons. Some even abhorred the prospect of gun ownership. However, they saw the need to protect themselves, so they gathered up as many firearms and boxes of ammunition as they could. Thus far, they'd not been approached by the criminal element ravaging the neighborhoods below their perch high above Maui.

Burgoyne abandoned his musings of life in the universe and considered his own plight. During a catastrophic event like the perfect storm, one's world became much smaller. It no longer mattered what was happening to the people stuck in New York City or the countryside of Pennsylvania. Burgoyne couldn't even concern himself with the plight of the Big Island of Hawaii. Even the population centers of Maui, such as Kahului or the touristy area of West Maui, seemed like half a world away.

Over the weeks during which chaos reigned on the mainland, naïve Hawaiians seemed to consider themselves insulated from the carnage. Certainly, like Burgoyne and his young charges, many hustled to the banks and grocery stores to stock up on everyday goods. The shelves, however, didn't empty completely until two weeks after the power grids suffered a cascading failure across the mainland.

Early on, there still seemed some sense of normalcy. Defiant in the face of certain collapse, many businesses remained open. Looting, on Maui anyway, was practically nonexistent as the locals worked together to weather the storm.

Then a series of events caused the dynamic to change. First, Hawaiian Electric suffered a power outage in Kahului. It was not as a result of the perfect storm but rather an error by one of the substation personnel. The outage only lasted an hour and a half, but it triggered the fears of the residents. The thin veneer of civilization was laid bare as the short-lived spirit of cooperation became an opportunity to better one's condition.

It began with price gouging by the retailers, who had a limited number of goods to sell. The locals who'd supported the businesses became irate. Tempers flared, and violence escalated.

The city of twenty-six thousand became a battle zone as neighbor fought neighbor for resources. Law enforcement was quickly overwhelmed, and many officers abandoned their posts to protect their own families. Despite Hawaiian Electric correcting its error by restoring the power, the fuse had been lit.

Survival of the fittest became the mantra of most.

A day after the power-outage debacle, ferry boats began crossing the Maui Channel from the Big Island to the desolate beaches located on the southeastern side of Maui. The influx of displaced refugees went unnoticed for several days until they began to walk into the rural communities at the base of the Haleakala Volcano summit.

The refugees were not welcomed with open arms. Maui residents adopted an us-versus-them attitude. The refugees banded together as well. The result was a type of primal warfare involving clubs, knives, and fisticuffs with rarely a shot fired from a firearm.

Every bowl of poi was fought over to the death. A can of SPAM, a favorite of islanders since World War II, was worthy of a brawl to gain possession of the commodity. Homeowners were killed, their bodies dragged into the dense forest, where they slowly decomposed. The squatters who took control of the properties immediately ravaged food supplies and then moved on to the next community like locusts in search of sugar-rich plant material.

Burgoyne had reluctantly allowed some of his braver students to descend the dormant volcano to conduct surveillance on the communities surrounding the observatory. Each day, they reported the violence to the group and warned that the marauders were getting closer to Haleakala.

Throughout the days and weeks following the perfect storm, Burgoyne wondered how long it would take for the madness to reach their doorstep. Soon, he'd find out.

CHAPTER TWO

Monday
Haleakala Observatory
Maui, Hawaii

Burgoyne had been part of the team at the Daniel K. Inouye Solar Telescope at the Haleakala Observatory. Known as DKIST, most of the facility was used for the study of the Sun. As the perfect storm was unfolding, the staff had been hyped up. This was truly a solar event for the ages, rivaling the often-cited Carrington Event of 1859.

The magnitude of the perfect storm surpassed the 1859 solar storm. Government agencies like NOAA had always reassured the public a solar event of this size would only happen once every five hundred years. This *reassurance* was not based on any scientific study other than one bureaucrat's hypothesis or the media's group-think. They were wrong.

It was difficult for his team to step away from the world's largest solar telescope in order to gather supplies for their anticipated prolonged stay at DKIST. After the weeks that had passed since the event, none of them regretted the actions they'd taken at Burgoyne's behest.

As the perfect storm dissipated and the heavens returned to relative normalcy, the residents of DKIST began to focus on their immediate future. Burgoyne's number one research assistant, Kelly Baxter, acted as a liaison of sorts between Burgoyne and the much younger members of the DKIST team who remained on top of Haleakala. She'd also become the de facto cat sitter for Yang, Burgoyne's adopted feral cat.

The sometimes-petulant cat was the least receptive of the residents to the change in diet and limited rations. His instincts wanted to hunt for mice and small lizards, both of which were in short supply on the high-altitude summit of the dormant volcano. Some of the students shared scraps from their own meals, which oftentimes resulted in Yang's bowels becoming disgruntled if not downright angry.

"Professor, our scout team has just returned. I think you should speak to them now."

Burgoyne had observed them making the long trek up the winding road to the observatory. He'd admonished everyone to preserve their fuel and resist the urge to drive up and down the summit road. Also, he didn't want to draw unnecessary attention to the observatory with activity that could be observed by prying eyes with binoculars or a small telescope.

"What is it?" he asked, lifting his aging body off his favorite rocky perch.

The fellow New Yorker paused and swallowed hard before responding, "Apparently, there is a gang forming in Kula. It's hard to tell whether they are locals or the refugees from the Big Island we've heard about. Anyway, they've stolen a large number of motor scooters for transportation and taken up residency at the Sandalwoods."

The Kula Sandalwoods was a small, boutique resort consisting of cottages and a modified main residence. Burgoyne had frequented the café for breakfast before he drove into Kahului to run errands. The owners of the Sandalwoods were *kama'aina*, a word meaning people of the land, often used to refer to native Hawaiians. Caucasians from outside of Hawaii, like Burgoyne and Baxter, were often referred to as *haoles*, which was pronounced as howl-ee. Haole was not necessarily used in a derogatory way unless a native Hawaiian felt it was necessary. One could tell the difference by their tone of voice.

Burgoyne gathered up Yang and held him in his arms. He snuggled the cat as they walked back to the observatory. The three young men who'd made the trek to the base of the dormant volcano were sitting just inside the observatory, chatting with the others while accepting food and water to renourish their bodies.

"Gentlemen," Burgoyne greeted them, "I understand there's news."

The three young men had stepped up to become the protectors of the group. They'd spent the most time patrolling the Haleakala Highway, toting camping gear and supplies in order to sleep along the way. Their trips to the base of the volcano generally took four or five days. The fact they'd returned after just three indicated there was a reason for concern.

"Yes, Professor," replied the leader of the trio, a native Hawaiian named Lopaka whose name, ironically, signified a bright flame, like the sun. Despite their new living arrangements, due respect was shown to Burgoyne. Somehow, the team, Baxter included, couldn't find a way to address their professor by his first name. Lopaka explained, "We touched base with a few of the residents at the bottom of the mountain before we ventured into Kula. Our usual sources of information wouldn't even come to the door. Only one peeked through the shutters on his window and told us to be careful."

"Careful?" said Burgoyne inquisitively. "Of what? Has the looting gotten that bad?"

The young man took another gulp of water before responding.

His eyes darted back and forth between Burgoyne and the other two scouts. "It's bigger than that. They claim Yakuza are on Maui."

Burgoyne rolled his neck on his shoulders to relieve the immediate jolt of tension that overcame his body. He hoped the information the scouts had received was an exaggeration of the truth.

A Japanese organized crime group known as Yakuza had been in existence for centuries, dating back to the early sixteen hundreds. While the number of Yakuza in Japan had dwindled to twenty-four thousand, the membership in Hawaii had grown as they successfully recruited locals to join their ranks.

The Yakuza operated primarily in Oahu, especially near Waikiki, where their money-laundering operations bought and sold real estate. Over the years, however, they'd entered the lucrative drug trade. Tourists to Oahu readily purchased everything from marijuana to synthetic opioids like fentanyl. Their gambling and prostitution operations gave them the reputation of being brutal enforcers of their illicit activities. One did not welch on a bet made through the Yakuza without expecting to lose a body part or two.

Burgoyne, through news reports, was aware of the Yakuza. From recollection, he knew their territory was primarily in Oahu. Maui was known to have a high crime rate because of drug abuse and chemical dependency. Burglaries and simple assaults had become commonplace. These were the crimes of the desperate, as Burgoyne would call them. A drug addict needed a fix, so he sought out a victim to provide the means to purchase drugs. The Yakuza were a different matter. They were organized, and they were known killers.

"In Kula? At the Sandalwoods?" asked Burgoyne.

Lopaka quickly answered to an audience that now included almost everyone at DKIST. "Many are at the resort, while others are taking people's homes to live in. If the owner doesn't leave willingly, they are badly beaten or even killed."

Burgoyne wandered the tile floor, which was covered in lava dust. "Okay. Okay. It sucks that organized crime has arrived on Maui. I imagine this bunch came from the Big Island to pillage the locals who have no way to defend themselves. I can't imagine they'd have any interest in a solar observatory, especially one that requires a twenty-mile drive to an elevation of ten thousand feet."

A murmur came over the group as they discussed their level of safety amongst themselves. Burgoyne needed a moment to think and chose his words carefully to avoid further frightening the young faces who looked up to him for guidance.

Lopaka, who'd become a leader within the group, made a suggestion. "Professor, I know we've avoided the use of our vehicles on the road leading to town. However, as we hiked back up on the Skyline Trail, the three of us came up with some ideas."

"Like what?" asked Burgoyne.

"Maybe, without drawing attention to ourselves, we could set up some kind of roadblock at the bottom. You know, a deterrent that might send the Yakuza off in another direction."

"You've made a good point," said Burgoyne. "If we make it difficult for them, chances are they'll seek out easier prey."

Baxter played devil's advocate. "Or they might wonder why someone would go through the effort to block a road that only leads to one place—a solar observatory."

Burgoyne added, "The question is what will be more effective? An actual roadblock as a deterrent, or leave it open, hoping the curious Yakuza don't see a need to drive up the face of the volcano."

CHAPTER THREE

Monday
Hogs & Hens
Gibson, Pennsylvania

Farmer Joe Sunderland had established somewhat of a routine while searching for his son's murderers. Like all farmers, he had a love for animals not just because they were a source of income but because they raised most of them from birth. Like the dairy cattle he raised on his own farm in McVeytown, his son's hogs and hens required attention.

The operation focused on free-range pig farming and the flock of chickens. Their care started with clean, safe living conditions as well as proper feeding. Water was important, too. His son grew crops around the hogpens for the sole purpose of feeding them. Corn, pumpkin, squash, and carrots were just some of the varieties of produce at his disposal. Just like humans, hogs were omnivores; they'd eat just about anything that was tasty.

After he cared for the hogs and hens, Farmer Joe would venture out into the surrounding communities in search of his family's killers. At first, he'd exhausted his son's stored gasoline as he traveled around Gibson and to other communities to the east, where the killers had seemed to flee towards.

When the gas ran out, he turned to his tractor. His son had an ample supply of off-road diesel to allow Farmer Joe six to eight hours of searching a day.

It was just before dawn that morning, and Farmer Joe was eating a meager meal of grits and Vienna sausages he'd found on the journey from McVeytown. Off in the distance, he heard the sound of gunfire. One particular farm run by the Cubbison family seemed to have been a magnet for trouble. He'd surveilled it several times, hoping to spot his son's killers. After the third time, he'd determined the Cubbisons had their hands full defending their place and didn't appear to be brutal murderers or thieves.

He continued to eat his meal, wondering if the Cubbison folks were having trouble. He wouldn't be much help in that regard, as he only had a shotgun in his possession that he'd found in his son's pickup. Nonetheless, the sheer volume of gunfire piqued his curiosity. He hopped on his tractor, shotgun cradled in his lap, and began the slow drive down the rural highway toward the Cubbisons' property.

He recalled the day he had been conducting a search when two vehicles had raced past him toward Harford. Then, shortly thereafter, he'd seen them gather at a nearby farm just past the Cubbisons' place before leaving again. These were all opportunities for him to determine the family was not a threat and not likely his family's killers.

Nonetheless, he headed toward the sound of the gunfire out of curiosity and as part of his constant search for the murderous bastards. As he rounded a bend, he came upon an abandoned roadside vegetable stand just as the sun was peeking up over the horizon behind him. Farmer Joe slowed the tractor to a stop when he noticed a car parked behind the small structure.

"Well, hello there," he muttered aloud, seemingly greeting the unexpected vehicle to the neighborhood. "What brings you here?"

He parked the tractor on the opposite side of the road and readied his shotgun. Undistracted by the gun battle raging down the road, he focused his attention on the car. He'd driven by the vegetable stand many times and had never seen it before.

Cautiously, he rushed across the road and entered the looted vegetable stand through the front doors. He swung the shotgun's barrel from side to side in search of anyone hiding in the place. After looking through the back storeroom, he exited to the rear of the building.

Tick. Tick. Tick.

It was the telltale sign of a car engine cooling down after a long drive. Farmer Joe walked at a low crouch, approaching the car slowly from the rear. He tried to avoid being seen in the side-view mirrors as he eased up on the exhaust pipe. He carefully held his hand up to the exhaust and felt the heat.

Farmer Joe's body tensed. Someone had to be close by. His mind raced. Were they attacking the nearby farm? He wasn't sure, as the exhaust still felt hot to the touch; however, the gun battle had been taking place for some time. Were they just onlookers, afraid to travel toward Harford for fear of getting involved in somebody else's drama? His mind was on high alert as it assessed the possibilities.

The sun had risen completely now, leaving him exposed to the owners of the car. He found a hiding spot behind a stack of hay bales near the produce stand and waited. He wasn't sure what he expected to see when the owners of the vehicle returned. They might have been innocent travelers trying to avoid the gunfire. They might have been active participants in the attack.

Regardless, Farmer Joe had to know.

CHAPTER FOUR

Monday
Near Cubbison's Farm
Harford, Pennsylvania

Farmer Joe waited patiently for the car's owners to return. His eyes searched the fields behind the produce stand. Then a sense of foreboding came over his body as he realized the owners might very well be across the road. They might be lying in wait for him, stalking the parked tractor, guns at the ready. An inner debate waged inside Farmer Joe. Should he stay, or should he go? Should he abandon his intense curiosity and look for safety?

Shortly thereafter, the decision was made for him as two men began walking briskly through the fields toward him. He couldn't make out their facial features; however, he saw that they were armed. Something told him they weren't part of the attackers. Their rifles were slung over their shoulders, and they didn't seem to be running from the direction of the attack.

As they got closer, Farmer Joe's tired eyes tried to assess their demeanor. Were they a threat? Were they curiosity seekers, like him?

The men slowed as they approached the produce stand. The bright sun shined on their faces. Farmer Joe squinted and then rubbed his eyes. Could it be?

His mind recounted the events the night he'd discovered his dead son. He pictured the two men who'd killed him, their facial features only illuminated by the blaze in the farmhouse.

Are they the same? Are these the men who killed my boy? What if I'm wrong?

No. I'm sure of it. Same build. Same hairstyles and facial features. I could pick them out of a lineup every time.

Farmer Joe gripped the shotgun and waited for the men to get closer. Just as they approached the front of the car, he jumped out from behind the hay bales.

"That's close enough! Another step and I'll put you down like a dog!"

The two men stopped in their tracks. One of the men raised his hands to shield his eyes from the bright morning sun. Farmer Joe sent a clear and convincing signal.

Racking a shell into a shotgun makes an unmistakable, metallic sound. Even in pitch-black darkness, an intruder could discern what to expect. Likewise, the two men who approached the car understood as well.

"Hands high!" he shouted at them.

The two men obliged. Farmer Joe studied their faces. They were similar, but he was not entirely sure.

"You! In the Eagles tee shirt. Slowly drop those binoculars and remove your rifle from your shoulder."

Farmer Joe's voice was stern and convincing. The man slowly dropped the night-vision monocular and eased the AR-15 off his shoulders until it fell in the tall grass.

"Good. Now you do the same!"

The other man hesitated. "You are making a mistake," he hissed.

Farmer Joe immediately detected his Middle Eastern accent. Once again, his mind tried to recall the night his son had been murdered. Did the men speak? Were they Arabic? All he could remember was their maniacal, defiant laugh.

He set his jaw and shouted back, menacingly pointing his shotgun at the men, "Drop the weapon, or you die right here, right now!"

The two men exchanged a quick glance. The second man slowly dropped the weapon. With Farmer Joe focusing on his movements, the other man eased his hand toward his back. Joe's keen, yet nervous eye didn't miss his sudden movement.

"Pull that pistol, and I'll shoot a hole in your gut!"

The man raised his hands before he was instructed to drop the gun to the ground. He heard the sounds of car engines starting in the distance. If these men were part of the attackers, they might be coming to the produce stand as a rendezvous point. He had to act quickly.

He glanced into the car and saw that the keys to the seventies model Oldsmobile Delta 88 were in the ignition. He eased around the back of the car while keeping a wary eye on his prisoners. He slowly retrieved the keys and then moved to the trunk, all the while keeping the shotgun pointed at the two men.

He knew the large sedan had ample trunk room. Most four-door sedans back in the day had been designed for comfort and road trips, especially the Oldsmobile models. He deftly popped the trunk and looked inside. It was empty.

"Now, both of you, get in the trunk. You two will have to get cozied up together."

Farmer Joe moved deliberately around the Olds until he was close to the men. He used the barrel of the shotgun to wave them around the sedan until they reached the trunk. He studied them closely, expecting them to make a move to overtake him. However, the shotgun kept them at bay.

With a few choice words in Arabic, the two men complied and

ended up spooning one another. With a hard slam that struck one of the men in the side of the head, Farmer Joe closed the trunk lid and breathed a sigh of relief. He'd caught his son's murderers. He was sure of it.

But now what?

CHAPTER FIVE

Monday
Kula Sandalwoods Inn
Island of Maui, Hawaii

Oh, how the mighty had fallen.

Tatsuki Goto had been described by the Federal Bureau of Investigation's San Francisco field office as ravenous, lethal, merciless, cold, and calculated. He had been a force to be reckoned with as he rose through the ranks of organized crime in the Bay Area.

Then he had been given a promotion.

For decades, Hawaii had been seen as a midway station between Japan and mainland America for the smuggling of methamphetamines into the U.S. with corresponding arms deliveries back to Japan. Similar to what America had experienced at its southern border, drug traffickers traded much-sought-after drugs to Americans in exchange for firearms.

Goto was born into a Yakuza family. His father had entered the country illegally as part of an influx of Yakuza recruits out of Japan.

His sons, all of whom were dead except for Goto, had taken up the family trade.

Goto had been approached by the organized crime's leadership in Los Angeles to take a senior position within their Hawaii operations. The gang's money-laundering operation had been turned over to corrupt lawyers, accountants, and government officials. The day-to-day operations involving drugs, arms trading, and prostitution required a proven foot soldier. Goto's experience in San Francisco had hardened him, making him an ideal choice for Yakuza leadership in Hawaii, which had faltered of late.

The island paradise proved to be too alluring for the longtime Yakuza leaders. They'd sampled too much product. They'd ruined too many prostitutes. They'd recklessly sold firearms to small-time hoods, who brandished them around Oahu and the Big Island. These criminals, when pressed, were more than willing to sell out the Yakuza lieutenants.

Goto had explicit instructions from his superiors based in Los Angeles. Clean up this *shitshow*. The Company, the name given to Native Hawaiian crime syndicates, were disciplined and determined. They'd made inroads into traditional Yakuza revenue streams, especially in the drug trade. Revenues were way down, and arrests of Yakuza soldiers were way up.

Unfortunately, the very traits that had earned Goto his new position in Oahu also led to his downfall. When the Yakuza who'd been entrenched in their positions across the state resisted his new approach to running the operation, he cracked down on their insolence. Perhaps, as it turned out, a little too hard.

He'd assembled a loyal cadre of lieutenants and foot soldiers who administered discipline on their fellow Yakuza who either didn't toe the line or who defected to the Company. The result was fear and paranoia within the ranks. The once mighty, steadfast Yakuza would get arrested and agree to a prison term rather than roll over on their brethren. Goto's heavy-handed approach changed that.

Dissension rose among the old guard. They'd made a decision. Quite simply, the new guy had to go.

None of the disgruntled Yakuza were willing to take Goto head-on. A contracted hit was not an option. Their best bet was to make deals with law enforcement. A federal investigation, as was often the case, took many months. You know, dot the i's and cross the t's in order to get an airtight conviction.

Goto sensed something was afoot, and he began to circle the wagons within his most trusted Yakuza. He also kept his girlfriend happy. Goto, a television-star-handsome man, dated a paralegal at the Department of Justice's offices in Honolulu. She fed him information regarding the investigation. He knew the indictments were coming, so he prepared an exit strategy.

The day the grand jury convened, Goto prepared to flee to the Philippines. However, something fortuitous happened.

The perfect storm.

Despite the fact the power outage had no direct effect on Hawaii, everyday life on some of the islands came to a near halt. Public events were cancelled. Government offices were closed. Businesses remained open for a while until eventually they ran out of product to sell. Banks ran out of cash to distribute to their customers, resulting in riots throughout the islands.

In effect, Goto was given a stay of execution.

An accomplished opportunist, Goto immediately plotted with his top lieutenants. They considered various ways to exploit the catastrophic circumstances to not only gain an immediate advantage over law enforcement, but also over rival gangs. Guided by his experiences learned from his father and in the trenches, Goto created his own gang within the Yakuza.

The Yakuza were renowned for their strict codes of conduct and organized hierarchy. This approach prevented those foot soldiers at the bottom of the organizational chart from being made aware of the gang's activities. In addition, the Yakuza took pride in their code of *jingi*—justice and duty. Goto's first step was to create an army loyal to him and eliminate others. The first seven days following the perfect storm was a bloodbath across Oahu and the Big Island. When it was over, Goto emerged unopposed in his leadership of the Yakuza and was now feared by other gangs throughout the islands.

Then, a week after the solar storm, four high-performance motorboats arrived from Los Angeles. After the twenty-three-hundred-mile journey, the boats carrying senior leadership within the Yakuza slipped into Kewalo Basin in Oahu. Goto's new reign as island king of the Yakuza was about to end.

Nervous and distrustful of the influx from the mainland, Goto and his newly formed gang went on the run. There were numerous defectors who assisted the Yakuza senior leaders as they attempted to purge Goto loyalists. Finally, with the heat too much to bear, Goto made the decision to reduce the size of his gang and flee Oahu for Maui and, he thought, greener pastures ripe for the pickin'.

CHAPTER SIX

Monday
Cubbison's Farm
Harford, Pennsylvania

Despite his wife's insistence, John Cubbison couldn't rest that day. Emma tried, without success, to get the weary warrior to rest. Let one of the young guys stand watch, she'd insisted. John simply kissed her on the cheek, shook his head no, and said *I love you* before he climbed into the saddle of his horse.

He squinted through his binoculars at the horizon from the east, toward Gibson, along the highway to the south, and then toward the west where the once serene forest witnessed so much death. Following the departure of Fred Stewart and his men, John hugged his family and told them to get some rest before they cleaned up the mess created by the bikers who had attacked them.

John's horse shifted beneath him with a shake of his head. He leaned forward and gently patted the stallion's neck for reassurance.

"Easy, old friend. I think we can catch our breath for now."

His horse stilled, and John returned to his task, his body sore from the gun battle the night before. He licked his lips and rubbed his face, which was covered with three days' worth of scraggly beard.

He sighed as a somewhat cool wind with a hint of moisture blew over him from the mountains nearby. It was a welcome respite from the excessive heat the region had endured through late summer. Moreover, the scent of rain brought a smile to his face, as well as a chuckle. His mind wandered to the many times in his life he'd visited the local feed store in the midst of a torrential downpour and heard his fellow farmers say we needed the rain. Only to lament days later that their fields had turned into rice paddies.

Such was the life of a farmer or rancher. They were entirely dependent upon the weather for their livelihood, an aspect of Mother Nature wholly out of their control. He'd come to expect severe weather and made his preparations accordingly. The one event he'd never contemplated was space weather in the form of a solar storm.

Off in the distance, a band of purplish clouds pulsed with the occasional flash of lightning where the peaks of the thunderclouds reached the sky. "Five or six hours," he mumbled to himself as he tried to gauge how much time they'd have to begin the cleanup process. Even then, considering the odd weather patterns they'd endured of late, the storm might spend itself before reaching Cubbison's Farm.

He raised his binoculars and studied a shape that was out of sorts along the roadside near the abandoned produce stand. It appeared to be the top of a tractor. He'd mention it to Grandpa Sam, who routinely ventured out in that direction for a mile or so in search of any human activity.

"Let's roll 'em out of bed." John spat and stopped at the dry sound of his voice. Talking to his horse was one thing. Holding conversations with himself was another.

John made a clicking sound from the corner of his mouth. His horse immediately responded and plodded toward the Cubbisons' home. The soft wind was the only sound he could hear besides the hooves clomping on the gravel driveway and the occasional snort.

He passed Emma's pride and joy, Cubbison's Market, which was largely intact despite being at the center of the firefight. As he rounded the clapboard building, he studied the familial home. It hadn't fared so well.

Its front façade was riddled with bullet holes. Few windows were left intact. The bikers, intent on taking the Cubbisons' property, had been undisciplined at best. It had been easier for them to destroy the house they coveted than shoot the human targets who defended it.

Thank God.

The gunshot wound to Emma's upper arm was superficial at best. The makeshift bandage torn from one of John's tee shirts had stopped the bleeding quickly. John suspected Emma's injuries would be more mental than physical. She'd put on a good front throughout the apocalyptic world they'd been thrust into. However, everyone has a breaking point.

Vida, the wayward Afghan girl who'd fled her family, had done her part to protect John's family and home. She, too, had been injured as a shard of glass struck her strikingly beautiful face. John could see why his son Luke was smitten with the young woman. She was very pretty and seemed to have nerves of steel. Yet there was still something about her that troubled John. He sensed she was holding back.

Then, as was often the case, the hand of God intervened. His son Matthew had been shot in the back of the thigh as he was rescuing a young girl whose family the Cubbisons had vowed to protect. Although it just grazed his flesh, the impact knocked them both to the ground just as the pyromaniac who'd tried to burn down their home lit a Molotov cocktail. If Matthew had not been shot, he would've been engulfed in the flames that killed the fire-loving maniac.

John dismounted and slowly walked his horse to the water

trough. He saw movement inside the house. Apparently, his family, with its new additions, were already stirring. He took a deep breath and sighed. Surely, he thought, there was more to this post-apocalyptic world than people shooting guns at one another. His eyes looked toward the heavens, and his raspy voice managed a few more words before he entered.

"We've had about enough, don't you think?"

CHAPTER SEVEN

Monday
Hogs & Hens
Gibson, Pennsylvania

Within seconds of arriving back at Hogs & Hens, Farmer Joe broke down into tears. All the emotions he'd tried to suppress following the killing of his son were coming out again. He'd convinced himself to remain focused on finding the murderers. He'd prayed for answers while searching for the men who ended his son's life. Now, he'd found them, and he asked God for strength to exact his revenge. But first, he wanted a confession.

He gathered himself before taking his shotgun and the men's rifles into the barn for safekeeping. Each of the men had handguns, which were now brandished by Farmer Joe. He planned on interrogating the two, and the handgun was more versatile for guarding the men.

He opened the trunk lid and quickly moved to the side of the car in case they planned to attack him. His foresight saved his life.

The moment the key turned, allowing the trunk lock to open, the two men mule-kicked the lid upward, slamming it to the top of its hinges before bringing it down hard against their backs. Their attempt to ambush Farmer Joe was quickly thwarted by the heavy trunk lid crashing against them.

Farmer Joe was not surprised; however, he was now angry. He fired into the trunk, sending a bullet through the thigh of one of the men. He screamed in pain and began to writhe around, fighting against his partner, who was desperate to escape.

"Don't move! I'm tellin' ya!" Farmer Joe growled.

The man didn't heed the warning. He came rolling out of the trunk and began to scramble on his hands and knees to get away from the sedan. Farmer Joe, with a slight, somewhat sadistic grin, shot the man in the buttocks. The man lurched forward, screaming in pain as he tried to cover the blood gushing out of the fleshy meat of his butt.

The ruckus caused by the gunfire and the men's screams brought the farm to life. Hogs snorted and barked as they rustled about their pens. The hens cackled and scurried about their coops as they sensed danger.

"I'll keep shooting until you talk! What's it gonna be?"

One of the men suppressed his pain to respond, "Talk? Talk about what? We don't know you!"

Farmer Joe got dangerously close to the man. He waved the handgun in the Afghan's face. Farmer Joe was incredulous as he screamed at the two men, "You don't remember me? You don't remember murdering my son and family right over there?" He waved his arm toward the burnt rubble of the farmhouse.

"We know nothing of this!" yelled the other man. "We killed no one!"

"Liars! You will admit what you've done! Get on your feet!"

Both men, who'd been shot in the lower extremities, struggled to comply. They begged for mercy; however, none was shown.

"We did not do what you accuse us of," pleaded one of the men as he helped his partner to his feet. They struggled to maintain their balance as Farmer Joe herded them toward an empty hogpen. The block building was full of mud and hog feces. The odor emanating from within immediately caused one of the men to retch.

He vomited for nearly a minute before Farmer Joe threatened them once again. "Confess what you did, and I'll show you the mercy you asked for!"

"We did nothing!" came the response in unison.

Farmer Joe scowled and shook his head. "Keep moving. Inside! Now!"

The bleeding men crawled and then managed to hobble into the pigsty. Once they were through the open doorway, Farmer Joe slammed the wood slat doors behind them and dropped into place the heavy, four-inch-by-six-inch beam designed to keep the hogs from busting through the door. It would've been seen as the perfect stockade if that were what its intended purpose was.

Distraught, Farmer Joe was growing impatient. He'd been searching for the killers, and now he was certain he had them. They were lying, and he intended to get answers. However, they had one more chance at telling the truth.

He looked into the pigsty through a hole in the wall the size of a cinder block. The men were stumbling around in the dimly lit enclosure, searching for a way out. The only other exit was a farm gate made of vertical steel slats leading to a smaller pen at the rear of the building. The men pulled furiously against the slats in an attempt to escape, to no avail.

"Admit what you did to my son and his family!"

"We did noth—" one of the men began to shout in response before the other man cut him off.

"Okay! Okay! We're sorry. We didn't know he was your son. We killed him, and it wasn't even on purpose. It was an accident, but we're sorry."

Farmer Joe exhaled, his shoulders visibly drooping as the two men tried to lie in order to save themselves. He didn't respond to the man's ruse. Instead, he walked to the large hogpen adjacent to the pigsty.

The highly agitated hogs were crashing against one another as well as slamming against their pen and the pigsty itself. Farmer Joe was surprised that the dozens of seven-hundred-pound behemoths hadn't knocked a hole in the wall.

He gripped the pistol and kept it trained on the pigsty door as he eased the slide lock open. The hogs rushed out, crashing into one another as they barked with excitement. Farmer Joe didn't hesitate. He rushed back to the pigsty where the two men were locked inside. He reached over the fence railing and flipped up the handle on the steel gate. It slowly opened inward, catching the two men by surprise.

The crazed hogs, however, smelled the fear and blood oozing out of the men and joined in a stampede as they rushed into the pigsty. The men's bloodcurdling screams caused Farmer Joe's skin to crawl. During Christmas dinner one year, he and his son had talked about the dangers of falling into the hogpen. The family had tried to suggest the young man was pulling their leg with the tall tale.

Farmer Joe tested the theory as several deranged hogs pulled and tugged on the legs of the wounded men until they were dismembered.

He alternated crying and vomiting as the men were eaten alive by the frenzied hogs. Their cries of pain would be forever embedded in his mind. However, justice and punishment were harsh at times.

He spoke to his son, confirming that justice had been served. "The bastards are dead, son. I got 'em. These killers will never kill again."

Unfortunately, it was a case of mistaken identity.

Sort of.

CHAPTER EIGHT

Monday
Cubbison's Farm
Harford, Pennsylvania

Emma Cubbison had fibbed to her husband. If he was going to defy her and refuse rest, she'd do the same. She watched until he'd ridden out of sight that morning, and then she began the cleanup process. In addition to being an accomplished business owner, she was proud to be a wife and mother. Times had changed, and she needed to keep her wits about her for the benefit of her family.

After surface cleaning the kitchen counters of glass and debris, Emma made a pot of coffee. Luckily, the barrage of bullets the home had endured hadn't damaged their generators or appliances. The family would have to adopt carpentry skills to put their humpty-dumpty of a house back together again.

That morning, Emma stayed busy, relieved that the rest of the household heeded John's admonition to get some rest. She needed some alone time to process the carnage and near-death experiences they'd all lived through. She didn't want to talk about it with anyone but herself.

All went well as she systematically cleaned up the front of the house until she reached the family room. It had been the gathering place of the Cubbison family for many generations. The furniture might have changed over the decades, but the love soaked into the walls was the same.

It was the destruction of the Cubbisons' curio cabinet that brought fits of sobs and tears from Emma. Every collected piece had a story. Each held a special place in the family's heart, both present and past. Most of the heirlooms had been needlessly destroyed by the men who thought they had a right to take what didn't belong to them.

Survival was one thing. Brazen thievery was another. Mindless destruction was unnecessary.

After the initial wave of sadness, anger rose within her. She marched toward the front door and flung it open. She wanted to scream. She wanted to curse the men whose dead bodies were still strewn about the farm. She wanted to grab her shotgun and put a load of double-aught buck in their rotting corpses, just for good measure.

However, she stopped herself. She took in a breath of fresh air that flowed through the Susquehanna Valley. She subconsciously rubbed her sore shoulder, still slightly throbbing from the bullet wound. She allowed the tip of her fingers to press the wound, and then she mentally measured the distance to the palm of her hand that rested over her heart.

"Six inches. Maybe," she'd muttered aloud. The bullet had struck barely six inches from her heart. Half a foot over would've meant certain death. "It kinda puts it all in perspective, doesn't it?" she asked herself, her palm pressed flat against her chest.

Emma took a glance around the farm, hoping to catch a glimpse of her husband. She contemplated retrieving her horse and riding in all directions to find him. Just to have a brief hug.

And a kiss. And a moment of solace away from the scene of the carnage.

However, she simply smiled and mouthed the words, *I love you*, to her husband. Wherever he was.

With a renewed sense of purpose and spirits lifted by a simple breath of fresh air, Emma returned to the task at hand. She hustled about, sweeping up shards of glass and slivers of wood. Several cardboard boxes full of debris sat near the front door to be hauled off by the boys when they awakened.

With the cleanup accomplished, she stood in front of a Federal mirror that had been in the Cubbison family since the late nineteenth century. The oblong, convex mirror was surrounded by a gold-painted frame and adorned with an American Eagle perched upon four arrows. Its design dated back to the early years of the United States government and was considered one of the oldest decorative pieces owned by the family.

Emma took a look at herself for the first time. Her hair was disheveled. Her clothing was bloodstained. And her face was gaunt from sleep deprivation. She shook her head and chuckled to herself.

"Hot mess express," she muttered aloud. She doted over her hair for a moment and licked her fingers to wipe a smudge of blood off her neck. Emma managed a smile. "Presentable, I guess. A genuine, apocalyptic *Susie Homemaker.*"

She let out a genuine laugh for the first time in days. It had the effect of washing away the angst she'd dealt with throughout the morning. It also motivated her to feed her family a hearty meal. It wasn't Thanksgiving yet. But, today, they'd all get the closest thing to it.

Emma began the preparations. She hustled back and forth to the refrigeration and freezer units in Cubbison's Market. She fired up the generator for a couple of hours, as had been her practice since the power grid collapsed. In addition to keeping their food frozen or cold, the generator allowed her to run kitchen appliances and to heat the water in the water heater.

Also, she made sure the lithium batteries for power tools were fully charged. There was a laundry list of things to do in the aftermath of the attack. Fixing the house that had been ripped to shreds by bullets was one. As she glanced through the kitchen door at the dead biker slumped at the entrance to the barn, she was reminded that there was the unsavory task of disposing of the dead as well.

Rotting corpses can present a significant health hazard to those assigned the job. Anyone handling the dead can be exposed to a myriad of diseases ranging from bloodborne viruses like hepatitis to gastrointestinal infections like cholera.

Emma had witnessed the rotting hulk of a cow in the past. Fluids were released through every orifice as organs, muscles, and skin became liquified. The bovine's corpse began to lose its mass as soft tissue decomposed along with bones and cartilage. Despite the loathsome task, it had to be done sooner rather than later. She rolled her eyes as she contemplated whether it would be best performed before her planned dinner or afterwards. She chose before.

Just as she was about to wake up the others, the front door abruptly opened. The silhouette of a man holding a rifle filled the entry. Emma lost all composure as she raced into her husband's arms and buried her head in his chest.

CHAPTER NINE

Monday
Cubbison's Farm
Harford, Pennsylvania

"Thank God you're home," she said in a muffled voice. Tears streamed down John's chest as Emma cried. He gently pushed her back to look into her eyes.

"Honey? Is everything all right?"

Emma managed a nod and a smile. She was embarrassed and quickly moved to wipe the tears off her face. Her eyes, however, refused to cooperate, and they welled up with moisture again.

"Yeah. Um, having a moment," she stuttered out in between sniffles. She laughed at herself. It hadn't been five minutes since she'd vowed to put on a strong, matronly façade for her family. Just like that, the waterworks opened up at the sight of her husband.

John smiled and kissed the tears off her cheeks. "I get it. We've been through a lot." He paused and looked beyond the foyer into their home. His eyes grew wide as he noticed the boxes full of debris. "Did you do all this?"

Emma nodded, puffing her chest out with pride. "I had to stay busy; otherwise I would've just lain in bed, staring at the ceiling," she replied. She changed the subject in an attempt to avoid further discussion of their damaged home. "Everything look good out there?"

John nodded as his eyes continued to assess the home's interior. They had a lot of work to do. "Yeah. Thankfully, very quiet. I did see a tractor I hadn't noticed before. I'll ask Dad about it."

Emma took her husband by the hand and pulled him into the kitchen. She explained her plans. "I think we all need a good, hearty meal. You know, Thanksgiving-style fixin's."

"Whoa! Sounds yummy, but are you up for it? I mean, it's a lot of work. Especially, um, how many are we feeding now, anyway?"

Emma counted aloud. "Immediate family is six. Add three for Asher, Lauren and Vida. That's nine under our roof."

"What about Jenna and her kids?" asked John. Over the course of their experiences following the collapse, they'd added several members to their extended family. There was Asher and Lauren Doyle, the New Yorkers who had been instrumental in protecting Grandpa Sam and Cat, the Cubbisons' young daughter, and Vida, the Afghan runaway, whom Luke had brought into their home.

Lastly, there was Jenna along with her daughters, Kay and Jewel, all of whom had been under the thumb of overbearing men. While they were given housing across the highway, they'd fallen under the protection of the Cubbisons during the gunfight. The three of them had slept on the sofa cushions in a back storage room following the gun battle.

Emma counted the mouths to feed. "Naturally, yes. That's twelve of us. I already have plenty of turkey that I started cold thawing earlier. I'm sure Lauren and Jenna will help me cook."

"What about Vida?" asked John.

Emma scowled and let out a deep exhale. "John, all of this had a profound impact on her. Especially at the end when Fred and his Marines were discussing their encounter with the men of Middle

Eastern descent. She tried to remain disinterested, but I could tell she was taking in the entire conversation. I wonder—"

John interrupted her thought. "At some point, we're gonna have a heart-to-heart conversation with her."

"I'll do it, John. Coming from a woman might be better. Plus, there's a complicating factor."

"What's that?"

Emma paused and explained, "She and Luke slept together this morning."

"Hold up. What?" John pulled away and wandered toward the door leading to the dining room.

"It's not what you think, honey," Emma explained. "It was more of a comforting-one-another kinda thing. They slept on top of Luke's bed with the door open."

"They're really close, aren't they?"

Emma nodded. "Trying times like these can encourage people to become close. I'm not sure how I feel about it." Emma looked past John to determine if anyone was eavesdropping.

"All the more reason to ferret out what she's holding back from us, right?"

Emma glanced at the wind-up timer she'd set on the kitchen counter, which reminded her when to turn off the generator. She needed to get to work, as did the guys. She patted her husband on the chest as she spoke.

"Go rally the troops except for the young ones. Ladies report to me. Guys report to you."

"Sir, yes, sir!" said John jokingly as he snapped a salute to his homestead field general.

She smiled. "I'll cook. You clean. Deal?"

"Clean?" asked John.

"Yup. Clean up our property of the dead vermin. I don't care if you drag them out into the road with the tractor to feed a wake of buzzards. Just get rid of them before supper."

"I'm on it," he said as he turned toward the center of the house.

"Hey, do we have any of those stupid masks from the pandemic? Those bikers stank even before we killed them. I can only imagine what they're like after lying out there all day."

Emma shouted after him, "Master bath closet. There are gloves in there, too. Be careful handling the dead. Full of diseases, you know."

John gave her a thumbs-up and walked up the stairs with a purpose. He was anxious to achieve some normalcy in their lives after yet another encounter with armed gunmen. Whether he truly believed it or not, he was going to take the approach their battles were behind them.

CHAPTER TEN

Monday
Cubbison's Farm
Harford, Pennsylvania

"How the hell did we pull this off, son?" Grandpa Sam asked as they worked with Luke and Matthew to gather the dead. Asher was dispatched to locate them all while the teens dragged the body onto a heavy-duty tarp affixed to the back of Sam's tractor. After six or seven dead were stripped of their weapons and ammo, they were dumped on the tarp and hauled through the woods to the back of Stanley's place. The burnt soil of Stanley's back forty acres was already ruined from the fire that almost took Luke's life. The funeral pyre for the dead bikers would only add to the charred ground.

"Fred Stewart and his merry mercenaries helped a lot," John replied.

"Still, we took them on by ourselves. We killed dozens of them before Fred arrived."

John shrugged as they exited the woods between the two farms.

His father had apparently forgotten about the fact the bikers had been closing in on the house.

Luke and Matthew walked dutifully behind the tractor, stopping just once to add a body to the heap. Asher was standing in the field, waving to get their attention. He pointed to three places in the field where dead bodies displaced the tall grasses.

Sam wanted to continue the conversation. "It was two parts planning and one part luck. We all dodged bullets."

"Literally," added John. They navigated the tractor toward the pile of dead bodies to add this load. After they were finished, they told the boys to take a break. Sam, John, and Asher worked together to gather up the last of the bikers' crew.

In a separate cart that was towed by a mule, Asher had gathered all the knives, guns, and ammunition from the dead. It was quite a haul. Because their attackers had no concept of ammo discipline and their shooting accuracy was horrible, the guns could be paired up with only a couple of dozen rounds per weapon. Nonetheless, it provided the Cubbisons with more firepower to fend off another attack.

"That's quite an arsenal, Asher," said John.

"Looks like the set of *Blue Bloods*." He laughed in response. Asher recounted an episode during which the NYPD discovered a large cache of weapons in an MS-13 gang stronghold. He retold the episode, which had been written almost exclusively by him for the show. As he finished, Luke and Matthew announced they were ready to light the fire.

Minutes later, flames lifted upward together with dark smoke caused by the diesel fuel they used as an accelerant. All of them were caught off guard by the stench of burning flesh. With their noses and mouths covered, they retreated from the fire and made their way back through the woods toward the house.

For the first time, the guys were able to recount their exploits during the gun battle. The conversation served to remind Grandpa Sam how close they had been to getting overrun. The bullets that whisked close enough to their heads to feel the air movement were fresh on their minds. These warriors were enjoying the memories of a hard-fought battle won.

As they approached the barn, John put a damper on the camaraderie and braggadocios bunch. "Listen up. Cat and Jenna's kids don't need to hear about this stuff. Time will tell how they were affected."

"That's right, son," added Sam. "Post-traumatic stress is the real deal. Let's try to avoid any conversations of what happened in the last twenty-four hours and focus on our future, such as it is."

"Agreed, Grandpa Sam," said Luke.

Matthew asked, "Dad, what about Jenna and her girls? They've been through a lot. I really believe she could be helpful to us in some way."

John and Sam exchanged glances. Asher was an outsider but completely accepted into the family. Vida was in a similar place as Jenna. To be sure, they'd proved their loyalty. However, John was unsure as to whether their allegiance was out of expedience for lack of better options.

He finally addressed Matthew's question. "For now, let's make sure Jenna and the girls feel safe in Ledbetter's place. We'll help feed them and protect them the best we can from afar. We're gonna have to teach Jenna to take care of herself, though."

"I'm sure she'll do whatever, Dad," said Matthew.

John sensed that Matthew was thinking with his heart. His teenage son was smitten with the woman nearly ten years older than him who already had two children. Not that the age difference was a determining factor. Just a consideration.

"Son, I'll continue to work with Jenna to teach her some self-reliance. And, if you're okay with it, I'll have Matthew involved as well."

John hesitated but agreed. "Everyone, I hope you understand. Winter is coming. We have a lot of work to do to harvest our crops and store them throughout the cold season. I don't want to put us in a position of having to forage on other farmers' lands or within their homes."

Asher spoke up. "Are there any homes left unsearched? We're weeks into the collapse. I suspect everything is picked over."

Sam responded, "You may be right. The only area of the county we haven't searched yet is toward the east and Gibson."

That sparked John's memory to ask, "Dad, do you recall an abandoned tractor near the old produce stand up the highway?"

"Nope. I was just up there a couple of days ago."

"Tomorrow, let's you and me check it out."

"Okay," said Sam. He slapped his son on the back and motioned toward the driveway. "Come on. I'm starvin'."

No, actually. It was just a figure of speech. The potential was there, however.

CHAPTER ELEVEN

Monday
Cubbison's Farm
Harford, Pennsylvania

The Cubbisons' home was full of life that early evening. Everyone cheerfully chatted as they performed their roles in the preparation of dinner. The sounds of chairs being slid up to the dining table and jovial conversation filled the air. The aroma of a hearty meal found its way throughout the house as Emma commanded her team of chefs.

John's team, led by Grandpa Sam, was in charge of logistics. The dining room table wasn't large enough for everyone, so as is typical in many households across America prior to the collapse, a kids' table was established. Cat happily decorated the table with flowers from the family garden and other mementos reflective of the holidays that hadn't been destroyed. Kay and Jewel, under the watchful eye of their mother, Jenna, assisted. Jenna gladly agreed to sit at the kids' table and assume the role of chaperone.

The dining table was set with a hodgepodge of dinnerware.

Most of the *fancy china*, as Emma called it, had been destroyed in the gun battle. The holiday serving pieces located in the bottom of the hutch had survived. The rest of the place settings, from glasses to dinnerware, was supplemented from the kitchen.

Luke and Vida were tasked with filling the glasses with wine, tea, and whole cow milk. The oldest adults enjoyed wine in stemware. The teens savored the flavor of fresh brewed sun-tea. And the children thought they were the cat's meow drinking fresh milk through a straw out of Ball jars.

John, who dared not enter his wife's domain during the meal preparations, carefully stuck his head through the doorway to announce that the tables were set.

"Perfect timing," said Emma, who'd quarterbacked the entire soiree. "Tell everyone to take their seats."

"Turkey's ready, Emma," said Lauren, who raised the serving platter as if presenting a gift to a king.

"Vida?" said Emma inquisitively.

"Mashed potatoes are ready except for one bite Luke snuck in and scooped up."

"Oh, really?" his mom said with a laugh. "When we pass the bowl around the table, make sure he's last." This drew a laugh from Lauren, who seemed to be studying Vida. Emma made a mental note to get her thoughts on the newcomer relative to her past and possible future relationship with Luke.

"Bread's ready, too," added Vida.

"Should we turn off the generator?" asked Lauren, who noticed Emma had allowed it to run past the timer's expiration.

"Oh, crap. Glad you reminded me," said Emma. "Start taking the food out and threaten anyone who touches it before the blessing with a wooden spoon across the back of their hand."

Lauren and Vida grabbed two of the largest spoons, which were to be used for doling out the potatoes and dressing, as they headed into the dining room. The rest of the family cheered their approval as the first of the supper fixin's appeared.

Emma bolted out the kitchen door toward the generator. She'd allowed it to run a couple of hours longer than planned in order to give everyone an opportunity to have a hot bath. None of the guys smelled of death after disposing of the corpses, but they did reek of smoke. The additional fuel spent to provide warm water was worth it.

By the time she returned, everyone was sitting respectfully at their seats in eager anticipation of the Thanksgiving-worthy dinner. Emma took her seat next to John on her right and Sam at the end of the head of the table.

"Okay. Thanks, everyone, for helping make this a special meal for us all," said Emma after catching her breath. She turned to her left and addressed her father-in-law. "Grandpa Sam, would you please say the blessing?"

He squeezed her hand and smiled. Then he bowed his head.

"We thank you, Father, for having created us and given us to each other as family. Thank you for being with us in all our joys and sorrows, for your comfort in our sadness, and your companionship in our losses.

"We thank you for our friends and family, for our health and our blessings. We ask that you send help to those who are hungry, alone, sick, and suffering. We open our hearts to your love and ask your blessing through Christ your son. Amen."

"Amen."

Grandpa Sam looked around the room and made eye contact with everyone. His tired, somewhat raspy voice was an indicator he'd aged substantially since the collapse.

"I want to thank all of our new friends, whom we consider to be our family. We've been brought together out of necessity but also to serve God's purpose. I don't know what the future brings. However, I do know that we can survive, and thrive, as a family."

"Amen to that, Dad," said John. He nodded and winked at his father. The two had always been close, but their quest to survive what seemed like a never-ending onslaught of criminal opportunists strengthened that bond.

"Now can we dig in?" Cat's question from the kids' table drew laughter from everyone.

"Okay, sort of," cautioned Emma. "We only have so much, so please be mindful of everyone getting a little bit. It's not that we're running out of food, but my kitchen was designed to feed so many mouths at once. I intend to put in a request to the contractor for a kitchen expansion after he plugs the holes in the walls and replaces the windows."

John laughed and leaned over the table to make eye contact with Grandpa Sam. "Sounds like a sizable change order to me, Dad. How about you?"

"You betcha. That reminds me. We need a signed contract, don't we?"

Sam was about to stick his fork in the sliced turkey when Emma jokingly pulled the platter away. "Would you like to eat, sir?"

Sam's eyes grew wide. He childishly nodded his head up and down.

"Are you gonna fix our house?"

He never stopped nodding.

Emma looked around the room. "Y'all are my witnesses. We now have a contract." She presented the platter to Sam, and he speared a piece of turkey in a blink of an eye for fear of further change orders to their agreement.

The food was passed around, and conversation ensued. Nobody discussed the events of the day, which had been commonplace in the past. Rather, storytelling seemed to be the topic of interest.

Emma asked, "Asher, during the production of *Blue Bloods*, you were primarily involved in the Sunday dinners, am I right?"

Asher had a mouth full of green beans but was able to nod and grunt out an uh-hum.

"Did you ever write a Thanksgiving dinner?"

Asher finished chewing and wiped his mouth with a sliver of paper towel, a luxury reserved for a special occasion like this one.

"You know, believe it or not, on a show known for the meal gatherings and willingness to allow Christian traditions to be portrayed, there has only been one Thanksgiving dinner. Well, sort of, anyway."

"What do you mean?" asked Emma.

"At the time, I was relatively new to the show and still trying to determine what my level of influence was over the series. After season one, a Thanksgiving special episode was discussed. The producers were adamant that it should be a plot that was outside the box, so I came up with an idea.

"The rest of the writers created the police procedurals aspect of the show. In that case, it was an investigation into whether a death was a murder or a suicide. Also, Erin had a new boyfriend who wasn't who he appeared."

John interrupted him. "How can you remember all of these details?"

Lauren laughed. "He has a younger wife to remind him."

Asher blushed and kissed his wife on the cheek. "Well, I have to, John. You see, we have, um, had a rabid fanbase who dissected every episode. If we repeated an investigation or subplot, they'd hammer us on social media. It was important for me not to repeat themes or dialogue."

"Was that the only Thanksgiving episode?" asked Jenna from the other table. "I'm sorry, but I never watched the show."

"That's okay," began Asher in his reply. "Yes, and here's what happened. Henry Reagan, the family patriarch much like Grandpa Sam is to the Cubbisons, was preparing Thanksgiving dinner when he suffered a heart attack. He was rushed to the hospital, where he had a brief stay in intensive care.

"Viewers loved Henry, so I had to give him a sense of humor and have him stay true to his role of family patriarch. When he woke up, the first thing he asked about was whether he could still have

Thanksgiving dinner with the family. This was a signal to the audience that he was gonna be okay.

"As the show progressed, the Reagan family was notified one by one and were advised that Henry would have to remain in the hospital through the Thanksgiving weekend. Undeterred, the family prepared a feast and brought it to the hospital cafeteria so they could have Thanksgiving dinner together."

John dropped his chin to his chest and tried to choke back his emotions. He tried to put out of his mind the subtle, unintentional reference to his father being similar to the fictional Henry Reagan. If something like that happened, the fictional Henry had access to a hospital. His father did not.

The family finished their dinner and complimented the cooks repeatedly. Cat let out a belch, and several others followed suit. The laughter was followed by a dessert of apple cobbler that Emma had canned for sale in the market.

After the dishes were cleaned and put away, the family gathered outside to watch the sunset. They retrieved rocking chairs and picnic tables from where special events had been held. It was resolved by family declaration that they'd start taking more meals outside as the weather got cooler.

As the conversation waned, Vida spoke to the group. "Please forgive me. But, um, I know nothing about Thanksgiving. My father refused to let me learn the American way of life. I am an American now, and I want to know everything."

Silence fell across the group as they contemplated Vida's request. They'd had the closest thing to a traditional Thanksgiving celebration they could, and one of the attendees knew nothing about why.

CHAPTER TWELVE

Monday
Cubbison's Farm
Harford, Pennsylvania

Emma leapt off the picnic bench and rushed to sit next to Vida, who'd remained joined at the hip to Luke. Emma felt genuinely sorry and guilty for not considering Vida's Afghan upbringing and relative newness to the American way of life.

"Oh, Vida, I'm so sorry. I just got caught up in the moment and didn't think—" Her voice trailed off as her eyes welled up with tears. It had been an emotional day for her, and Vida's revelation seemed to trigger Emma's feelings.

"It's okay. Everyone was having so much fun. I guess I just have this need to know."

Grandpa Sam stood and wandered about the group as he spoke. "Well, maybe I can help. Now, I may be the oldest, but I'm a ways off from the Pilgrims."

Everyone laughed, but Vida was still in the dark as to his meaning. She provided some background into what she'd experienced before leaving Afghanistan.

"We have a similar tradition called Shab-e-yalda, which celebrates the longest night of winter. It's a time for family gatherings, big meals and storytelling."

"Kinda like what we did today?" asked Luke as he nuzzled a little closer to Vida.

"Yes. Our celebration is observed at the winter solstice. Many refer to it as the night of the forty, which represents the first forty days of winter. It's the toughest period of the year for many Afghans who don't have heat sources. It's a symbol of the resilience and perseverance of our ancestors."

Sam shoved his hands into his pockets and smiled. "Well, our Thanksgiving is not that much different other than the time of year and the history behind the traditional holiday. Do you wanna hear about it?"

Vida nodded, but it was three children who voiced their approval, led by Cat, who enjoyed listening to Grandpa Sam.

"Yes, please!"

"I love stories," said Jewel, the youngest of Jenna's daughters.

Sam was happy to oblige. "Thanksgiving in America was a time to celebrate the good fortune of the fall harvest and to give thanks to God for our health and safety. Certainly, other ancient cultures celebrated the harvest. Egyptians, Greeks, and Romans had comparable celebrations. Even before the Pilgrims landed at Plymouth Rock four hundred years ago, the Indians held large feasts in honor of their crop harvests.

"One of the most famous Pilgrims aboard the Mayflower, William Bradford, kept a detailed diary of the early Thanksgiving celebration in the New World. Bradford invited the local Indian tribe to join them in celebration. Around a hundred of the natives joined fifty Pilgrims for a massive feast coupled with contests and games.

"That first feast, the earliest Thanksgiving, was far different from what the Pilgrims found when they'd arrived in the New World the year before. Half of them died of disease and starvation. By the time spring came, the numbers were greatly reduced, and those who survived the harsh Massachusetts winter were barely alive.

"The Indians had assisted them by helping them plant corn and other crops. They showed them how to hunt beaver and fish for cod. The community survived, and as a result, the first Thanksgiving became a celebration of their accomplishments and an opportunity to thank God for their blessings."

Vida smiled. "Thank you. Our cultures share a common tradition for all the same reasons. They are simply celebrated on different days of the year."

Emma added, "My guess is that there are many things we have in common even if our religious beliefs differ. I look forward to learning from you, as I hope you'll learn from us."

"I agree," said Luke cheerily. He was pleased his family was engaging Vida so intimately. He really liked her and wanted their relationship to continue.

Everyone began talking among themselves as the sun, ablaze in an orangish glow, sank below the horizon. The rainstorm John had predicted never materialized.

Emma approached Vida and gently placed her hand on her back. She leaned in to speak to her. "Will you take a walk with me?"

"Um, okay," she replied. The trepidation in her voice was not unexpected. "Is everything all right?"

Emma smiled and wrapped her arm around the young woman's shoulders, pulling her close. "Absolutely. It's just, um, well, I need to talk to you about Luke."

"I like him very much," Vida blurted out as if she was aware of where the conversation was going. She had never been allowed to date boys in her community; however, she imagined her father would've spoken to her suitors in a similar manner.

"I can see that, and he's certainly smitten with you as well," said

Emma. "Vida, I don't want this to be an awkward conversation. I hope you understand that I'm a mother who loves her kids very much."

Vida swallowed hard before she spoke. "My mother was very similar to you. Yet she was held back by my father and the ways of Afghan men. Women are treated poorly in my culture. Luke was the first boy, um, man who treated me with respect and—"

She stopped and became emotional. Emma reached out and took her hand to support her. "What is it, Vida?"

Embarrassed, she wiped away the tears with her free hand and laughed at herself. "Adoration," she finished her thought. "Luke adores me. He puts me on a pedestal. He doesn't treat me as if he owns me. Or that I owe him something. He has always been a gentleman. It's so much different from my old world."

Emma hesitated for a brief moment. She hated taking advantage of Vida's emotional state. However, the young woman had let her guard down, and perhaps now was the time to pry open the steel doors that blocked her inner thoughts from the rest of the group.

"Vida, you used the phrase *my old world*. Is it? I mean, are you truly prepared to leave your family and community behind to live with us?"

Vida nodded and sheepishly kicked at the gravel of the driveway. "Emma, my mother could not protect me. And my father would've followed the way of our community, not that this matters anymore."

"Because you've left them for good?" asked Emma.

"Yes, and because my father is dead. I believe Matthew killed him."

Emma was stunned. "What are you talking about?" Her tone of voice had changed, and Vida immediately picked up on it.

"This morning, after the men were killed, the soldiers were talking with Grandpa Sam about the car. You know, the GTO."

"What about it?" asked Emma, who'd adopted an interrogation tone.

"It belonged to my father."

Emma allowed the words to sink in for a moment. If it was Vida's father behind the wheel of the GTO the night of the altercation at Picatinny Arsenal, then it was likely Matthew had unknowingly shot and killed him.

An awkward silence had fallen over them. Emma wasn't sure what to say other than to defend her son.

"Matthew had no idea."

Vida nodded and provided Emma a reassuring smile that could barely be seen in the coming darkness. "I know this. When I first heard the conversation, I was stunned and unable to keep my composure. That's why I went inside so suddenly. I went into Luke's bedroom to comfort myself, and I even cried for a moment. Then I remembered why I ran away to begin with.

"He beat my mother. He allowed my uncle to rape her as well. He would soon condemn me to the same fate. That's why I left and vowed never to return.

"As soon as I calmed myself, Luke came in. He was loving. Gentle. He consoled me and reassured me without having any idea what was in my mind. That's when I knew I had found someone to share my life with." She paused and turned to Emma.

"Please do not doubt me. I will never go back there. My life is here, with Luke, and you. If you'll allow me to stay."

Emma took Vida in her arms and held her close. The two shared a moment, but Emma's mind wandered. Matthew had killed her father. The dynamic between Vida and the Cubbison family became much more complicated now.

CHAPTER THIRTEEN

Monday
Kula Sandalwoods Inn
Island of Maui, Hawaii

In the nine days that Tatsuki Goto and his entourage had taken up residency at the Kula Sandalwoods, they'd swept across that part of Maui like locusts devouring the soft leaves of a fruit orchard. They were patient, and they had a plan.

Most importantly, they needed a base of operations that was far away from the population centers of Kahului and Wailuku. Their archenemy, the Company, had a stronghold in Kahului. His contingent was too small to take them head-on. The boutique café and inn in the center of the island fit the bill.

There were numerous cabins to assign to his foot soldiers, and his top lieutenants could occupy the main house. Because it was perched atop a hill overlooking the western, more populated areas of Maui, as well as the highway below, he and his men could stand guard to fend off law enforcement or the island's criminal element.

The inn's vast property on the hillside provided ample storage for their ill-gotten gains. Immediately following the solar storm, Goto realized the new currency would not be American dollars and especially not cryptocurrency. Gasoline, food, guns and ammunition would be highly sought after. Not to mention the illicit drugs for the addicts and pharmaceuticals for the infirm.

Their initial foray into the island's resources was highly successful. The more rural parts of Maui located to the eastern part of the island provided little in the way of interest. Any homeowner who dared raise a weapon to his soldiers were dealt with swiftly, and their weapon was added to Goto's arsenal.

Vehicles across the Hawaiian Islands continued to operate, as they were unaffected by the electromagnetic pulse generated by the solar storm. Gas, however, was a precious commodity. Upon arrival on Maui, Goto commandeered a variety of vehicles ranging from fuel-efficient motor scooters to his so-called battle vehicles, large pickups. Every empty fuel can was taken and filled with gasoline siphoned from any available source.

His soldiers operating the scooters were dubbed the *makika*—the Hawaiian word for mosquitos or stinging flies. They would swarm into a neighborhood and terrorize its occupants. While men and children were openly held at gunpoint, the Yakuza would force the women to turn over their food and supplies. If anyone challenged the *makika*, they'd be beaten, and they'd witness their loved ones being brutally murdered.

Goto also recruited new soldiers into his new Yakuza gang. There were initiation procedures, the most important of which was leading Goto to something of great value. Then they'd have to commit an act of murder to prove they were capable of brutality. Even then, because he'd been betrayed before, the new recruits were kept at arm's length, which had always been the way of the Yakuza.

Goto was getting settled into his war on Maui. However, even after a short time, he was growing weary of his accommodations at the Kula Sandalwoods. The Yakuza leaders of old, located on Waikiki, were known to commandeer the most lavish properties for themselves. Luxury homes on Maui were often clustered together and provided little protection. Goto had once quipped that the *haole* mansions were perfect for his *makika* raids; however, he wouldn't want to live there.

That afternoon, while he was wandering the grounds, assessing his vehicle inventory, he considered an outside-the-box alternative to a traditional residence. One that, despite its unique attributes, would be befitting someone of his stature. He would be king of the hill, insulated from the mayhem that ensued daily across the island.

Perched high above the island to the east behind the Kula Sandalwoods, the Haleakala Observatory stood like a castle on a mountain. One fit for the new king of Maui.

PART 2

———

Tuesday
Change is hard, then messy, but courageous.

CHAPTER FOURTEEN

Tuesday
Kula Sandalwoods
Maui, Hawaii

Morning came much too quickly for Goto as gunshots near the Sandalwoods compound rang out just after sunrise. He pushed the woman, a local seeking protection, off his muscular body and rushed to get dressed. He was still slipping on his shirt with one hand and gripped his Kel-Tec PLR-16 in the other. The pistol-sized weapon, a version of an AR-15, used the same ammunition as its larger counterpart. It was easily hidden and was ideal for the type of close-quarters combat Goto experienced on the streets.

The moment he entered the lobby, he shouted, "Where's that coming from?"

"We're on it, Boa!" exclaimed one of his lieutenants. His closest associates often referred to him by the Hawaiian word for warrior.

Several men rushed past Goto and took up positions outside the door. Seconds later, the high-pitched whir of the scooters could be heard behind the main house, tearing down the driveway and onto the highway in the direction of the gunfire.

Several more shots rang out, and then a car horn began blaring incessantly. Goto walked onto the veranda overlooking the western side of Maui. Everything appeared still, and the gunfire ceased. He walked down the grassy slope to get a better look at the highway. A bright reflection caught his eye, causing him to spin around and look toward the sun rising in the east. It had reflected off the shiny dome of the massive Inouye Solar Telescope. He'd never noticed the reflections before and considered it a sign to act on his thoughts from the day before.

The sounds of the scooters and a large truck heading toward the resort brought his attention back to the highway. He raised the PLR-15 to his belly, prepared to engage anyone who dared attack them. He was pleased to see his men leading a liquor truck toward him. The blood dripping off the truck's door instantly revealed the fate of its driver. The smiles on his men's faces reflected their jubilant mood at scoring a truckload of alcohol.

Goto didn't share in their enthusiasm. Too much liquor could be a problem within the compound. Despite their early successes in sweeping across east and central Maui, basically having their way with the citizenry, Goto was keenly aware a small contingent of Hawaii National Guard forces were patrolling the cities beyond. If his men were too bold, they might bring the heat upon their somewhat vulnerable location.

He turned to his lieutenants. "Secure the cargo. Promise them a luau tonight after the day's work is done. Also, prepare a truck with three of the men. We're going on a drive."

"Where to, Boa?" his top man asked.

Goto lowered his weapon and walked toward the east, squinting his eyes to make out the silhouette of the observatory. Then he turned to address his subordinate.

"First, I want to drive into Kihei. The properties along Maalaea Bay are our next targets." He paused and looked to the top of

Haleakala again. He pointed his rifle barrel toward the summit. "After that, I want to go up there."

"Um, the only thing up there is the observatory and maybe some park ranger buildings."

Goto smiled. "Exactly."

CHAPTER FIFTEEN

Tuesday
Haleakala Observatory
Maui, Hawaii

At Haleakala, Professor Neal Burgoyne felt on top of the world. The ten-thousand-foot peak was the highest on Maui and afforded him a view across the entire Hawaiian Island chain. In a few spots, with a small, portable telescope, he could catch a glimpse of Kahului. At night, he found the once vibrant medium-size city to appear increasingly dark. Fires were more prevalent. Vehicular traffic was almost nonexistent. During the day, he could barely make out pedestrian traffic. It was if the city was dying day by day.

"Yang! Up and at 'em. I'm going on an excursion, if you'd like to join me."

The insolent cat made no movement from his perch atop a cushioned chair sitting in the corner of Burgoyne's one-room apartment. He didn't really expect Yang to join his planned adventure toward the bottom of the mountain; however, he felt compelled to ask.

Despite the infamous tantrums Yang would throw when Burgoyne left, the cat seemed to live by the axiom *there's no place like home.*

Burgoyne fed Yang and loaded his backpack for a planned day away from the observatory. Hiking boots, extra water bottles, binoculars, a small first aid kit, and a handgun given to him by one of his students would supplement a few energy bars out of the group's food supplies.

Since his return from New York, Burgoyne had lost a substantial amount of weight. By his own estimate, since there wasn't a scale anywhere on the premises, he was down ten pounds or more. "You can always tell in your clothes," he'd said to himself one morning when he tightened the belt on his khakis another notch or two.

His family used to make fun of him for storing away smaller sizes of his favorite clothing when he began to gain weight over the years. He vowed to drop a few pounds in order to wear them, but the anticipated weight loss never happened. When he moved to Hawaii, he thought he'd force himself to reduce the size of his waistline because he didn't want to embarrass himself at the beach. However, his busy life atop Haleakala didn't allow for much beach time, and his love of Hawaiian cuisine only added inches to his belly. Now he'd apparently given back all that he'd gained and then some.

His reason for cutting back on his share of the food rations was out of concern for his students and assistants who'd followed his advice and remained at the observatory. Late one evening after most of the young people had turned in for bed, he and Baxter had entered a storage room turned into a food pantry. They'd studied the clipboard that was used to keep track of their supplies and daily consumption. Their assessment was grim. Burgoyne expected them to run out of food within two or three weeks.

What troubled him most about this was his miscalculation concerning Hawaii's ability to weather the catastrophic event. He knew the islands relied heavily on products delivered from the U.S. mainland and countries in South America. He was shocked how quickly the ships would stop delivering. South America was unaffected by the solar storm's impact. However, each of the countries hunkered down to protect their own citizens and stopped exporting foodstuffs to other nations.

The Hawaiian Islands were known for growing sugarcane and pineapple, moneymakers for large plantations, to be sure. However, they were of little nutritional value. There were some local farms that grew fruits and vegetables to be sold in island grocery stores, but not near enough to feed the population. Greenhouses were filled with papayas, macadamia nuts, and coffee, mostly for export purposes.

Years ago, Hawaii could've sustained its entire population with its rice growers. However, the antiquated techniques of utilizing hand labor could not compete with California's mechanized production technology.

While both Burgoyne and Baxter reached the same conclusion, neither had a ready solution that didn't involve risking the lives of the observatory's refugees. Rather than join the growing number of looters and profiteers across Maui, they chose to hunker down in the days and weeks following the collapse. Both Burgoyne and Baxter agreed, adding to their food supplies would most likely require the use of weapons. And loss of life.

He entered the observatory and made his way to the cafeteria. Everyone was awake and quietly munching on a meal of eggs and rice. He was immediately offered a bowl and politely declined. He'd make do with a protein bar.

Baxter approached him and whispered in his ear, "The patrols didn't see anything out of the ordinary. I instructed the day shift we'd make our way down to the park headquarters."

The park headquarters and visitors' center were approximately ten miles down the mountain. In the weeks since the group had holed up at the summit of Haleakala, none of them had taken the time to explore the complex in search of supplies. This would be the group's first, albeit safe, foray into scavenging for survival.

"I need to fill these water bottles and grab a couple of protein bars; then we'll head out," said Burgoyne as he slid the backpack off his shoulder.

"Let me, sir," said Baxter. "Um, nobody knows we're leaving for the day. What do you want me to tell them?"

"I'll take care of it." Burgoyne turned over his backpack to Baxter and wandered into the middle of the small cafeteria. He cleared his throat loudly to garner their attention.

"Everyone, would you mind listening up for a moment?" He paused to allow everyone to finish eating and turn toward him. A few of the students wished him a good morning. He managed a smile. He hoped it would be.

"Okay. Thanks. Baxter and I are going to head out for the day. Our first stop will be the park administration offices and the visitor center. Honestly, I feel bad that I haven't personally started these trips into the community sooner.

"As you all know, we send out scouts from time to time to gauge what life is like in the neighborhoods and small towns that surround Haleakala. Lately, the reports haven't been so good. The islanders are suffering from lack of food supplies and medical attention. Plus, not unexpectedly, there has been a criminal element that has taken up residency in the area."

Their concerned voices rose to a crescendo as they fired questions at Burgoyne, and their eyes sought out the scouts, who clearly had held back some information from the group.

"Whadya mean?"

"What kind of criminals? Thieves? Killers?"

"Do you think they'll come up here?"

"Do they have guns?"

All valid questions, and Burgoyne would have to speculate to provide answers. Instead, he quickly tried to assuage their concerns in order to keep them calm. Now was not the time to panic.

"These are the types of questions we intend to get answers to over the next several days," he began. "After we determine whether the park headquarters has any useful supplies for us, I want to examine ways to set up a series of roadblocks restricting access to the summit.

"Here's the thing. A roadblock is nothing more than a deterrent. Criminals tend to follow the path of least resistance. A burglar will avoid a home with a fence, motion lights, and a barking dog on the property. There are easier houses to rob. I hope the same will be true of the road leading up to the observatory."

One of his students interrupted him. "It's twenty miles to the bottom. Why would they even bother?"

Burgoyne shrugged. He'd asked himself that same question over the last several weeks. Curiosity was the only logical answer. Nonetheless, the curious can be a threat, too.

"Well, I don't know. However, I'd like to give them plenty of opportunities to turn around and go back down. That's part of what I have planned for today."

A young woman raised her hand. "Professor, if we block others from coming up, aren't we basically preventing ourselves from going down? I mean, um, you know, to get food and stuff."

Burgoyne, Baxter and a few trusted graduate assistants had access to the food supplies. He wanted to believe they were tight lipped. However, the students were all bright and had to be aware their supplies were dwindling. As evidence of their supposition, they'd all commented on Burgoyne's rapid weight loss. People don't stay chubby during the apocalypse unless they have a lot of food stashed.

Burgoyne nodded as he spoke. "These are all considerations that I'll have in mind as I assess our options. Like I said, today is the first of a series of scavenging trips I plan to lead. Step one is to secure our mountain. Step two will be to restock our pantry."

"We trust you, Professor," said a voice from the back of the room. "What can we do to help?"

Burgoyne studied the faces of his charges. None of them had lost faith in his leadership. That time could come in short order if they get overrun by criminals or if they run out of food. For now, his promises to keep them safe would have to do.

"Carry on with your usual duties," he replied. "Those of you assigned to moving the rock barriers to the entrance of the parking lot, see if you can recruit some help to speed up the process. Stack them into a double row if possible. The width of the entryway only needs to be the size of our pickup trucks."

"Yes, sir."

Baxter returned from the storeroom and handed Burgoyne his backpack. Before he left, he provided one more admonition to the group. "It's very important for all of you to have a keen sense of awareness as you go about your duties. Keep your eyes on the road and trails leading to the observatory. Take nothing for granted. Got it?"

"Yes, sir!"

Burgoyne made eye contact with several of the students and smiled. Regardless of what their immediate future brought, he was certain they'd give it their best.

CHAPTER SIXTEEN

Tuesday
Cubbison's Farm
Harford, Pennsylvania

"Okay, demo is done," said John as he stepped away and surveyed the pile of destroyed wood siding, broken glass, and window casings. The first rainfall they'd experienced in weeks had finally dissipated, enabling John to put his construction crew to work. Everyone except Lauren and Emma were involved. Emma couldn't bear to watch the family home taken apart, so Lauren invited her to patrol the perimeter with her.

"What's the plan for all this, Dad?" asked Luke. He and his brother had undertaken the most dangerous duties, which involved climbing extension ladders to remove Dutch lap siding from the second floor. Asher had handled the lower level by himself while Sam and John removed the windows, working from the inside. Vida had volunteered to tote debris to the pile.

"Grandpa Sam and I talked about it. We might as well utilize the trail to the Stanley place. We'll start a burn pile where the fire has already ruined the ground. And, because that house was built at around the same time as ours, it'll serve as our lumber supply."

"You can't get more efficient than that, right?" asked Sam rhetorically.

Asher studied the sky. While the sun had displaced the rain clouds, he noticed more white clouds forming to the west.

"Whadya think, John? Do we have a few hours?"

"Hopefully," he replied. "I think we should focus on pulling the siding off the addition at the back of Stanley's house. It most likely has some type of sheathing under the siding. We'll strip the addition down to the studs. Then we'll nail on the siding to fill our gaps and use the sheathing to cover the window openings."

"Why don't we just pull out Stanley's windows today?" asked Matthew.

Sam walked up to Matthew and put his arm around his shoulder. "Your dad and I might be able to extract a few windows today. However, removing them to use as replacements will be far more time-consuming than tearing out the broken ones like ours."

The group worked together to load the construction debris into the back of the horse-drawn trailer. They used hammers to back out any nails that hadn't been bent during the demolition process.

The Cubbisons were like most homeowners when it came to building supplies. When a project arose, they'd go to the local hardware or home improvement store to buy what they needed. The Ace Hardware and lumber supply was on the other side of Harford, making it far too dangerous and costly to scavenge for a box of nails or lumber. Their approach was more labor intensive, but it prevented them from exposing themselves to possible trouble away from the farm.

An hour later, the wagon was unloaded, and everyone began the process of dismantling the addition to the Stanley home that had been built just twenty years ago or so. John asked Matthew to work with him on the window extraction while Sam supervised the meticulous deconstruction of the addition. After his conversation with Emma about Vida, John decided to probe Matthew to determine what he might know about the girl.

"It seems your brother and Vida have become very close," he said in a way that encouraged Matthew to weigh in on the subject. As they spoke, John used a flat pry bar to remove the interior trim from a window, which provided them access to the wood casement.

"For sure," said Matthew as he tossed aside the wood trim. He readied the DeWalt cordless reciprocating saw, commonly referred to as a Sawzall. The power tool's blade would jut in and out, causing a sawing motion. The tool came with interchangeable blades capable of cutting through wood and nails. "They're never apart."

John chuckled. "Have you heard Luke say the L-word?"

"No, Dad. Geez. I mean, who knows? I haven't even seen them kiss each other. Who knows? They're always patrolling together, so they could be in the pasture somewhere making out."

John was embarrassed at having asked the question. He could've made that assumption for himself.

"They seem inseparable, so I know there is something between them," he said before pausing for a moment. He took the Sawzall from Matthew and began cutting through the nails that held the window frame to the surrounding studs. When the last nail was detached from the wall, the window shifted slightly, indicating it was ready to be removed.

He continued, "How do you feel about her? Do you think she'll fit in as part of our family?"

"Yeah, I think so. She hasn't done anything that might cause me to dislike her or even not trust her. She's quiet. She seems to want to pitch in. And from what I saw, she was very helpful during the attack the other night."

John couldn't disagree with any of those statements. He needed Matthew, of all people, to be comfortable with Vida. He was most at risk of her deciding to take revenge against the family for her father's death.

The two worked together to remove the window and set it to the side. They moved to the next bedroom and started on another. John thought about Vida's behavior since the moment she'd learned it was Matthew who killed her father. He tried to recall anything unusual in her demeanor or attitude toward his family. Especially toward Matthew. Based on their interaction during the special dinner Emma had made as well as her assistance today, he would've never known that she was aware of who killed her father.

He asked Matthew, "What about since the attack? Any change in her attitude or the way she treats any of us?"

Matthew thought for a moment before responding, "No, um, not at all. Dad, what's this all about?"

"Nothing, son. Really. It's just that your mom and I are trying to look to the future. We wanna believe all of this fighting-for-our-lives crap has passed. That means allowing the newcomers into our family, whether as friends or, possibly, a lot more in the case of Luke and Vida."

"Well, if you're talking near future, I haven't overheard any talk of love, marriage, or babies in a carriage. Long term, who knows? Dad, the way things have been going, I wonder if we'll even have a long term."

His comment struck John as odd. It was somewhat fatalistic that his teenage son would discuss the end of their lives before that proverbial ripe old age, whatever that looked like.

"That's kinda pessimistic, isn't it?"

"Realistic, Dad. I believe there'll be more groups trying to take what we have. They may not be as large or organized as the bikers. They might be better armed and well trained. Things could've gone much differently the other day if Fred and the other guys didn't show up. Sure, we might've won the battle, but some of us would've died. I don't know how I could live with that."

John gulped. It saddened him that his teenage son thought this way. Then he reminded himself he and Matthew had been side by side throughout the trip to New York and then during the attack on their farm. All of these events had occurred in the first several weeks of the collapse. Odds were high that armed conflict with marauders would happen again.

And again. And again.

CHAPTER SEVENTEEN

Tuesday
Cubbison's Farm
Harford, Pennsylvania

Emma and Lauren rode the perimeter in a hub-and-spoke pattern. They'd ride away from the main house, patrol a half mile of fence line, and then return to the house located near the center of the farm. The next trip out might be in the opposite direction to view another section of the property. The idea was to take a haphazard approach to the surveillance while always maintaining a constant eye on the main buildings and their supplies.

Emma and Lauren had become close throughout the ordeal, almost like sisters. Naturally, Emma appreciated the Doyles' heroics and sacrifice as they'd protected Cat in New York. Lauren had saved Sam's life by returning for him after everyone had become separated. A bond had formed between them, and Emma trusted Lauren implicitly.

They'd patrolled for over an hour before Emma worked up the courage to broach the subject of Vida and the death of her father.

"Lauren, I've got to talk to you about something that is only known to John and myself. Naturally, you can discuss it with Asher. We need you to be very careful about, well, um, let me explain."

"Gosh, Emma. What is it? Is everything okay?"

Emma let out a deep sigh and stopped her horse. They were near the eastern fence line where the bikers led by the pyromaniac nicknamed Blaze had entered their farm. Had he not been stopped, the entire family would have died as their house burned. Being that close to death created strong bonds between relative strangers. She shifted in her saddle and explained.

"When all of you ran into trouble at the arsenal that night, Matthew shot the driver of that Pontiac you brought back to the farm. That car, as it turns out, was being driven by Vida's father."

"Oh no!" exclaimed Lauren as her body tensed. Her reaction caused her horse to become skittish. For a moment, she struggled to calm the horse. "Wait, how would she know this?"

In response, Emma relayed the part of the conversation between Sam and Fred Stewart that Lauren wasn't aware of.

Lauren nodded as she added, "That explains Vida's sudden emotional crash. We thought she'd just gotten caught up in the moment. In reality, it was the realization her father was probably driving that car and his killer was Matthew."

"That's right. Naturally, John and I are concerned about what's gonna happen next, if anything."

"Have you talked to her about it?" asked Lauren.

"I have, and her attitude was basically that her father had it coming to him. If not by Matthew, then by her or her mother."

"Do you believe her?"

"I want to, Lauren. I really do. Yet people have time to calm down and think things through and maybe act impulsively. I don't want my son to die because I didn't do the right thing."

Lauren glanced toward the west and noticed the skies darkening. Rain might be coming for a second night in a row. She pointed in that direction, and Emma nodded. They began riding back to the house.

"Well, let me say this. Both prior to the attack and afterwards, I haven't seen any indication from Vida that she's homesick or cares one iota about her father. I do believe she loves her mom very much and probably would like to be reunited with her at some point. However, not back at the compound and under those circumstances."

"I appreciate your opinion. I actually feel the same way. My protective nature puts me on guard, that's all."

Lauren reached out to take Emma's hand. She provided her a knowing smile. "I'll keep my eyes and ears open. If I see anything unusual from her, or even Luke, I'll come to you immediately. Those two have a romance of some kind. It might be a teen crush on one another or something more. They don't appear to be physically lovey-dovey in a PDA sort of way."

Emma smiled. She hadn't noticed any overt public displays of affection between the two, either. Perhaps Luke was respecting Vida because of her experiences as a young Afghan woman and the abuses they typically suffered. She loved her son for his restraint and obvious respect for Vida.

She wanted to feel better about the situation, and Lauren seemed to help her. Yet it would be some time before she'd not think about reaching for her pistol in the event Vida made a threatening move toward Matthew.

CHAPTER EIGHTEEN

Tuesday
Haleakala Park Headquarters
Maui, Hawaii

Baxter wheeled the car into the parking lot of the park headquarters, where the scout team, consisting of three men and a woman, greeted them nonchalantly as if they were about to hike the trails together. None of them were carrying their weapons or appeared to be concerned about their surroundings. Burgoyne would take the time later to remind them the world had changed and was much more dangerous.

Burgoyne exited the vehicle first and addressed the group. He didn't want to break their spirit. However, leadership required being tough on his people from time to time for their own good.

"Hey, Professor," one of them greeted him casually. "We just got here, too."

Burgoyne nodded, his eyes darting around the parking lot and the building within view. "Well, I'm glad that guy over there with a rifle didn't shoot you," he said sarcastically.

They all spun around in the direction of the administration building located behind the visitors' center. One of the men pulled his pistol and pointed toward the entrance before swinging it wildly toward the windows.

"Where? Where is he?"

Burgoyne shook his head in disbelief. Keeping these young people alive was going to be a challenge. It was also a reminder that armed conflict with looters or desperate refugees needed to be avoided. His soldiers were anything but.

"Guys, do I have to remind you that there are people with guns out here and no law enforcement to protect you? You always have to assume that someone might be hiding out in any building you approach. Remember, first you clear, and then you explore. Right?"

Dejected, the foursome agreed. The unarmed scouts hustled off to their pickup and grabbed their weapons. Under Burgoyne's direction, they fanned out to clear the compound, which was far more extensive than he realized. In all his years at the observatory, he never realized that there were so many other buildings making up the park headquarters. Storage sheds, residences, and garages were scattered about behind the two buildings visible to the public parking area.

"Let's start with the cars. Make sure they're empty. Don't bother going through them now. We'll have time for that later."

The group of six methodically approached one vehicle after another, looking inside windows and open doors. Burgoyne found it odd that so many vehicles had been abandoned.

"Where'd they go?" he asked aloud as he and Baxter inspected the last car.

"Hiking, I guess? It's strange they didn't return to get their cars, though."

Burgoyne scowled. *Very strange.* It caused him to conclude they were holed up in the buildings somewhere. Probably scared and hungry. Therefore, dangerous.

"This way," he instructed, pointing toward the visitors' center. "I

BOBBY AKART

need someone to guard the exits while Baxter and I enter through the front door."

"We noticed it had been broken into when we arrived," said one of the scouts.

Burgoyne nodded. It was possible the compound had already been picked over, but it was worth a look.

They entered through the glass doors, stepping through the aluminum frame. Shards of glass broke under their feet as they moved into the darkness.

"Lights don't work," said Baxter as she flipped the switches on the wall several times.

"Damn. I didn't think about a flashlight."

Without the benefit of the sun's warmth, Burgoyne shivered in the dark building. Daytime temperatures at Haleakala averaged in the low fifties at that time of year. At night, they dropped to around thirty-six. However, in the last couple of weeks, several nights were below freezing.

Baxter bumped into Burgoyne in the dimly lit conditions, startling the professor. He abruptly stepped forward and tripped over a toppled chair. Burgoyne landed hard on the concrete floor, moaning in pain as his knees took the brunt of the impact.

"Sorry, sir. I guess I'm a little on edge."

Burgoyne pulled himself onto his feet. The commotion could've easily been heard by anyone hiding in the building, so he took a chance. He gripped his weapon.

"Hello? Is anyone here? I'm Professor Burgoyne. We mean you no harm. We're, um, just looking to help survivors."

He held his breath and listened for any type of response whether verbal or the sound of movement.

Nothing. So he tried again. Louder this time. The result was the same.

He turned to Baxter. "See if anyone has a flashlight or even a lighter. Worst case is we'll create a torch of some kind."

Baxter left, and Burgoyne took a calculated risk based on the

82

lack of response he'd received. Using the outside wall of the window-less space, he moved past the informational vignette located near the doors. The entry hallways were broken up by displays and seating areas. There were two small offices at the sides of the building, filled with simple tables and chairs. A bathroom was the only other confined space. All were empty with no signs of looting other than the broken glass at the front door.

Baxter returned with a lighter. He illuminated the space, and Burgoyne was able to confirm what his cursory search had indicated. There was no evidence of looting.

His hopes of finding useful supplies rose on their discovery although the fate of the visitors whose cars dotted the parking lot still nagged at him. With a final look around, he and Baxter exited through the front doors and gathered the rest of their team.

With caution, they approached the administration building, a structure that resembled a small residence. Burgoyne chuckled as he compared the two structures. Visitors were treated to a simple, rectangular building with no windows. The park administrators' offices were reminiscent of an upscale neighborhood.

He stopped the entourage just short of the pathway leading to the solid wood door entry. He studied all the windows in search of movement or a prior breach. Everything looked secure except the curtains or blinds were all closed. This concerned Burgoyne. Perhaps this was where the owners of the vehicles were hiding out.

He turned to his group. "Everyone, fan out around the building. Look for movement, broken windows, or breached doors. Anything that might be out of the ordinary. Then circle back to here."

The scouts nodded and hustled off to surveil the perimeter. Baxter remained with Burgoyne, who was anxious to approach the building but resisted the impulse. He needed to be patient in order to avoid making a mistake.

Minutes later, the four scouts returned and reported the same thing. No activity. No evidence of a break-in. Curtains and blinds closed.

Despite the cool temperatures, beads of perspiration appeared on Burgoyne's forehead. For a reason he couldn't put his finger on, entering the administration building was more dangerous than the visitors' center. Regardless, it had to be done. He turned to Baxter.

"Are you ready to do this again?"

The brave graduate assistant nodded. "I have the lighter, but I think we'll have more ambient light through all these windows."

Burgoyne agreed and turned to the others. "Okay, same routine. I want one of you posted on every side of the building. If you see movement in the windows or someone leaving, shout out your location so we know. And, all of you, don't shoot unless fired upon. Baxter and I might come through an exit, and we'd rather you not plug us with a bullet. Fair enough?"

"Yes, sir."

Burgoyne looked into Baxter's eyes to assess her readiness to enter the unknown once again. With a nod in response, the two walked shoulder to shoulder toward the front doors and tried the knobs.

They were locked. Burgoyne stepped back and studied their options. There were two plate-glass windows on either side of the doors that, if broken, allowed them sufficient space to slide in. For a brief moment, they'd be vulnerable to attack, however.

Baxter seemed to sense the concern, so she came up with a suggestion. "We'll break through the glass at the same time. They can't shoot us both simultaneously, right?"

Burgoyne nervously laughed at her nonchalant approach. Baxter had become the female equivalent of a mini-me of her old professor. He was proud of his protégé.

"Let's roll," he said.

Seconds later, the two heaved softball-sized stones through the plate glass and stuck their heads inside to see what greeted them.

It was death.

CHAPTER NINETEEN

Tuesday
Federal Emergency Management Agency
Region 3 Office
Philadelphia, Pennsylvania

The FEMA regional headquarters in Philadelphia had been bustling with activity following the addition of investigative personnel from the Federal Bureau of Investigation. Offices were packed with temporary seating and tables. Laptop computers were used to access the remaining operable Starlink satellites that provided sparse internet connectivity. Turf wars over jurisdiction were waged, as was often the case.

The president had ordered a full investigation of the bombing that had taken place at the Viewmont Mall a week ago. Officially, the usual marching orders had been issued to the Department of Justice and the Department of Homeland Security. Leave no stone unturned. Find the perpetrators and bring them to justice.

Unofficially, the president's directives used his martial law declaration to suspend the constitutional protections ordinarily afforded

American citizens. In his tirade to the DHS undersecretary assigned to FEMA Region 3, the president demanded in no uncertain terms for the National Guardsmen to kick down doors if they had to. Confiscate operating vehicles that they come across. Forcibly take any weapons when they find them. And, as he put it, if "some smartass says anything about the Second Amendment or spews any *molon labe* garbage, feel free to execute them for treason."

The president had gone off the rails. He was unrestrained by political concerns, as the martial law declaration gave him the power to assert his will over Americans struggling to survive. The bombing provided him the impetus to crack down on his opposition. Years of preparation within the U.S. government provided him the human assets willing to carry out his orders.

John Smith, who went by the first name of Jack, was a longtime Department of Justice employee who handled both legal affairs of the federal government as well as enforcement actions against so-called domestic terrorists. After the perfect storm brought the nation to its knees, the president called upon his ally and political supporter to handle special assignments as events warranted. Until now, he'd been working by the president's side out of the bunker located beneath the East Wing of the White House known as the Presidential Emergency Operations Center, or PEOC.

Smith had led a handpicked team of administrators to Philadelphia to take command of the investigation. Once they'd gathered the facts available from eyewitnesses, they started to follow leads. One of them involved a shootout involving vehicles full of armed men along Interstate 81 north of Scranton.

There were ten exits off the interstate between the mall and the Susquehanna River, which marked the boundary with New York State. To get adequate investigative coverage, he created five squads of guardsmen. Each squad consisted of twenty armed personnel riding in hardened Humvees. They were instructed to move systematically up the highway, taking one exit at a time, in search of the bombers or their accomplices.

Tensions were high as the teams arrived at Exit 201, a rural area with a smattering of farms and elderly residents. The guardsmen showed no mercy as they began their interrogations of the local residents. The owners of the Messimer Dairy Farm suffered the worst fate as they attempted to stand up for their rights. The response was swift and deadly.

All thirteen members of the family, including women and children, were executed. Their dairy cattle were seized as well as their operating machinery. Their immediate neighbors were brought onto the property to witness their execution. They were instructed to advise their neighbors not to resist the guardsmen or they'd suffer the same fate.

News traveled slowly in a post-apocalyptic world and certainly not nearly as fast as the National Guardsmen who swept through Susquehanna County. By the time they reached the Harford exit, many of them had forgotten their purpose. The raids were less about searching for information about the bombers and more about thrusting their boots on the necks of the American people.

Until now, they'd been met with limited resistance, and for those who did, it never ended well. However, this would be their first encounter with Fred Stewart and his close-knit group of ex-Marines.

CHAPTER TWENTY

Tuesday
Haleakala Park Headquarters
Maui, Hawaii

Both Burgoyne and Baxter recoiled from the stench of decaying corpses. Baxter retched uncontrollably in the gravel landscape bed while Burgoyne wandered around in a circle, violently rubbing his nose and looking upward toward the sun.

Two of his graduate students rushed toward them, with their weapons pointing at the entry door. They weren't sure if Burgoyne and Baxter had been poisoned or possibly pepper sprayed. As they drew closer, the putrid smell of over eight hundred chemicals emitted by the decaying corpses escaped into the beautiful Hawaiian day.

"What the hell?" asked one of them as he recoiled away from the evidence.

"God-awful," said another as he pulled his green University of Hawaii sweatshirt over his nose and mouth.

Baxter's stomach had emptied itself of its contents, yet it

continued to convulse from the shock. Burgoyne, who was now on his knees in an attempt to fight back the vomit, ordered his assistants to break out the windows.

"Which ones, Professor?"

"All of them!"

The four scouts moved around the first floor of the two-story structure, breaking out the windows with rocks and the butt end of their rifles. They located a shovel near a small garage and used it to pull open the curtains and tear down the blinds. Soon, a slight breeze was flowing through the downstairs of the park's administration building, carrying the sickening odor of decaying bodies with it.

After several minutes, Burgoyne and Baxter were able to wash the taste out of their mouths with bottled water. They eventually recovered and gathered the courage to look inside once again. What they found shocked their consciences.

Beyond the double wood doors was a large open space, a common area, designed for gatherings of staff and perhaps dignitaries. Large photos adorned the walls of the park's accomplishments and scenic vistas, as well as aerial photos of DKIST.

In the center of the space were several couches, chairs and mattresses, all of which were occupied by more than a dozen bodies in various states of decay. Using the daylight shining through the southern exposure, Burgoyne was able to see the entire room. With half his body stuck through the broken plate-glass window, he was able to slowly look for the cause of their demise.

There was no blood. No indication of a gunfight or a brutal beatdown. Nobody had empty glasses near their bodies as if they'd joined in some type of mass suicide or succumbed to a poison.

Puzzled, he continued to search for answers without actually entering the room. Then he saw the killer. Lifeless. Inanimate. Motionless. Yet it was merely the weapon. The silent killer had long since dissipated.

Carbon monoxide.

Toward the back of the room was a gas-powered generator.

Nearby, several space heaters were plugged into the portable generator. Apparently, the visitors, who'd elected to stay at the park administration complex to stay safe, had grown cold when the buildings
lost their power. They'd used the generator for power and the space
heaters to create a warm environment.

Then, as they slept, they breathed in the carbon monoxide
spewed out by the generator. The high concentration of the poison
replaced the oxygen in their bloodstreams. Within an hour, their
hearts, brains and bodies became starved of precious oxygen. Death
came quickly and silently.

Burgoyne pulled his head back out of the window and turned to
his team. He explained what had happened to the refugees. Then he
asked the tough question that he wasn't sure how he would answer.

"Clearly, they planned on living in this building to survive.
Although we'll need to search the rest of the compound to confirm
this, I presume they brought anything of value to this building." He
paused and glanced inside again. He rolled his head around his neck
and shoulders to relieve some tension.

"Is anyone willing to go in there with me to retrieve food or
supplies of value? If the answer is no, I fully understand. No judgment here, trust me."

Nobody backed out of the task. Baxter slid through the broken
window and unlocked the door. The stench of death had dissipated
somewhat, but everyone used their shirts and sweatshirts to cover
their faces.

A quick glance through the common area revealed nothing of
value to them, not even weapons. The doors to the offices on the first
floor were mostly closed. The group seemed to have compartmental-
ized the administration building by storing like-kind supplies in each
office. Cleaning supplies and personal hygiene products were in one.
Water and other drinks were in another. Nonperishable foods were
in a third. An infirmary, of sorts, had been established, complete
with the first aid supplies kept within the administrative complex.

Systematically, the group brought their finds to the parking lot before going on a building-by-building search of the complex. To Burgoyne's surprise, there were several cabins on the premises used by the park rangers to live when they were on duty. They were about the size of a large efficiency apartment. They'd been abandoned and cleaned out of any items of value.

The maintenance sheds yielded some items that the observatory did not have. Tools. Gas cans. Search and rescue supplies. Camping equipment.

With everything piled in the parking lot, Burgoyne performed some mental calculations. He assessed their two pickup trucks and the items to be toted back up the mountain. He came up with an idea. However, it required a gut-wrenching task. In fact, he didn't even advise his team of his plans.

He handed his gun to Baxter. "Guys, give me a minute. I forgot to check something." Burgoyne reached into the pile of camping gear and grabbed a pair of gloves. He walked briskly back to the administration building and steeled his nerves for the difficult task. After pulling his shirt over his face and donning the gloves, he went back inside.

Puzzled, the rest of the search team waited anxiously at the edge of the parking lot, wondering what their esteemed leader was doing. After several minutes, Burgoyne emerged with his pants pockets bulging away from his thighs. He was out of breath when he reached the parking lot. He quickly removed the gloves and flung them onto the rocky soil.

"Sir, what did you do?" asked one of the scouts.

Burgoyne caught his breath and began removing car keys from his pockets and handing them to his team. "Match the keys with the vehicles. Pick the four with the most fuel in them. Then take all of this stuff and fill up our two pickups and the vehicles with the most fuel. We'll take these up to the observatory."

"Great idea!" exclaimed Baxter.

"Yes, sir. We're on it," said another.

Another asked, "What about the other vehicles?"

Burgoyne looked around the parking lot and assessed his options. "If the Jeeps and that Ford Bronco aren't in the top four, move them up the hill well beyond the entrance to the visitors' center. Otherwise, bring me the keys to the rejects."

"Okay!" a couple of the students shouted in unison.

"Also," added Burgoyne, "check under the seats and in the glove boxes and consoles for anything of use."

"Got it!"

The group scurried about to identify the four cars or trucks with the most fuel. They loaded up their trunks and pickup beds with the supplies they'd found and created a caravan on the other side of the entrance. Only the Ford Bronco was low on fuel, so it was parked on the side of the road in the midst of some rubble.

Burgoyne watched the activity and wandered toward the highway. Just above the entrance to the complex were two swing gates that were padlocked at night to avoid people accessing the road leading to the observatory. There was a similar set of gates approximately a mile from the observatory parking lot.

"Okay, Baxter, let's you and me barricade the road. Hopefully, it'll be enough to prevent anyone from passing."

"If we prevent others from coming up, will we be able to get out?" she asked.

Burgoyne held up the keys. "We can always unblock the road. Besides, I think the four-wheel-drive Jeeps will allow us to drive up and down the trails. You know, kinda like a gravel road through the Adirondacks." The fellow New Yorker smiled as her professor provided her the perfect visual.

"Do you think it will work?" she asked.

Burgoyne shrugged. He'd soon find out.

CHAPTER TWENTY-ONE

Tuesday
Haleakala Park Headquarters
Maui, Hawaii

Burgoyne sent the scout team and their overloaded vehicles back to the observatory. A couple of them voiced concern that he and Baxter needed assistance to position the remaining cars to fulfill Burgoyne's plan. However, what he had in mind required some thoughtfulness and time.

"Okay, Baxter, first things first. Let's stage an accident."

Baxter, who was in the process of looking through the breaker boxes located on the inside of a utility shed, shouted back to her professor, "Just one more thing!"

She'd been perplexed as to why the power had been disconnected to the park administration complex. The solar storm had had no impact on the facility, and their scouts had not reported any power outages at the base of Haleakala. It must've been an intentional act by the park rangers before they left the facility unattended to return home.

Burgoyne could hear loud clanking emanating from inside the shed as he waited somewhat impatiently for Baxter to assist him. After a few more hard whacks, she shouted, "Yes," followed by the sudden restart of the heating and cooling units nearby.

Baxter emerged, swinging a small sledgehammer back and forth. "I had to bust the lock off the breaker boxes. This may or may not be the case, but I believe cutting the power off indirectly led to those people dying."

Burgoyne, who wanted to go through the buildings again at a later time, nodded his approval. He was certain their hasty rummaging through the darkened spaces might've overlooked something of usefulness. First, they needed to wind it up to join the others.

"Good. Great. Now, turn it back off. Let's not make this place inviting for others. Besides, we still have work to do."

Baxter frowned and returned to the utility shed. Now that the shed was illuminated, she spied a heavy-duty chain attached to steel tow hooks. She also noticed a large, commercial fire extinguisher. After killing the power, she dragged the chain out of the shed and grunted as she lifted the fire extinguisher. Burgoyne noticed her struggling and rushed to her side.

"Baxter, we can come back, you know," he said as he relieved her of the tow chain.

"Yeah, I know. I'm just afraid somebody else might come along and take the stuff we left behind. You know, like the generator."

Burgoyne hadn't thought about the portable generator that had caused the deaths of the visitors holed up in the administration building. He'd simply looked at the power source as the cause of their deaths. Besides, he hadn't fathomed losing power at the observatory although it could happen.

"You're right," he said as he draped the chain over the side of the open Jeep Wrangler. He arranged the boxes and duffel bags to create a fairly flat surface. "Do you think we can pile the generator on top?"

Baxter set the fire extinguisher down with a thud. "Yeah. It's got handles. I've got room for a couple of the space heaters. Also, there are several long extension cords in the supply shed. We don't wanna end up like them." She nodded toward the administration building.

The two worked together to top off the already overloaded Jeeps. They moved them just above the visitors' center entrance and then addressed the remaining vehicles.

"Which of the cars has the least amount of fuel?" asked Burgoyne.

"The brown KIA."

"Good. It's worthless to us, anyway," Burgoyne said as he explained his plan. "I'm gonna take that Subaru just below the entrance. I need you to pull the KIA straight across the center lane and park it in the middle."

"Are you gonna wreck it?" asked Baxter.

"With pleasure," Burgoyne said with a smile. He wasn't sure why he disliked KIA automobiles. He'd never bothered to analyze it.

Minutes later, Baxter abandoned the car and stood off to the side as Burgoyne drove up the hill at a steady speed. He didn't need to hit the small, lightweight car with great force to accomplish his purpose. He tried to keep his speed under ten miles per hour to prevent the airbags from deploying in his face.

Just as his car was about to strike the KIA, he let go of the steering wheel and covered his face with his arms. The right front fender pushed its way into the KIA, causing the driver's door to collapse inward slightly. It was sufficient to lend the appearance of an accident to avoid looking like a barricade.

"Are you okay?" asked Baxter.

"Piece of cake. Now, let's block the rest of the road with these last four cars. I'm gonna raise the hood on the KIA and another vehicle to make them look disabled. Look, the whole idea is to block the road without making it look intentional. I mean, if someone wants to come up the mountain, they can on a bicycle or a scooter, like those thugs apparently have. At least this might slow them down. Meanwhile, we'll still be able to get around the scrum of cars with the two Jeeps."

It took them fifteen minutes to position the vehicles in a way that looked natural while also giving them the ability to dismantle the mess if they needed to. They placed all the ignition devices in a Ziploc bag and stored them in Burgoyne's Jeep.

The two of them casually strolled through the center of the complex, pointing out buildings to be searched at a later date. They neared the last building when Baxter grabbed Burgoyne's arm.

"Did you hear that?" she asked.

Burgoyne spun around and focused his senses toward the road. He heard the faint rumbling of an engine seeming to strain.

"I think it's coming from the bottom. We need to go! Now!"

He broke out in a run and turned to glance at Baxter, who hesitated at first. She was soon in pursuit, easily outpacing the older Burgoyne, who was twice as old as she was. She broke out into the open space between the visitors' center entry and the road leading to the observatory. There was no doubt a vehicle was arriving, as the sound of the engine grew louder.

"Hurry!" she hollered, waving her arms to encourage Burgoyne to catch up. Despite his many years at the observatory, the high altitude continued to put pressure on his lungs, making it difficult to breathe when he overexerted.

Burgoyne's chest was heaving when he arrived next to his Jeep. Baxter had already started it for him. He'd barely closed the door before throwing it into drive to scurry up the dormant volcano. A series of S curves just beyond the visitors' center immediately shielded them from view.

They continued up the mountain about a mile when they came to one of many points where the hiking trails crossed the road. Burgoyne slowed and pointed his arm out the window toward the left. He turned quickly onto the paved trail and sped up, checking his mirrors to confirm that Baxter followed.

Years ago, Burgoyne, excited about his new position at the observatory, had frequented the trail to get to know Haleakala and to become acclimated to the high altitude. Unfortunately, his exercise program had ended a long time ago. He did, however, recall that the trail provided an overlook of the highway near the park administration complex.

Just before they'd doubled back sufficiently to get a clear line of sight, he parked the Jeep, taking a moment to point the vehicle toward the observatory. Seconds later, Baxter had done the same, and she quickly joined his side.

"What are you thinking?" she said breathlessly as anxiety overtook her.

"Come on," was his reply as he half-jogged down the hill, crouching as the visitors' center came into view. They slowed their pace and lowered their bodies as they sought out two boulders to crouch behind. After catching their breath, they rose in unison to observe the vehicle and its occupants.

What Burgoyne saw confirmed his worst fears.

CHAPTER TWENTY-TWO

Tuesday
Kula, Maui, Hawaii

Goto was unfamiliar with the southwest shore overlooking Maalaea Bay. It was primarily a community for locals, as the tourist resorts were located near the forest reserve on the far western beaches of Kaanapali. He marveled at the beauty of Lanai, a tiny volcanic island with only a few resorts. He'd have to consider that as a possible refuge for his gang, although resources would be limited.

Not surprisingly, retailers and grocers had been looted as well as restaurant operations. This made their task of resupplying the crew more difficult, but not impossible. As they'd done in the Kula community, his vicious soldiers would go door-to-door, cleaning out each residence of any useful supplies while killing anyone who resisted.

The primary purpose for surveilling Wailea was to gauge the level of law enforcement protection. He was pleased to see the island's government continued to protect the areas around the largest population centers on the north side of the island.

After clearing out a group of refugees at a small shopping center filled with restaurants, they fed themselves and loaded up one of the pickups with nonperishable foods. He sent the truck back to the compound at Kula Sandalwoods, and he instructed his driver to prepare to take a ride toward the observatory. He wanted to get there before sunset to take in the views.

As they made their way toward the highway leading to the summit, Goto tried to envision what lay in store for him at the top of Maui. He couldn't imagine that anybody was still there. His understanding from one of the local men who'd joined his gang was there was limited staff on the premises in the form of college kids, most of whom were from out of town. It had been years since he'd driven to the summit, but he never recalled seeing any security personnel at the top. Most of the occupants who worked on Haleakala, he recalled, were nothing more than park rangers who manned the visitors' center halfway up the mountain.

Goto was growing impatient as the shadows grew longer and the sun began to lower itself on the horizon. The heavy, four-door Ford F-350 weighed nearly seven thousand pounds. Despite its strong motor, the behemoth struggled as it lumbered up the mountain, navigating the S curves toward the park administration halfway point like an elephant winding through a thick jungle.

His spirits lifted as a brown sign indicated the visitors' center was just ahead. He instructed his driver to have his weapons ready in the event it was occupied by someone foolish enough to take them on. The driver slowed his approach as he rounded the last curve. Then he suddenly jammed on the brakes.

"What the hell?" grumbled one of the rear passengers.

"A car wreck? Here?" questioned Goto dubiously.

"They must've been in a hella-hurry to crash up here."

Goto adjusted himself in the front seat and leaned forward. "Let's walk from here. Let's spread out on both sides of the road. Eyes wide open."

Seconds later, the men were making their way up the rise toward the entrance. In a near-perfect military-style formation, their heads were on a swivel, studying the surrounding terrain. Their guns were partially raised, ready to fire upon the slightest movement.

Goto raised his fist in the air, indicating that his fellow Yakuza should halt. He intently listened to the near silent surroundings, with only the faint sound of an adult Hawaiian petrel moaning its distinctive call, oo-ah-oo, as it returned to its nest for the evening.

Goto lowered his eyebrows, squinting to block the sunlight reflecting off the volcanic rock. He searched for movement around the vehicles.

Nothing.

He issued his instructions to his team in a loud whisper.

"Shock and awe," he began. "Let's hit the vehicles first, clearing them of targets. Then run quickly toward the visitors' building. Remember, stay spread apart. No easy targets. Maopopo?"

"I understand," his man replied.

On his signal, they rose out of their crouches and stormed up the rise toward the wreckage. They raced around the vehicles, looking in all the windows while keeping a watchful eye on their surroundings. Then, without wasting a moment, they rushed across the parking lot toward the visitors' center, fanning out to avoid being bunched together.

As Goto led the way through the compound in search of targets, he was unaware that he was being watched from above. He didn't take the time to study the vehicles to determine the pileup had been staged. He didn't listen to the slight ticking sound coming from the Subaru, nor did he notice the dripping of fluids coming from the Subaru's dislodged radiator hose.

By the time they'd finished searching the compound and examined the dead souls within the administration building, Goto had missed his opportunity to watch the sunset from atop Haleakala at the observatory. He vowed to come back in a few days after they'd looted the bayside community they'd just left.

It was a decision that enabled Burgoyne and his group of astronomers to get ready.

CHAPTER TWENTY-THREE

Tuesday
Harford House Motel
Harford, Pennsylvania

Fred Stewart slid down in the Adirondack chair that was always left open for him when his men gathered around the fire at night. It had become an evening ritual for the group of misfit Marines who'd found their way to Harford. Even with a threat of rain, and despite the heat index, the men enjoyed an evening of camaraderie.

Their early days in the small, unremarkable town were spent preparing the motel to be a long-term residence and stronghold for the group as they survived the collapse together. Many in the community feared the men although they'd never performed any act of violence against them. Their gruff, menacing appearance coupled with the weaponry they wielded was sufficient to send local residents scurrying into their homes and locking their doors.

Businesses, however, didn't fare so well. At first, Fred instructed his men to loot national concerns that had locations in and about

Harford. After that, out of necessity, in his opinion, he moved against some of the locals. This drew the ire of the small-business owners who lived in the community. However, out of fear, they dared not speak out against Fred or his men.

Fred used the locals' trepidation to his advantage. They systematically swept through the town, gathering anything of value. Some items were of greater value than others, especially in light of the collapse. Then he made it known he was prepared to barter these stolen goods for items of value.

Out of mutual necessity, a truce was formed between the residents of Harford and Fred. Food was a valuable commodity to maintain the presence of the ex-Marines at Harford House. So were operating vehicles, which seemed to appear out of nowhere as the locals became desperate for hard-to-find items. Life-sustaining prescription medications and other essential household goods were of particular interest to the locals. Fred never traded away guns or ammunition unless absolutely necessary. The flow of weapons into Harford House had grown in recent weeks to the point travel trailers had been towed upon the property as housing units for displaced Marines whose motel rooms were used for the burgeoning arsenal.

Fred and the men who had assisted in the battle at Cubbison's Farm took the remainder of that day to tell stories to the other ex-Marines about their exploits, which had lasted less than an hour. Regardless of the ease with which Fred and the other men had dispatched the bikers, to a man, the others lamented the fact they'd missed out on eradicating the biker gang from the county. All of them longed for battle.

Tuesday was a day of looting as Fred took a squad up to the next interstate exit to peruse the businesses rewarded to them by the truce with the bikers. They found everything to be picked over. The hotels at the exit had been stripped of anything of usefulness, including sheets and pillows. Refugees making their way up and down the interstate between Scranton and Binghamton either stopped over when tired or took the bedding to find a car to sleep in along their route.

The big prize of his negotiated truce with the bikers was the Pennsylvania State Police post on Harford Road. Located a mile or more from the interstate, it drew little attention from the refugees. The bikers had not been interested in taking the extraordinary effort required to breach the fortified building. Fred and his men looked at it as a worthy challenge, so they took it on.

The single-story, block and brick building had a dozen rectangular, fixed-glass windows, three steel security doors, and a glass-door entry, which was the logical point of entry. Others had tried to break through the glass with high-powered rifles, only to be disappointed. The bulletproof glass was designed to withstand .50-caliber ammunition.

Fred, however, had made a whale of a deal with a quarry operator whose wife was pregnant and in need of lifesaving medication. He not only provided the family the drugs to save mother and unborn child, but he also provided them a newborn starter pack of formula and feeding accessories.

His benevolence had been rewarded with a supply of ANFO, ammonium nitrate fuel oil, a substance widely used in mining operations. Also, he had been provided the special primers used to detonate the ANFO together with instructions on how to avoid blowing himself up in the process.

The challenge for Fred as he took on the task of blowing a hole in the wall of the staties' building was how much of the ANFO was required to accomplish the task. If the building contained an arsenal with accompanying ammunition as he suspected, he'd prefer not to destroy it in the process. Or, worse than that, trigger a massive explosion that killed his squad.

After he and his men cleared the perimeter and set up armed security, on a hunch, he searched the abandoned cars for keys that might unlock the facility. No such luck.

The next step was to create a presumed layout of the structure.

Using an overturned steel drum found behind the building, his men looked through the one-foot-by-six-foot fixed-pane windows located near the roofline. Offices and meeting rooms with windows were located in the front half of the building, while the back half was solid block.

Fred decided to blow through the front of the building, presumably the farthest point from the arsenal and supply rooms. Perhaps, he thought, they could rummage through the debris and find the keys to the vault doors he assumed were in place to protect the weaponry. Plus, it would give him an opportunity to test the quantity of ANFO necessary to open the weapons storage area.

Because they had no knowledge of the complicated formulas for the use of ANFO, the group reached a consensus. With a shrug and a prayer, they set the first explosives and corresponding detonation requirements. Once Fred cleared the area, he took up a position behind their vehicles on the highway and initiated the blast.

"Shit, too much," were the words he muttered as the entire front façade of the sixty-foot-wide building blew in all directions. The red metal roof peeled open like a flip-top can of Vienna sausages. The block walls, poured solid with concrete, threw a million pieces of rock and block skyward, eventually raining down on the heads of Fred and his men.

The battle-hardened ex-Marines were awestruck by the massive destruction of the ANFO that was on par with any of the armaments at their disposal during their tours of duty in the Middle Eastern theater. All of them equated the destruction to be equal to that of a shoulder-fired Mk 153 used by the Marines. The shoulder-launched multipurpose assault weapon was the U.S. military's version of the Russian RPG, or rocket-propelled grenade.

After the dust and debris settled, the men moved in while the security detail kept a wary eye on any looky-loos drawn to the sound of the explosion. If there was anything of value in the offices and storage rooms at the front of the building, it had been obliterated by the blast.

The back half of the building, however, was not. It remained intact, protected by the double steel doors and solid block wall separating it from the administrative side of the structure. Fred grimaced as he stared at the barrier between him and the presumed arsenal the state police building contained. He'd have to reduce the amount of ANFO used to a very small amount to prevent destroying the prized possessions on the other side of the wall.

Later that evening, as Fred and his squad of looters retold the events to those who had remained at the Harford House during the operation, he said, "Sometimes, it's better to be lucky than good."

One of his men had become fascinated by the roof, which had peeled backwards yet remained remarkably intact. Steel trusses ran from the back of the building to the front, holding onto the standing seam metal roofing with long screws. The former Marine had been assigned to the logistics units in Afghanistan for a while and had been involved in the expansion of Marine installations throughout the country.

He brought Fred's attention to the gaps running between the steel trusses that rested on the solid wall. The wall not only protected the items stored behind it, but it also acted as support for the roofing system. The ex-Marine pointed out the spacing between the top of the wall and the peeled-back roof. The men could enter the space from above without the use of explosives.

The squad worked together for hours, scaling the solid partition wall to retrieve weapons, ammunition, and tactical gear, including body armor, night vision, and ballistic protection. The state police's vault of weapons and gear was so extensive, Fred questioned what the purpose would be for storing that much military-grade gear in a single location.

Regardless, it took several trips for his men to haul the fruits of their labor back to Harford House and find a place to store it. Each man was outfitted with Level IV body armor capable of stopping .30-06 steel-core armor-penetrating rounds. They were all assigned fully automatic weapons similar to those issued to them by the military. They donned tactical vests capable of holding two handguns and utility belts for their weapons' magazines.

Fred and his men were now prepared for war, if one came their way.

He wouldn't have to wait long.

CHAPTER TWENTY-FOUR

Tuesday
Cubbison's Farm
Harford, Pennsylvania

Lauren traded patrol shifts with John so she could spend more time with her husband. She also needed an opportunity alone with Asher to discuss the revelations about Vida. Asher took in all the facts before commenting.

"Any reasonable person would understand that Matthew had no idea who was shooting. He was simply defending himself and his own father. It seems, on the surface, Vida understands that. However, that said, it does insert an uncertain dynamic into our group. Should we ask her to leave out of an abundance of caution?"

Lauren was taken aback by his suggestion. Emma had never insinuated that Vida should be expelled from Cubbison's Farm. "Do you think that's necessary?"

Asher directed Lauren to a gate along the east fence line. Before he answered, he dismounted and opened the farm gate before motioning for her to ride through. As she did, she looked down to him.

"Where are we going?"

"Sam and John asked me to check out a vehicle or tractor of some kind up the road. It's two in the morning or so, and it's been very quiet. This will be a chance for us to check it out without anybody seeing us approach."

Lauren shrugged and waited for Asher on the shoulder of the road. They rode along the grassy shoulder to avoid their horses' hooves from creating a racket. Once they were on their way, Asher responded to his wife's question.

"It's a tough call. Fortunately for you and me, it's one that we do not have to make. It's John and Emma's place. Matthew is their son. We have to respect their wishes."

"Okaaay," she began, stretching out the word. "I take it you think Vida should go, right?"

Asher swayed back and forth in the saddle as if he were symbolically on the fence regarding the matter. "What if I had been the one who shot her father? How would you feel?"

Lauren didn't hesitate. "Either she'd have to leave, or we would. I can't imagine having to sleep with a pistol under my pillow because one of our own was holding a potentially serious grudge."

"See?" asked Asher. "Now, consider this. If I was able to confirm that it was her father who shot you in the back with the intent to gun you down, I might've tracked him down myself. That certainly might put me at cross purposes with Vida."

"Resulting in her getting kicked out of our group?" asked Lauren.

"If I was concerned that my need for revenge put us in a potentially hostile situation, yes. She'd need to go. Or we would."

Lauren slowed to allow Asher to take the lead. They were barely a hundred feet from the abandoned produce stand. Asher led his horse down a slight embankment and brought him to a halt. The two dismounted and tied their horses to an old fence post.

As he drew his handgun, Asher whispered to his wife, "I'll check it out."

"No," she shot back. "We will check it out. I'm not leaving your side."

"I need you to guard the horses," he argued, to no avail.

"You need me to have your back. That's the deal, cowboy."

Asher chuckled. "You're so stubborn."

"Nope. Helpful."

The two spread apart, each of them walking along the solid white line separating the highway from the gravel shoulder. As they approached, Asher's eyes studied the level area around the abandoned building. He didn't see any type of vehicle, much less a tractor. After a quick look around, they confirmed the building was uninhabited, and began walking back toward their horses, occasionally looking over their shoulders to confirm nobody was following them.

Lauren revisited the subject of Vida and worked in the topic of their future. "I vote we leave the decision regarding Vida up to the Cubbisons. I don't consider her to be the enemy, nor do I think she's a threat to our safety. I believe Matthew should know, however."

"Probably. Yes. Again, that's not our call."

As they rode back in silence, Lauren began to think of their future. "Do you ever see us going back to New York?"

Asher sighed and then responded, "I seriously doubt it. Think about it, our jobs are gone. I don't think they're gonna be producing *Blue Bloods*, or any other prime-time television show, for a lot of years."

Lauren laughed. "After this shit, I don't believe anybody will be interested in post-apocalyptic fiction. I'll have to take up editing chick lit. You know, something less stressful."

Asher became serious. "Lauren, it's gonna take many years to fix this. I can only guess, but it may take years to get the power restored to the entire country. Think about it. All of our transformers, computers, and infrastructure related to the power grid comes from China. They'll demand a king's ransom to help us fix things."

"We'll just print more money and send it to them," quipped Lauren.

"Yeah, except the dollar is probably worthless. I wouldn't be surprised if the gold standard returned. That's why I used the reference to a king's ransom. China can name their price, in gold or something else of value."

"Like what?"

"Real estate, maybe? I dunno. My point is this. For quite a long time, this is our best option, and we're darn lucky the Cubbisons like us. I believe we contribute, and they appreciate us being here. That said, we're not family, which means we'd be encouraged to leave if times got rough."

Lauren shook her head and fought back tears. "Asher, I'm not cut out for hitting the road like some kind of *Walking Dead* character. Hell, zombies would be easier to fight than these lawless thugs who have no remorse for killing others. We need to make this work."

"We'll be fine. One day at a time."

PART 3

———————

Wednesday
Fight or flight.

CHAPTER TWENTY-FIVE

Wednesday
Harford House Motel
Harford, Pennsylvania

It was before dawn that morning, and the night patrol at Harford House was giving way to the early morning contingent. The four men stood nonchalantly outside the front entrance, smoking cigarettes. During their idle conversation, one of the men, a former sergeant, held his right hand in the air and made a fist. The rest of the men immediately stopped talking.

"Do you hear that?" he asked the other men as he wandered away from them.

"Are you kidding? I'll never forget it."

"Where's it coming from?" another asked.

"More than one," mumbled the ex-sergeant. "From the interstate."

The unique sound of the large, military Humvees was etched in the ex-Marines' brains. The massive six-point-five-liter engines chugged along, barely heard over the roar of the oversized all-terrain tires on the pavement. Their approach could only mean one thing. The National Guard was coming to Harford.

"Get Fred! Now!" the ex-sergeant shouted. "The rest of you, wake up the men in the trailers and take up positions along the perimeter. Weapons hot, but do not engage. Understood?"

"Roger that!"

The men were suddenly scurrying in all directions as the sun began to peek over the wooded area along Leslie Creek.

Within minutes, the ex-Marines had poured out of Harford House, wearing all the ballistic protection they'd been issued following the recent raid of the state police facility. Despite the fact they hadn't prepared for a battle since their return stateside, the disciplined ex-Marines hadn't forgotten their training.

The sun was shining brighter as the caravan of tan-colored Humvees slowly approached the intersection about two thousand feet north of Harford House. Fred's men remained hidden behind a variety of barriers that had been put into place around the perimeter of the triangle-shaped lot where Harford House stood.

Without the need for binoculars, they could see the National Guardsmen exit their Humvees and slowly walk into the center of the intersection with their weapons shouldered. Within a minute, a dozen men had accumulated there, looking in all directions, as they waited for their commanding officer to issue instructions.

Fred, with his newly acquired Sig Sauer P227R handgun drawn by his side, moved quickly at a low crouch along the barriers of ostensibly stranded vehicles, piles of debris, and various types of lawn equipment. Unless the guardsmen were poorly trained or oblivious, it wouldn't take them long to notice the makeshift barricade around Harford House.

He approached his top lieutenant, who rested his .308 Winchester sniper rifle across the seat of a golf cart surrounded by bales of straw. He was intently studying the guardsmen through his scope.

"Talk to me," whispered Fred as he dropped to one knee.

"A dozen men. Three, maybe four Humvees. The house on the corner is blocking my view. I only see one CO."

"Small squad but large enough to—"

"Wait!" he whispered excitedly. "Two civilians. Um, sure 'nuf. They're wearing FBI jackets."

Fred stood and reached into his kit for his binoculars. He squinted to block out the bright morning sun. He was able to quickly confirm his lieutenant's assessment.

Suddenly, the entire contingent began scrambling back to their Humvees. The powerful engines roared to life and lurched forward in the direction of Harford House.

Fred and his men were born to do battle. They'd just never envisioned fighting their fellow Americans. He backed away from the barricade and shouted to the rest of his men in earshot.

"Everyone stand down! Pass it along! Stand down unless fired upon!"

Fred quickly retreated to Harford House as the first two Humvees roared past him toward the front motel entrance. The other two Humvees veered toward the west to flank the rear of the Harford House buildings. He shouted orders to his men as he rushed to the main entrance.

"If they try to come onto the property, warn them off verbally. Do not engage unless fired upon. Let me see what they want."

The Humvees screeched to a halt when their drivers discovered the entrance to the motel was blocked by parked vehicles. Armed guardsmen poured out of the vehicles and fanned out along the barriers with their rifles raised. They were unaware that Fred's men were hiding just on the other side of the barricade as the guardsmen were taking up positions only a few feet away.

"I am Sergeant Frank Pierce of the Pennsylvania National Guard!" a man bellowed through a loudspeaker affixed to his Humvee. "I want everyone within this compound to make yourself seen."

None of the ex-Marines moved.

"I repeat, make yourselves seen with your hands up, or we will enter with all due force necessary!"

"No, you won't," said Fred calmly but loud enough for the men in the Humvees to hear. Fred had holstered his weapon and held his hands to his sides to avoid any overt hostile act that might escalate the situation.

Two of the guardsmen stepped toward the parked vehicles and pointed their rifles at Fred. "You heard our sergeant. Hands up and call anyone else out of the buildings. Don't make this difficult. It won't end well."

Arrogance. Fred stifled a laugh. He liked arrogance. They were usually the first to die in battle. Besides, after seeing their lack of situational awareness on display, he was comfortable putting up his dozen against their dozen anytime.

"I don't think so," Fred replied. "Let me speak to your CO. And might as well bring out the two feds who came along for the ride."

Nobody moved for what seemed like a long minute. Fred continued to stare at the vehicles while allowing his eyes to scan the movements of the guardsmen who'd taken up positions behind the barricades. He gave himself an imperceptible nod of approval as his men continued to hold their positions out of sight of the guardsmen.

The rear doors of the lead Humvee swung open, and the two federal agents exited. They both wore khaki pants, white shirts, and the signature navy blue windbreakers with the letters FBI screen-printed on the back in gold. They also wore dark sunglasses. He imagined they'd introduce themselves as Agent Jones and Agent White.

The sergeant who led the guardsmen bellowed at Fred, "Do not mess around with us! Call everyone out into the open. They should be unarmed, and their hands need to reach the heavens, or they'll meet their maker."

Another smile crossed Fred's face, one that he couldn't obscure. If the guardsmen were arrogant, their commander was *ultra arrogant.*

"That won't be necessary, Sergeant," interrupted the taller of the two FBI agents. "There's no need to be afraid, sir."

Fred burst out laughing. He simply couldn't contain himself. He tried to stop laughing, but the humor in the federal agent's statement generated a sincere outburst.

"You think this is funny, pal?" bellowed the sergeant. "We'll show you funny! You can start by slowly removing that handgun from its holster and placing it on the ground in front of you. Hell, don't do it slowly. Make a move! I want you to try something!"

The guardsmen's attitude spoke volumes to Fred. They were undisciplined and a bunch of cowboys. During the brief standoff, he surmised the FBI was probably investigating the bombing at the mall. The guardsmen were using their peon power to muscle the local residents around.

Also, Fred knew and understood this method of operation Most likely, there was another element to the visit besides the investigation of the bombing. One that involved enforcement of the president's martial law declaration.

Sometimes, he hated it when he was right.

"I'm Special Agent Johnson, and this is Special Agent Williams."

Jones and White. Johnson and Williams. All the same in Fred's mind. *What are these two afraid of? That I'm gonna Google them to see where they live?* He smiled again at his inner wit. Oddly, he was enjoying the confrontation.

Agent Williams spoke next. "We are investigating the bombing at the Viewmont Mall in North Scranton several days ago. Do you know anything about that?"

Fred thought for a moment. There were two ways out of this predicament. Cooperate and hope they'll go away. Or fight their way through this bunch of wannabes.

Fighting would bring a tremendous amount of heat on them later. More, he knew, than his group could handle. However, he doubted cooperating would satisfy them. The FBI, perhaps. But not the mouthy, undisciplined guardsmen.

"I might be able to help you, but the sergeant needs to tell his men to stand down."

"We will not! I give the orders here! Unholster your weapon!"

His men moved closer to Fred. He could see his loyal gunners tense to his left and right. This would be a bloodbath within seconds.

"Hold on! Hold on!" shouted Special Agent Johnson. "There is no need for this."

"I agree," added Fred. "Let's talk it out. Deal?"

"No promises," shouted the sergeant.

"Let me hear what you have to say, and then we can—"

"That's not what I said," interrupted Fred. "I have valuable information you need about the mall bombing. However, we want assurances from you, and him, that we'll be left alone. In fact, put in writing that the entirety of Harford Township and the surrounding areas will be protected from what that guy has in mind." Fred pointed his finger directly at the National Guard commanding officer.

"That's it!" shouted the sergeant. He turned toward his men, when Special Agent Johnson took control of the situation.

"Enough! Sir, do you have specific knowledge of the bombing at Viewmont Mall? I have to know the value of the information before I waive any rights of the Pennsylvania National Guard to enforce the edict set forth in the martial law declaration." He caught himself and gulped as he finished the sentence.

Fred allowed his grin to show. *Oops. Slipped up, didn't ya. Now, you can bet your collective asses I want it in writing.*

"Sorry. The offer stands. I can assure you, as an honored former United States Marine, that the information I have will be useful. However, I need assurances from all parties involved."

The two FBI agents whispered back and forth before motioning the National Guard sergeant over to join them. Meanwhile, Fred locked eyes with the two men who were pointing their weapons at him.

He wasn't afraid to die. Since his return stateside following the botched withdrawal from Afghanistan, he'd wished death upon himself a thousand times. Things had changed now. He had a squad to lead and a community to protect.

He was willing to take a stand.

CHAPTER TWENTY-SIX

Wednesday
Harford House Motel
Harford, Pennsylvania

The National Guard sergeant summoned one of his subordinates over and issued his orders. The subordinate passed the directive on to the rest of the squad. They slowly pulled away from the barricades, keeping their rifles pointed as they prepared to respond to any movement within the Harford House property. They withdrew to the other side of the street and took up positions behind trees or parked cars. They did not leave.

Special Agent Johnson spoke to Fred. "I'm going to take this to my superiors and then return. I can't go empty-handed. So let me ask a couple of questions, and you can provide me as much information as you're willing. Okay?"

The man seemed sincere, so Fred agreed. Besides, it was the only hand he had to play. "Sure."

"Did you witness the actual bombing?"

"No."

"Did you observe any suspicious people prior to the bombing?"

"No."

"After?"

"Yes."

Special Agent Williams joined his partner's side. "Do you believe you could provide a description of the suspicious person or persons you observed?"

"Yes. Vehicles, too."

The FBI agents' reaction to this revelation clearly told Fred he'd given them the breakthrough they needed to find the bombers.

"Thank you, um, Mr.—" Special Agent Johnson's voice trailed off, hoping that Fred would fill in the blank.

"Just call me Fred. So are we done here? For now, anyway?"

Special Agent Williams replied, "Yes, of course. Naturally, we'd ask that you not go anywhere."

"My squad will see to that," said the bellicose sergeant.

Fred raised his chin and set his jaw. He'd had about enough of this guy. Without responding to the agent's question, he turned around and marched into the front of Harbor House, where several of his men waited for him.

It didn't take long for his men to weigh in on the standoff.

"We can take 'em, sir."

"Fred, just give us the word. These guys will run with their tails tucked."

"Guaranteed," added another.

"I don't trust any of them, feds or the Guard."

Fred agreed with all of their statements. However, he had to decide whether to let it play out or find a way to escape. He began to pace the floor when one of his top lieutenants entered through the back doorway.

"Fred, can you fill me in?"

Fred ordered one of his men to relieve his other top advisor, the ex-Marine sniper who'd first observed the arrival of the National

Guard contingent. He needed to make a decision with a clear head and not among the hyped-up jarheads.

The three of them met in the converted attic of the main house that afforded them views of the entire perimeter through fixed-glass windows. A map of the county was hung on the wall near a small dining table. Another map was rolled out onto the table and held in place by several dusty books. Fred leaned over the map as he spoke.

"During the conversation, they let me know that the National Guard has another purpose for being here. Certainly, they are the muscle to lend an assist to the FBI agents, who are primarily interested in investigating the bombing. My guess is the president is pissed this happened during a relief effort.

"However, what I saw was a bunch of thieves bullying American citizens under the cover of martial law."

"I believe it," said the ex-sniper. "This was one of the things I wanted to tell you. After the guardsmen fanned out around our perimeter, I continued studying the road leading from the interstate through my scope. In fact ..." He cut himself off and moved to the attic window facing east. He turned to Fred and pointed over his shoulder.

"What is it?" Fred asked.

"Take a look for yourself."

Fred cupped his hands over his eyes to block out the glare. He studied the two-lane road leading into Harford. There were three M35 series cargo trucks. The two-and-a-half-ton, six-by-six trucks had been a staple of the US military vehicle fleet since World War II.

"How many men were in each?" he asked.

"Only the drivers, Fred. I believe they're being used to haul confiscated supplies, food and weapons. They could even tow vehicles that still run, like ours."

Fred pounded the wall and walked away from the window. "Sergeant asshole isn't gonna walk away from this even if the feds tell him to. Once we give up the information they need, initially he may leave peacefully. You know he'll be back."

"With an even larger force," said one of Fred's lieutenants. "We can hold our own to an extent. They could also outgun us with double the rifles."

"Or more," said the other lieutenant. "We'd never survive a prolonged assault. And who knows, if they have an MRAP, we're toast."

An MRAP was an acronym for a mine-resistant, bulletproof military truck designed to break stalemates like this one. Fred knew their makeshift barricades could easily be breached by an MRAP, followed up by a full-frontal assault of guardsmen.

"Dammit!" Fred exclaimed out of frustration. "Man, we had it goin' on here. Now, these assholes are gonna tear it all down?"

"We can haul ass out of here." One of the men stated the option Fred was also mulling. He laid out a simplistic plan. "We're up to seven operating vehicles, all of which are close to the building. We'd have to move quickly to get them to the rear of the main house, using the left wing of the housing units as cover. We'll load them up and bust through the north exit into the neighborhoods and the apartments. From there, we'll split up and head in different directions. If they open fire, we'll light 'em up."

"It's doable, sir," his other lieutenant suggested. "If we move quickly, we can pull this off while they're undermanned. Personally, I feel like the moment they take on fire, they'll tuck tail and hide."

"Roger that!" The two lieutenants exchanged high fives.

"Then what?" asked Fred.

"We can regroup out in the country somewhere. I really don't think they'll follow us. At least not this skeleton squad left behind."

"They'll come looking later," added the sniper. "We're good, though. I'm sure we can bury ourselves in the woods where they'll never find us."

Fred paced the floor and moseyed from window to window to study the location of the guardsmen and the positioning of his human and physical assets. However he felt about the prospect of running, the intentions of the National Guard sergeant were obvious. What they'd built for themselves at Harford House was doomed.

But where will we go?

He answered his question aloud. "We have a friend who owes us a favor."

CHAPTER TWENTY-SEVEN

Wednesday
Harford House
Harford, Pennsylvania

Fred patted his men on the back and sent them downstairs. He needed time to think alone. For several minutes, his mind wandered as he paced the floor of the attic that had once stored antiquities purchased by the Hollywood star who'd lovingly restored the property to its former glory. Now the space held a few pieces of molding, a couple of mirrors, and the small desk and chairs that Fred used from time to time to brainstorm with his guys.

It was midmorning, but the skies had suddenly turned gray. The gloom seemed to cast a melancholy feeling over Fred. He'd suffered through so much following his return stateside. Rejection. A feeling of abandonment. Mockery. Bullying. As a veteran and a wounded warrior, he deserved better.

He'd made the best of his life, such that it was. Then along came the great equalizer. The solar storm from hell, or the heavens, depending upon how you looked at it. Suddenly, things began to fall into place. His survival instincts were greater than those around him. His knack for taking advantage of a bad situation served him well. His keeping in touch with his former unit allowed him to draw like-minded people around him.

In this small town, he'd found a way to make a life for himself. Now, ironically, the very government he'd fought for, but was then abandoned by, now threatened to knock him down once again. It would've been expected that someone in Fred's position, based upon his experience following his military career, would be consumed with anxiety and a feeling of doom.

Fred, however, was a fighter. He would find a way out of this predicament, even if it meant a firefight against fellow members of the United States military.

"That'll be up to them," he said to himself with a sigh. "I need a distraction that keeps the shooting to a minimum. One that won't cause those guys to overreact." He pointed angrily toward the window overlooking the front lawn.

Then he heard it. Slow at first, like the ticking of an old windup alarm clock.

The sound grew louder and more rapid. Fred looked toward the rafters and focused on the sound of raindrops pelting the galvanized roof. The insulation served to muffle the sound; however, Fred confirmed the rain was falling by looking out each of the windows.

He rushed to the window overlooking the front of Harford House and the street separating his men hidden behind the barriers and the sparse cover afforded the National Guardsmen. One by one, the part-time guardsmen ran from their positions toward their Humvees. They hunched over, looking at the ground, as if the rainfall was going to muss their hair or cause them to drown. Fred might've found their retreat to be comical if it hadn't been for the opportunity he'd just been given.

The rain turned into a sudden torrential downpour. The guardsmen raced for cover. However, his fellow ex-Marines remained in the trenches, protecting their stronghold. He'd never been prouder of the men he'd served with overseas.

Fred had to act quickly and decisively. He ran across the attic floor to the spiral staircase leading to the second floor of Harbor House. He was shouting orders as he descended the narrow steps.

"Everyone gather in the lobby! Now!"

Most of his men were already there. The sound of heavy feet running from the main house toward the motel rooms located in the two wings could also be heard. By the time he entered the lobby, all of his men except for those holding their posts in the rain were awaiting his instructions.

"Okay, listen up. There's no time to explain my reasoning. I'm asking you to trust me. We have to leave."

There were a few moans and groans from his men, but none of them challenged his decision. Fred expected this. However, he needed his men to rally behind him to achieve a hasty exit from Harford House. He summoned his two lieutenants to his side.

"We're gonna divide this unit into two squads. One will be responsible for pulling our vehicles to the two porticos at the sides of the building connecting the guest rooms. I want you to fill them up with weapons and ammo first, medical supplies second, and don't forget to leave room for your own asses."

"Sir, we'll have a helluva time loading all the armaments. Plus, a lot of what we traded for is small caliber with a limited supply of ammo."

Fred thought for a moment. He thought of the defenseless town. He wasn't prepared to risk the lives of his men to stay and defend them. However, he'd provide them the tools to protect themselves. Their leaders would have to decide whether they wanted to live on their knees or die on their feet.

He then turned to the two men who'd spent the most time patrolling the community. "Do you remember where the mayor and the other town leaders live? You know, city council, law enforcement, etcetera."

"Yes, sir," replied one of the men before adding, "All are within walking distance in the neighborhoods behind us.

"Good. Grab your kits and body armor. Go to the mayor first and then the next closest public official. We don't have time to make a day of it. Maybe an hour or two at best."

"What do you want us to do?" he asked.

A meek voice interrupted the conversation from the dark hallway leading to the motel room wings. "Um, my name is Phoebe. The mayor's my dad. I might be able to help."

"Come here," said Fred.

"I can help, too," said another female voice from behind Phoebe.

"Me too," said a third. "I'll fight them if we need to. I swear."

Fred was overwhelmed by the women's willingness to join in their battle. His mind raced back to his years in Afghanistan. The people of the small town had wanted nothing to do with the brutal Taliban. They wanted to live their lives, raise their children, and worship as they pleased. Some of them joined the Afghan army and fought alongside the Marines as they rooted the Taliban out of their strongholds. He wondered if these women, and the others in the community, would do the same.

"Sir?" asked one of the lieutenants. Nobody left as they awaited Fred's instructions.

He began to wander through the lobby, rubbing his temples, occasionally glancing toward the front lawn to gauge the rainfall. It was still coming down steadily. At this moment, he had the group of guardsmen bunched together inside their Humvees.

Fred's inner debate spilled over into a vocal outburst. "Dammit! Fine!"

"What's that, sir?" asked the lieutenant.

Fred sighed. "Okay, change of plans. Sort of."

He motioned for Phoebe and the second woman to join his side. They slowly pushed their way through the room full of men. Fred addressed the two scouts who knew the town the best.

"Escort these ladies to the mayor's home first. I want it to look like they are being ushered out of Harbor House. Do you follow me?"

"Yessir," one of them responded. "Do you want us to relay a message?"

"You bet," began Fred. "Tell them hellfire is about to rain down on their tiny little hamlet, and if they hope to have a roof over their head by day's end, they'd better rally the town. Tell them they have an hour, maybe less, to get here. We'll arm them. We'll give them the balance of our supplies. And protect them from what's likely to come next."

The men nodded and hastily escorted the women through the rear exit closest to the neighborhoods. The others focused on Fred, curious about what he was referring to. Although, most had an idea.

Fred turned to the other lieutenant. "Pull every man off the perimeter and post them up in the dry along the outside of Harbor House. Have them hold their weapons at low ready. I want those wannabes hiding out in their Humvees to see we have just as much firepower as they do."

"What about the vehicles?"

"Leave them where they are for now. However, move our weapons, ammo, and tactical gear to the porticos. Same with the medical supplies, focusing on what you'd put in your field trauma kits. Get ready to load up any MREs we have in stock. We may be displaced for several days."

"Roger that."

The lieutenant and his hand-selected men quickly entered the dark hallway leading to their storage rooms. Fred turned to address the remainder of his crew.

"Devil dogs, are you ready for some action?"

The men didn't hesitate in voicing their excitement.

"Damn straight!"

"Oorah!"

CHAPTER TWENTY-EIGHT

Wednesday
Harford House
Harford, Pennsylvania

After Fred ran into the attic to get eyes on all three Humvees that remained parked in the vicinity of Harford House, he returned to the lobby to join the men, who were all adept at special operations. He led them through the rain to a four-door Ford sedan parked at the rear exit of Harford House, just out of view of the Humvee that had now retreated to the intersection where they first arrived. The other two remained positioned across from the front entrance to the property.

Once they were in the Ford, Fred looked around. He turned sideways in his seat and told the men what he hoped to accomplish.

"I have no doubt we could take the guys left behind. We might lose some people, or we might not. We would definitely end up killing a lot of guardsmen, who are most likely here following orders. What I have in mind is a win-win, but we've gotta move lightning fast."

"Shock and awe, Marines," said the driver as he gripped the steering wheel, itching to get started.

"Exactly," said Fred, appreciative of his enthusiasm. "We'll start with the Humvee that isolated itself back toward the intersection. We're gonna taunt them and see if we can draw them away. Then we'll either neutralize them or eliminate them altogether; that'll be their choice."

The driver started the car and goosed the gas pedal to keep the old clunker running. It wasn't able to outrun much of anything, except for the behemoth Humvee.

"What if they don't chase us?" asked one of the men in the backseat.

"All the better," said Fred. "We'll approach them from behind and take them out of the game without bloodshed."

They pulled out onto the street and moved quickly toward the Humvee. Fred turned in his seat to study the other Humvees parked closer to the front entrance. Neither seemed to make a move to engage them.

"Sir, I see headlights. They've started their engines."

"What if they have comms?" asked one of the men in the backseat. "We'll have the rest of their squad up our asses in a flash."

Fred had thought about that. He suspected operating communication devices between the National Guard units came at a premium. He doubted they were issued to these search squads; otherwise the two FBI agents and the sergeant wouldn't have left to get the necessary approvals to grant the amnesty Fred sought for his men.

"No worries, gentlemen. It'll just make it a fair fight."

"Oorah!"

They raced past the Humvee. Fred wanted them to give chase. He and his men knew the local streets better than the guardsmen. Plus, if they could commandeer the Humvee, it would make the next step in his plan go smoothly. To encourage the guardsmen to fall into his trap, Fred rolled down his window and shot them the bird as they drove past. Not surprisingly, the Humvee gave chase.

"Where to, sir?" asked the driver as his eyes alternated between the empty road and the pursuing Humvee. Before Fred could answer, one of the men in the backseat sounded the alarm.

"Weapons hot! The front passenger laid his rifle outside his window. He plans on firing on us."

"Don't panic," said Fred. "The fairgrounds are up ahead. When we get there, drive past the first driveway to the parking lot on the right. Then take the second entrance."

"Yessir."

The man sped forward and then suddenly slowed to turn the wheel hard to the right. The tires skidded on the wet pavement, and the back end of the Ford started to slide around. However, he deftly adjusted, whipping the steering wheel back and forth until he regained control. He turned into the parking area, which was filled with stalled vehicles destroyed by the effects of the solar storm.

"Nice driving," said Fred.

"I did the power slide on purpose, sir. I used to do a lot of street racing before I signed up. I figure the Humvee driver will slow his roll as he approaches the entrance, giving us time to get into position."

Fred smiled and nodded, internally praising himself for picking the right man for the job. He pointed through the windshield.

"Stop! Park it sideways to block their access. Everyone take positions on both sides of the entrance. They'll come to a stop, and we'll be there to greet them."

Seconds later, the Ford was blocking the drive, and the four men were scurrying for cover to intercept the Humvee as it entered the parking lot.

The driver of the Humvee, despite observing the Ford's difficulty in turning, came in hot and overshot the entrance. He put the big truck into reverse and spun the tires to get in front of the entrance. He then pulled directly toward the parked Ford.

Fred and his men didn't hesitate. They rushed the Humvee, pointing their automatic weapons at the heads of the driver and his passengers. The men were caught in the confined quarters of the Humvee without the ability to maneuver their rifles in response. They raised their hands in unison, and the fight was over before it started.

Fred shouted first, and then the rest of his men joined in.

"Out of the truck!"

"Now!"

"Hands up! Don't try anything!"

The guardsmen complied although the driver tried to argue Fred and his men were making a big mistake. After interrogating the men, Fred realized he was doing exactly the right thing.

In the few minutes he quizzed the guardsmen, he realized they'd been issued a license to loot in exchange for assisting the FBI with its investigation. Furthermore, Fred learned, the president was cracking down on those who resisted by stripping them of their freedoms and their worldly belongings.

For their participation in this scheme, Fred sentenced the four men to humiliation. He stripped them of their uniforms and zip-cuffed them to the door handles of the stalled vehicles. Then he and his men donned the National Guard uniforms, ill-fitting as they were, and returned to Harford.

There was still work to do.

CHAPTER TWENTY-NINE

Wednesday
Harford, Pennsylvania

Fred's driver had to push the Humvee to its limits to take the circuitous route around Harford to get into position behind the three M35 cargo trucks that patiently awaited orders from the sergeant who had left with the FBI agents. A plan was starting to unfold for Fred and his men that might be the best-case scenario for all concerned, except the U.S. government.

"Ease in behind them so they can see it's a Humvee approaching," Fred instructed. "When you park, tuck yourself behind the last truck. As soon as he pulls to a stop, everyone move deliberately and with a sense of purpose toward the drivers. Weapons at low ready. I'm sure they're armed, but not likely to engage. Why would they bother, right?"

The rain had slowed to a gentle trickle from the skies. It had served its purpose by bunching the guardsmen together while distracting them from their assignments. Now Fred was going to turn the tables by commandeering their transport trucks.

Within a minute, the drivers were thrown against the large wheel wells of the M35s and held at gunpoint while Fred decided what to do with them. The activity had drawn a crowd of locals, so he was hesitant to tie them to a tree or something equivalent to that.

He thought fast and decided to perpetuate the narrative being told to the mayor. "Folks, we need you to stay back. These men are under arrest for treasonous activities. They, and others like them, have been using their authority to loot local towns like yours. Please stand back, and we'll be out of your way."

The M35 drivers immediately protested.

"He's lying!"

"They're imposters!"

Fred shoved one of the drivers into the side of the truck. "Nice try, traitor. Men, load them into the back of the Humvee after you cuff them. You traitors are under arrest."

Fred's men did as instructed. It took over five minutes of pushing and shoving, coupled with the guardsmen jawing over their innocence. Once they were tucked into the backseat of the Humvee, Fred explained what he hoped to accomplish next. He used the rainsoaked hood of the Humvee to draw a crude map of the streets around Harford House with his fingers

"I'll lead the way, pulling directly in front of the entrance. Our guys will stand down." He paused and pointed toward the dark patch over his missing eye. "One eye has its advantages sometimes."

The men laughed while glancing around to make sure the locals weren't eavesdropping.

Fred continued, "I need you to form a semicircle around the two Humvees that are here, across from our entrance. They're backed into a driveway and flanked on both sides by a brick column with lanterns on top. If they suspect something, they'll have no place to go but backwards in their trucks or to bail out and take us on. If all goes as planned, we'll surprise them before they can make that decision."

"If they're gonna fire on us, that will be the time," said one of his men.

Fred nodded and slapped the hood of the truck. "Agreed. Eyes wide open, and heads on a swivel. We need to avoid killing them because that will bring the damn Army to Harford. If we simply embarrass them, like those ass clowns half naked at the fairgrounds, they might stay away."

"Let's roll!"

So they did. With Fred leading the way, the convoy pulled out and headed toward the intersection where the National Guard squad had first appeared. Without stopping, and while ignoring the belligerent guardsmen who were handcuffed together, Fred turned the Humvee toward Harford House, checking his side mirror to confirm the heavy M35s were keeping pace.

The rain picked up again, which was a plus. If the rain had stopped completely, the men in the Humvees might've exited the trucks to avoid the stuffy interiors. The continuous rainfall held them in place.

However, Fred did not consider the reaction of the guardsmen upon seeing his approach. They must've assumed the Humvee Fred was driving belonged to their superior officer and contained the FBI agents. The sight of the M35s tagging along only confirmed their assumption. By the time the convoy pulled to a stop at the front driveway at Harford House, the remaining guardsmen were spilling out of their trucks, and Fred's captives were screaming at the top of their lungs.

Then chaos ensued.

The M35s arrived just as the guardsmen were walking into the center of the road. Rather than slow down, the lead driver ploughed through them, causing them to scatter in all directions. None of the guardsmen had expected hostiles to approach them, so their weapons weren't ready for the unexpected attack.

Fred quickly exited his truck, with the barrel of his automatic weapon moving back and forth, alternating between the three targets on his side of the M35 caravan. He shouted at them to raise their hands and slowly remove their weapons.

Dumbfounded, the three didn't move. It didn't help that the three men held captive in the backseat of the Humvee were all screaming instructions and hurling expletives at Fred.

When a burst of automatic gunfire sent bullets flying into the pavement on the other side of the M35s, Fred decided to fire a volley at the three guardsmen in an attempt to force them to comply with his demands.

The men were shocked and immediately raised their arms again. Fred wasn't sure if they did so in response to his gunfire or because of the screaming leathernecks who poured out of the lobby of Harbor House. He took a second to glance beyond the Humvee and saw a dozen of his men racing toward the driveway entrance with their weapons pointing in his direction.

Fred stepped sideways so his guys could make out his face while keeping his rifle trained on the three men. On the other side of the transport trucks, gunfire was being exchanged between his ex-Marines and the remainder of the guardsmen.

"Hold these three!" Fred shouted as the first of his men arrived through the vehicle barrier. "The rest, come with me."

He and four men circled around the troop transports to get into position behind the guardsmen. They were pinned down between their Humvees, taking on sporadic friendly fire from his guys.

"Give it up!" he hollered during a break in the gunfight. "Nobody will get hurt. Stand down!"

"You have no authority—!" one of the guardsmen began to shout back to Fred before being cut off.

"I do today! Last chance. Drop your weapons and raise your hands high over your heads. Come out one at a time, and you won't be harmed."

Fred used hand signals to his men to hop the fence and circle around the Humvee. When he saw they were in position, he raised his hand and motioned for them to move in.

"Raise your hands or prepare to die! Your choice!"

When the guardsmen saw the two men standing behind them with automatic weapons, they quickly complied.

The standoff was over.

CHAPTER THIRTY

Wednesday
Harford, Pennsylvania

With great power comes great responsibility is an old adage often misattributed to politicians and other people of historic significance. In actuality, it first appeared in a Spider-Man comic book in 1962. Comic aficionados often refer to it as the Peter Parker principle. Fred Stewart was unaware of its historical background as being part of American pop culture. However, he certainly felt the weight of its significance on his shoulders.

He had set into motion a series of events born out of necessity and survival. He never had any intention of taking on the U.S. government, especially in some kind of armed conflict. Yet just a little over an hour ago, he'd found himself standing alone, facing half a dozen rifles and a contingent of National Guardsmen who were a little too overzealous in performing their duties.

When the power grid collapsed, Fred, who'd been increasingly bitter over the years, as he felt his government and society had abandoned him, saw an opening to make up for many lost years. Like so many others across the country, Fred looked at the perfect storm as an opportunity to better his lot in life. He moved quickly and decisively to create a home for himself, surrounded by his comrades, and well stocked with supplies.

To be sure, he broke laws of man and civility to enrich himself. His hardened attitude to outsiders served his self-interest well. Then he gradually softened. From the initial interaction with the Cubbison family when their son was hurt, to the benevolence of Dr. Quinn, the veterinarian who saved his man's life, he began to sense his role in the remote Pennsylvania town was something more than squatter and looter.

When he and his men were able to come to the rescue of the Cubbisons as they faced certain death at the hands of the criminal biker gang, he realized that he could be a force of good in the community.

With the change of circumstances, he could have enjoyed his role as the protector of the town and surrounding areas. He had slowly opened himself up to the local residents following the gun battle with the bikers at Cubbison's. He began to feel better about himself and his future. And then, once again, his government let him down. So he took action.

As a result, he'd commandeered three Humvees, three M35 cargo transports, and a dozen half-naked National Guardsmen, who stood before him in the rain. Fred managed a chuckle as he muttered the acronym *FUBAR*.

He prided himself on being fluid in his planning, adapting to conditions on the ground, as they used to say in Afghanistan. He'd just bottom-lined the only possible scenario for his men as they spoke at the front of Harford House. They had to roll out. Quickly, in fact.

They expected the FBI agents and their National Guard escort to return at any time. Most likely, with reinforcements sufficient enough to dislodge Fred and his men from Harford House. He intended to leave the impression for the locals and the returning guardsmen that he had fled to New York. He would allow the men held captive to believe that as well.

The first order of business was to load as many of their acquired supplies and weapons cache into the M35s as possible, leaving just enough of the weapons for the locals to defend themselves.

Second, all operating vehicles were topped off with fuel and the rest stored in gas cans to be hauled in one of their vintage pickup trucks. Each vehicle was assigned to a two-man team, while the rest would be prepared to leave in the three Humvees.

Finally, the hostages would be blindfolded and crammed into the back of an old Ford Econoline van. Fred and another man would drive them north toward the state line, dropping them off sporadically and miles away from one another. It would take them many days to find their way back to Harford, once they clothed themselves.

The plan was designed to give them a head start on their quest for a new home. Each of the vehicles would set out in a different direction on a mostly northerly route to facilitate the ruse. However, he wanted them to regroup at a place that was familiar and free from confrontation—Cubbison's Farm. He instructed his men to drive north and begin a roundabout turn that led them back to Cubbison's. They were all supposed to arrive at the farm near simultaneously, just after dawn. His top lieutenant, a man who'd assisted in the defense of the farm, would drive the Pontiac GTO and arrive at the Cubbisons' front gate just before dawn. The car would be easily recognizable to any patrols the family had on duty at that hour. His lieutenant would explain that the Cubbisons should expect company to arrive as the sun did that morning.

As his men hustled about their duties, Fred paced the parking lot, his mind wandering between his days living in his car, to the out-of-the-box thinking that built this compound, to what an uncertain future held for them.

His thoughts were interrupted when he noticed the mayor and his daughter approaching. They were leading a sizable group of local residents. Some were carrying umbrellas while others let the rain pour over their heads. All of them had a look of concern and uncertainty on their faces.

The mayor, whom Fred had previously met under less amicable circumstances, spoke first when the group gathered in front of the steps of Harford House.

"They tell me you're leaving. Is that true?" he asked.

A man standing next to him also asked, "All of you?"

Fred took a deep breath, ignored their questions, and got right to the point. "You may or may not be aware of the bombing at the Viewmont Mall in Scranton recently. The FBI is investigating, and they're using the National Guard as escorts to visit communities like Harford. On its face, it appears to be noncombative. While I believe the federal agents' intentions are good, the guard, or at least this unit, have ulterior motives."

"Like what?" the mayor asked.

"Are you familiar with the martial law declaration issued by the president?" Fred asked in response. The group nodded. "Well, that declaration gave the National Guard authority to confiscate pretty much anything they wanted. Even if it didn't, I believe they'd take it by force."

"They wouldn't do that," countered a woman in the group.

Fred grimaced. "Actually, ma'am, I think they have been, and that was their intention for Harford after the FBI interviewed you. They said as much during my conversation with the agents and a sergeant who threatened me more than once."

The mayor pointed at Harford House and the surrounding grounds. His voice reflected his contempt for Fred and his men.

"It's because of what you've done here. They know this is some kind of fortress. They want back what you took."

"Maybe," said Fred. "We were their first stop but certainly not their last. Regardless, they left a small contingent here, and we've taken them into custody. I plan on releasing them once we get to New York."

"New York?" asked a man in the back.

"That's right. We are pulling out in just a matter of minutes. I believe we've become a lightning rod for the National Guard, which in turn puts this town and you people in the crosshairs. With us gone, they might redirect their resources in search of us rather than turning this town upside down to confiscate every last bread crumb for the government's redistribution."

The mayor continued to question Fred. "Why are you telling us this? Just go already."

His attitude began to upset Fred, who was trying to protect the town in his own, unorthodox way. *Would the mayor rather I turn our weapons on the Guard and vice versa?* There would undoubtedly be collateral damage to the residents of Harford. Fred forced himself to suppress his dismay and continued.

"We are going to leave you weapons, ammo, medical supplies and other items that can be used to better your lives. I suggest the moment we pull out, you gather them up and leave the grounds. Except, of course, for the town leaders. You should greet the National Guard when they return."

"And say what?" asked the mayor.

"Answer their questions, and be truthful. You can tell them as little or as much as you see fit. Just keep in mind that, although you may not see it at this moment, we are doing you a favor. We're leaving and drawing them away from you."

The townspeople began talking among themselves. Several approached the mayor to whisper their thoughts into his ear. He seemed to be receptive to their advice, as his tone softened.

"Okay," he began after a long pause. "We'll follow your suggestions under the condition that you not return to Harford. I mean, not that we can stop you if you did. It's just, we want our town back."

"You have my word," said Fred.

It was time to go. He raised his hand over his head and rolled it around in a circular motion. His men hustled off to their vehicles and began to head out of town on the four roads leading north.

After one final look around Harford House, Fred headed west toward US 11. Every ten miles, he planned to drop off a captured guardsmen until they were spread all over Northeastern Pennsylvania. Further, he and his men never planned on returning to the small town, although they would always be watching in case the residents needed their help.

CHAPTER THIRTY-ONE

Wednesday
Lake Wallenpaupack
Wayne County, Pennsylvania

Abdul Rahimi was growing increasingly impatient. It had been four days since his scouts had been dispatched to the area surrounding the small town of Harford. The men he sent were his most adept at conducting surveillance. Not that he considered their job to be easy, he certainly expected a fast result considering they'd virtually pinpointed the location of the wayward Pontiac GTO.

After evening prayers, he abruptly walked away from the others in their compound on Lake Wallenpaupack to be alone. He strolled the shores, recollecting the events that had led to the death of his best friend, Jamal Khan. He'd somehow managed to blame Khan's daughter, Vida, for weighing on her father's mind, leading to his being distracted during their attack on the Picatinny Arsenal. Therefore, following his warped logic, Vida might as well have pulled the trigger herself.

Of course, he knew that was illogical to an extreme; however, his built-up anger began to cloud his judgment. Before his trusted soldiers left, they'd discussed the approach they planned to take during their search. He was keenly aware the American FBI and their military would be searching for the bombers. It was likely his vehicles had been spotted on the interstate leading north out of Scranton.

Abdul allowed the possibility that his two scouts, despite their attempts to hide their Afghan identity, had been caught. He began to believe he was sitting around their community waiting for men who were unable to return.

He made the decision to take a group of men to search on his own. He'd follow the same route into Harford, searching for the GTO and his two scouts. It shouldn't be that difficult to find what they sought, he'd convinced himself.

He felt the pressure in other ways. Abdul was keenly aware that Afghan communities like his would soon be the focus of the Americans' investigation. He'd forbidden anyone from leaving the compound without his permission. He wanted to remain out of the public eye until the emotions had died down. His leaving the compound was risky as well, especially since he wanted to take a highly visible group of men to assist in the hunt.

Yet his obsession forced him into a decision. The life of Jamal Khan must be avenged. Khan's daughter, the insolent teen Vida, must be returned to the compound to suffer her just punishment. Any infidels harboring these fugitives must be punished.

Abdul set his jaw and marched back to the compound, where several of his men quietly waited. After prayer, it had become part of their routine to assess and reassess their community's safety and future. The men were silent as he appeared near the fire they'd gathered around.

Abdul's face was gaunt and tired. His eyes were the color of steel, almost lifeless. He spoke in a low tone of voice, with a hint of a growl. In less than a minute, he exuded the frustration and anger that had built up within him as he rallied his men to pray, sleep, and prepare to do battle.

CHAPTER THIRTY-TWO

Wednesday
Cubbison's Farm
Harford, Pennsylvania

"I just need one more!" Luke yelled to the guys on the ground. "Make it fifty-six inches, ripped down to six even!"

The guys had spent the day finishing the repairs to the Cubbison home. The first order of business was to remove the plywood sheathing used as a temporary covering for the window openings. Then, because the replacement windows salvaged from the Stanley house didn't match the broken ones exactly, they had to modify the stud walls without harming the structural integrity of the wall. This resulted in some of the windows being off center, much to the chagrin of Sam and Emma.

With the windows installed and functioning, they turned their attention to patching the last of the holes in the siding. Once again, because the siding removed from the Stanley house didn't match the Cubbisons', some precision cutting was required. The length was easy. The height of the board in relation to the opening required a lot of skill. Sam was the expert cut man, as they called him. After painting the boards with white exterior primer, from the ground it was difficult to discern which boards were the replacements. Most importantly, cosmetics aside, the home was secure for the upcoming winter months.

Inside, Emma recruited Vida and Lauren to help her use Super Glue to repair as many of the ceramic family heirlooms as they could. Certainly, the cracks and chips were obvious even after successfully piecing the decorative tchotchkes back together. In the early days of the Cubbison family, many of these pieces had been used in their day-to-day lives. Over time, their value as a part of the family's history outweighed their intended function, landing them a prized spot in the family's hutches.

Many had been destroyed, causing sadness for Sam and Emma. It was Emma who refused to be beaten by the now-dead bikers who'd carelessly shot up their home and belongings. The ladies banded together and repaired what they could. As they did, they discussed the plight of Jenna and her girls.

"Vida, you and Matthew have spent more time with Jenna than any of us," began Emma. "Can you tell us where her head's at right now?"

Vida held two parts of a serving piece together to allow the glue to set up as she replied, "She definitely appreciated Sam helping her get started. But, um, he's a guy and doesn't really understand women." She paused for a moment and then apologized. "I really didn't mean for that to come out that way."

Emma and Lauren burst out laughing. Emma explained, "Sam is old school. As far as he was concerned, she had a roof over her head and a stocked pond out back. Then it was like, *have a nice day.*"

Vida gingerly set the serving bowl down and slowly removed her hands, allowing them to hover near the rim as if she planned on catching the piece of fine china if it fell apart again. It held, and she managed a smile.

"He didn't do much to get her set up, you know? I've gone over there frequently, and Matthew has, also. He's gone to the neighboring farmhouses and gathered up basics like kitchen items, sheets, blankets and pillows. For my part, I've spent time with her cleaning. The man who lived there was a pig."

"In more ways than you know," added Emma under her breath.

Vida continued, "In fact, after we're done here, I planned on going over to Jenna's to help her decorate. She doesn't have much to work with, really. If anything, there are things she wants to throw out. Plus, there's an attic and garage full of stuff. She's afraid of going in the attic after what happened, you know, with the fire bomber."

Emma put her decorative piece onto the table, and the ladies inspected their work. The delicate heirlooms were holding together with the Super Glue, although the tube was almost totally flat. She'd have to search for some more or put it on her wish list she'd started at the beginning of the collapse. Thus far, the Cubbisons had not ventured out to abandoned homes or businesses in search of items of usefulness. There had been several conversations within the group regarding foraging versus looting. Emma expected that time would come.

She was about to speak when Cat entered the room. "Mom, don't we need to check on the mama cow?"

Emma pushed her chair away from the table and stood. "That's exactly what I was about to suggest. Vida, you can head over to Jenna's anytime you'd like. Don't forget, we're gonna eat at dusk."

"I'll remember. I'm on patrol with Grandpa Sam this evening."

Emma turned to Cat. "Let's go check on that cow. Lauren, would you mind straightening up before one of our clumsy men comes in and destroys a morning's work?"

"Not a problem," she replied and then asked, "Is there anything I can do to prepare for dinner?"

"Nope. Leftovers tonight. They'll be easy to warm up during our generator hour."

The group split up and went their separate ways. Emma and Cat saddled up and moseyed across the pasture until they reached a pen with a small barn specifically used for birthing calves. The Cubbisons had designed and built the calving barn to replace an old chicken house with dilapidated runs.

The calving barn was located just north of the main house at the top of a small rise. The structure's size was bigger than necessary considering the size of the Cubbison herd at the time. However, after they'd incorporated the Stanley herd into their own, they learned they had two pregnant cows within weeks of giving birth.

Emma and Cat dismounted and made their way to the swinging farm gate that led into a five-foot-wide alley. Another gate separated the alley from each birthing pen, commonly known as a jug. The alley was also used as a confinement alley leading to the hospital corral, or pulling stall, as many cattle ranchers called it. On the other side of the pulling stall, connected by a narrow calf-sized chute, was a post-birth stall where the newborn calf could be processed before reuniting with its mother.

Emma and Cat had barely entered the confinement alley when she heard one of the cows acting restless in her stall. Sam had instructed the guys to feed the pregnant cows once daily between five in the afternoon and ten at night, hoping this would result in the mothers calving between five in the morning and midnight when activity around the farm was near normal.

Emma rushed ahead and looked into the first jug. The pregnant cow was milling about but not acting unusual. The next jug was two corrals down. There, Emma found the pregnant cow stumbling through the hay until she finally dropped onto her side.

"Oh, boy! Here we go!" she exclaimed before grabbing Cat by the shoulders. "Honey, hurry. We'll need Grandpa Sam, your dad and probably Luke, too. This baby's comin'!"

CHAPTER THIRTY-THREE

Wednesday
Cubbison's Farm
Harford, Pennsylvania

The guys raced through the pasture, with Cat in hot pursuit. The group arrived all at once. Luke didn't bother opening the gate. He simply took a slight leap and catapulted over the gate. Likewise, the next gate was nothing more than a hurdle to fly over.

"How's she doin', Mom?" he asked as he skidded to a stop in front of the jug. Luke had taken a personal interest in these cows since he'd rescued them from exile at the back of Stanley's farm. Caring for those cattle had almost killed him, literally.

"Fine, son. You know, we never actually knew when she bagged up. It could've been eight weeks ago or right before you discovered them. We knew she was due, though." The term bagged up referred to when the cow's udder filled with colostrum. Had modern veterinary technology been available to them, Dr. Quinn would've brought a portable ultrasound to determine how far along the two cows were.

Instead, the Cubbisons had to work off their knowledge of their cattle and Sam's wealth of experience. He was out of breath as the rest of the entourage arrived, remaining respectfully outside the jug to avoid stressing the cow.

"Emma, have you checked for positioning? Where is the calf in the birthing canal?"

"I haven't," she replied. "I've just tried to keep her calm."

"Good. Good. Let me in to take a look."

Sam eased into the jug and dropped to his knees at the side of the cow. He began to feel her abdomen, with a focus on the pelvic canal. He looked up to Emma and asked, "Has she pushed since you discovered her?"

"No. She was staggering somewhat, her knees buckled a little, and then she seemed to flop over on her side."

"She fell over?" Sam asked.

"No. It was more like a not-so-graceful sit and flop."

"Hmm," Sam mumbled without explanation. *At least she's on her left side*, Sam thought to himself, glad the cow's largest stomach compartment was under and not on top of the calf.

"What does *hmmm* mean?" asked Cat.

Sam laughed. "Well, Cat, I have this mental checklist that deals with the cow's female parts. I don't know if your mom is ready to teach you about reproductive anatomy."

"Keep it simple, Grandpa Sam," Emma suggested.

"Okay, well, there's a part inside called the cervix. I checked to see if it has dilated, gotten larger, to allow the calf to come through. It has. Then it's easy to confirm her water sac has broken. See the hay underneath her?" Sam picked some of it out and showed Cat.

"I see," she said. "Does that mean she's ready?"

Sam grimaced. "I'm not sure her calf is in the proper position. That's why I want your dad and brother to be ready to pull. We may have to assist her calf by pulling her out."

"Ewww." Cat's childlike reaction was not unexpected.

"Well, kind of, Cat. But remember, it's part of the miracle of birth. Mama and baby will be just fine."

"What can I do?" asked Emma.

"I think we are about to start a long labor," Sam answered. "I would've preferred to have guided her into the birthing room in the back, but this'll do. I don't want to stress her by forcing her onto her feet. We can do it right here if you don't mind keeping her calm."

"Absolutely," said Emma.

"How can we assist while we wait, Dad?" asked John.

"Well, as you know, cleanliness is a must," replied Sam. "We need buckets of warm water, some clear and some with a light mixture of mineral oil. We'll need a bucket of water with antibacterial soap to keep our hands and arms clean. John, I'll have you help pull her."

"I wanna help pull, too," insisted Luke.

Sam understood why. "Okay, if necessary, you guys will pull, and I'll give you direction. We've done this many times before." He thought for a moment, and then he added, "I'll need a birthing kit from the hospital corral. It'll have the equipment we normally rely upon plus the lube to assist the calf out the starter gate."

Everyone followed Sam's instructions and prepared for the new addition to the Cubbisons' herd. Much to Sam's surprise, and delight, the calf began his journey into life faster than expected.

It had been three hours, and the calf had made steady progress through the birth canal. Because of the calf's positioning, Sam decided it would be best to help birth the calf by pulling it out when the cow was pushing.

Sam preferred to use a sixty-inch chain to assist the calf through the birth canal. Rope wasn't sufficiently sanitary, in his experience. He carefully wrapped each chain around below the dewclaw and above the hooves of the front legs in order to avoid injuring the newborn.

As the cow pushed, John and Luke alternated pulling on a leg to bring the calf through the pelvic opening. When the cow rested, they rested. Within an hour, the guys were walking the shoulders out by alternating the legs they pulled. Once the head and shoulders were free, Sam worked with the guys to rotate the calf slightly to aid in the passage of the hips.

When the calf was free, all three Cubbison men fell simultaneously onto their backsides, their chests heaving as they gasped for air. The calf found its footing and stood on wobbly legs for a moment. As he did, the group spontaneously burst out in applause and exchanged high fives.

A new life was brought into the world under austere circumstances. It didn't matter that it was a calf rather than a baby. It was a sign that they all had a future ahead of them. A future full of life.

CHAPTER THIRTY-FOUR

Wednesday
Ledbetter Place
Harford, Pennsylvania

Vida arrived later than planned. She stuck around to help Lauren clean up their restoration project, and as she began walking toward the highway, she heard Cat call for the guys. She desperately wanted to view the birthing process. However, she didn't want to break her promise to Jenna and her daughters.

As soon as she arrived, she told Jenna and her daughters about the big news. Naturally, the children wanted to race to see the new baby cow, as they called it. Vida had to tamp down their enthusiasm.

"Let's give him a day with his mommy first. Okay?"

"Aww, we wanna see him," the girls whined in unison,

Vida knelt down next to them on the front porch. "Maybe tomorrow. I tell you what. I promise to come back over when the time's right."

"Are you coming back tomorrow, too?" the oldest, Kay, asked.

"I think so, yes. It depends on what Mr. and Mrs. Cubbison need me to do."

Jenna intervened. "Come on, girls, stop badgering Miss Vida."

Vida stood and smiled. She appreciated the friendship she'd developed with Jenna and her girls. She turned to Jenna.

"It'll depend on what the day brings. It's been nice to avoid the kind of drama we've dealt with in the last couple of weeks."

Jenna shooed the girls inside. She motioned toward the steps, where she led Vida toward Ledbetter's garage. She made small talk as they walked along.

"I knew that deal at the farmhouse wasn't going to last," Jenna began. "Those men were losers, and it was a matter of time before things got out of hand."

"I felt bad for leaving you and the other women behind like that," said Vida. "It's just, well, I've been through a lot."

"I get it. I kinda look at this as a fresh start, even though it's a hand-me-down. It's really hard to look at this place as our new home. I'm not sure how long we'll live here."

Vida stopped. Jenna's attitude had changed for some reason. "I'm not sure I understand. You've fit in well with the others. You have a place you can call home. I realize it's a challenge, but ..." Her voice trailed off, hoping Jenna would explain herself.

She didn't. Instead, she walked ahead and opened the garage door. She'd sorted through the contents and stacked them into neat piles.

"This is my version of a department store. Over here, you have men's apparel. This is housewares. This section is hardware. And finally, the liquor store."

Vida marveled at the cases of wine and liquor of all varieties that had been stored in the garage. The prior occupant of the home certainly placed a high priority on remaining inebriated from one hallucinogenic substance or another.

She rummaged through the boxes of housewares. "Is there anything here that you didn't already have?"

"No, not really," Jenna replied. "It was almost like he had a second home and brought all of its contents here. The décor is older. Kinda old ladyish."

"It's better than the cowboy stuff he had inside the house," quipped Vida as she sorted through the vases and artwork. She turned her attention to the pile Jenna had identified as hardware. There were multiple toolboxes, with nails, screws, and hand tools. She spied an opened tube of Super Glue and snatched it up to give to Emma.

"The clothes are mostly for hunting, it appears," said Jenna. She picked up a pair of camouflage pants to show Vida. "Didn't you and Sam say the guy who lived here was really big?"

"Yes. If he wore these, it must have been twenty years ago. They look more like they'd fit Luke."

"Or Matthew," added Jenna. "Pretty much the same thing, right?"

The two women laughed. Vida had speculated internally that Matthew was attracted to the much older Jenna. He spent an inordinate amount of time at her place, trying to act like a father to her girls while shamelessly flirting with Jenna.

His relationship to Jenna was one of the many complicating factors impacting the inner strife Vida felt as she processed the fact that Matthew had killed her father.

"You know he likes you," said Vida suddenly.

"What? You mean in a romantic sort of way?"

"Yes. Surely you've noticed."

Jenna blushed and turned away. She'd been forced to grow up much too quickly. She hadn't had the opportunity to learn about teen crushes and romances. She had been forced to become a woman. Despite the fact she was eight years older than Matthew, she'd found herself open to the possibility of a relationship with him.

She tried to blow it off. "Come on. He's just lonely. Besides, is he even eighteen yet?"

Vida smiled as she picked out a few items of home décor. She placed them in a U.S. Postal Service bin until it was filled.

"I don't think stuff like that matters anymore. However, since you asked, Luke and Matthew just turned nineteen in June. They're technically legal."

"Shut up, Vida!" protested Jenna playfully. She'd never admit that the edgy teen was exactly the kind of man she'd been attracted to as she grew up. "Besides, I don't think his family would approve of me as a potential girlfriend."

The two exited the garage and headed toward the house. Jenna's daughters ran out to greet them. They took the postal bin out of Vida's hands, and each grabbed a handle. They skipped away, chattering between themselves.

Vida pointed toward the girls. "They're getting settled in, aren't they?"

"They're real troopers," replied Jenna. "They also don't understand the fact we are in a life-or-death situation."

"Come on, Jenna. Don't be so negative."

"We all could have died the other day, Vida. It's a matter of time before some bunch of killers who aren't morons like those bikers show up to take everything. I'm not sure I wanna be here when that happens."

"I don't know. Surely, we've had our share of trouble. Besides, where would you go?"

"Into town, maybe. Those soldiers who helped us seem pretty cool. They live in a motel, but they seem to have a decent life. And they are professionals at protecting people. I worry about my kids, you know?"

Vida scowled. She considered the Cubbisons to be pretty good at defending themselves as well. Then again, she wondered if things might've ended differently if the former Marines had not arrived just in time. The main house had been close to being torched by that one maniac.

They changed the subject and spent the rest of the afternoon making the Ledbetter home a better place to live for Jenna and her girls. Vida hoped that Jenna would learn to like her situation better. After all, like Vida, she was an outsider. It was nice to have someone to talk to without fear of saying the wrong thing.

She said her goodbyes and shoved a short grocery wish list into her jeans. Emma had committed to feeding Jenna and her family. However, Vida knew that Jenna would need to stand on her own feet soon.

The sun was lowering in the sky as she made her way across the long field toward Cubbison's Farm. She wondered to herself how she'd find a way to survive if she was forced to strike out on her own again. The more she considered the difficulties associated with being alone in this violent world, she realized how lucky she was to be with this family.

Then again, there was a dark cloud hanging over their relationship. It was the fact that her father, her flesh and blood, as flawed as he was, had been killed by Matthew Cubbison. Vida questioned whether she could let it go because, days after learning the truth, it still bothered her.

Vida closed her eyes and sighed. She looked toward the setting sun for inspiration. Suddenly, she was engulfed in darkness.

CHAPTER THIRTY-FIVE

Wednesday
Northeastern Pennsylvania

One by one, Fred dumped out his hostages. The men were becoming increasingly belligerent, exacerbated by the fact they were released with their hands zip-tied behind their backs and wearing nothing but their boxers or briefs. Despite their protestations, every ten miles or so, when Fred came upon an appropriately desolate location in the Pennsylvania countryside, he'd drop off another half-dressed guardsman. On the bright side, Fred had said to his armed companion, the rain had stopped so they'd be less uncomfortable. However, nightfall was coming quickly.

It was near midnight when the last hostage awaited his fate. Just ten minutes prior, Fred had driven across the overpass of Interstate 81 just south of the New York State line. The deserted stretch of country road ran alongside State Game Lands Number 35, a heavily wooded area that suited his purposes for the final release.

They broke through a barrier and rode along a gravel road that caused the old Econoline van to bounce back and forth, tossing their last captive across the cold, steel floor. He complained and cursed Fred, but wasn't provided any relief until Fred pulled to a stop in a clearing atop a hill.

"All right, you're the last one out, but we need to have a conversation first," said Fred as he exited the van. He and his man flung open the rear doors of the van and dragged the man onto the cold grass. He rolled over onto his knees and tried to push himself upright, but Fred brusquely forced him back down with his hand. "Not quite yet. I need you to listen to me carefully."

"Fine," the guardsman hissed. "It's freezing."

"No, not really," said Fred before adding, "Besides, you'll work up a sweat finding your way back to Scranton."

"Where am I?" he asked as he settled into a cross-legged position on the ground.

"Near the New York State line."

"Jesus! It'll take me days to walk back to Scranton. Are you gonna give me any clothes?"

"No," replied Fred. "I am, however, going to give you some valuable information to pass on to the FBI."

The guardsman nodded and tried to study Fred's face in the pitch darkness. "I'm listening."

"Okay, I'm going to tell you this because I am a man of my word and an American patriot. The people responsible for the bombing need to be brought to justice. However, whether you want to admit it or not, your sergeant had plans for us and Harford that were outside the bounds of law and decency."

"No comment."

"Well, I didn't expect that you would since you're part of it. Nevertheless, you need to pass along what I know."

"Okay. Go ahead." The tone of his voice changed. He was defeated and ready to get back to his barracks.

Fred explained, "After the bombing, I was with three of my men, taking a drive down I-81 with no particular destination. We'd just acquired a vehicle and wanted to see what the rest of the area looked like after the grid went down.

"On the other side of the highway, heading north, we saw two groups of men speeding away. In the backs of their pickups, men sat on the sides with their rifles pointed into the air. All of us reached the same conclusion."

"What was that?"

"They looked like Taliban or some other terrorist bunch riding through Afghanistan or Iraq or Syria. You pick."

"How would you know that?" he asked.

"I just know. Anyway, we continued on toward Scranton and saw the massive flames and smoke coming up from the mall location. The next thing we knew, for God knows what reason, these guys were firing upon us. They chased us back toward town until we ditched them. I'd be willing to bet money they had something to do with the bombing."

"Middle Eastern?" he asked.

"No doubt in our minds."

"How many?"

"Six or eight. Maybe nine. Also, the pickup truck beds were full of long guns and ammo cans. They must've hit an arsenal of some kind."

"And that was the last you saw of them?"

"Correct."

The guardsman seemed to run out of questions, and Fred was tired of talking to him. He walked beside the man and hoisted him off the ground.

"Are you gonna cut me loose?" the guardsman asked, turning his back to Fred and raising his arms. Fred wasn't willing to take the risk.

"No. You'll manage. Good luck."

He and his companion got back into the Econoline and slowly drove down the rut-filled dirt road until they reached the highway. Then, going from his hours of studying the maps of the area, he began to make his way to their destination. As he did, he contemplated the day's events.

Mostly, he tried to assess the viability of the wild-goose-chase ruse he'd created for his pursuers. He wanted to believe the National Guard had more important adversaries to catch, like the perpetrators of the bombing. At the very least, he hoped the FBI would keep the National Guard focused on their investigation rather than chasing Fred. Heck, Fred thought, if the locals didn't volunteer any information, it could've looked as if the National Guard squad left in Harford went out on their own.

The possibilities as to what might happen next were endless. He was glad that he was able to think things through on the fly, especially his self-restraint in not feeding the details of the bomb suspects to the mayor or the other locals. He planned on saving that tidbit of information for last so the FBI would continue to focus its available assets on searching for the perpetrators.

He and his companion continued to drive in near silence, both contemplating what their future looked like. Certainly, Fred could've led his men into New York and the unknown. However, they'd be starting from scratch. The ability to take up residency in a small town or rural area had passed with time. Shelter, fresh water, food, and medical supplies had already been picked over. He and the ex-Marines weren't farmers. They had seeds but were unsure whether they could grow anything. Besides, they didn't have enough food in their cargo trucks to last the winter.

No, Fred knew that he needed help to survive the coming months of harsh Pennsylvania winter weather. Under the pressure he had endured earlier that day, he could only think of one place to ride out the possible search while setting themselves up to survive with a minimal amount of food.

Right after dawn, he'd know if he'd made the right decision.

CHAPTER THIRTY-SIX

Wednesday
Cubbison's Farm
Harford, Pennsylvania

Vida kicked, struggled and attempted to scream. All to no avail. The brute who had caught her off guard had his powerful right hand covering her mouth while his left arm was wrapped under her arm and squeezed against her chest. He easily dragged her along like an oversized rag doll being hauled to the curb to be tossed on a pile of trash. The hood pulled over her head smelled of sweat. Musky. As if it was used by a man who rarely bathed.

Although she was unable to see, Vida's eyes grew wide as a sudden realization came over her. The men of her community bathed infrequently, and none used deodorant, as they deemed the ingredients to be impure. She was in the hands of one of Abdul's men. In fact, based on the strength of his grip and the size of his arms, which she continuously tried to pull off her, she knew exactly who he was.

She fought harder, as she expected she'd die very shortly but only after she'd suffer all kinds of indignations and torture. She'd be treated like a piece of meat. Lower than animal life. Subhuman. Her last moments on earth would be brutal and painful. She'd wish to die throughout the ordeal.

As she tired, she began to give up the fight. Her mind wandered to Luke. She'd never opened up enough to tell him how she truly felt. She was too guarded, and he was too much of a gentleman. She fantasized about kissing him. Holding his body close to hers. However, that never happened. Now she begged Allah for forgiveness, and she asked God for help.

None would come.

Minutes later, Vida was pulled into a building of some kind and was thrown onto a dusty floor. The wind was knocked out of her, so her attempts to scream only produced a large gasp. By the time she filled her lungs with oxygen, the hood was removed, and a gag was forced into her mouth. A man tied it roughly behind her head. Another man quickly bound her wrists.

Her eyes were wild from fear as she tried to focus on the dark surroundings. She tried to focus on the silhouettes of the four men who stood over her, menacingly pacing like wolves ready to attack their prey. Eerily, none of them spoke. They didn't threaten her. They made no utterances that might give away their identities. This raised her anxiety and level of fear to heights she'd never experienced in her life.

And then she felt the hot breath of a man on the back of her neck. The hair stood on her neck as the tiny muscles near her hair follicles reflexed in response. His whisper was guttural. Animal-like. Sincere. Familiar.

It was Abdul.

"I should beat you like the dog that you are before I let all of my men take you. You will beg to die, but I will not let them kill you. You will suffer as your family and their community have suffered. You will feel pain that your dead father, our brother, felt as he was murdered by the infidels. The infidel scum that you have joined."

He grabbed her hair and forced her head backwards. She felt the cold steel of a large knife against her throat. For a moment, she wished he would end it. Slice open her throat so she could die without enduring the brutality they had in mind for her. A slight smile came across her face. It grew wider. She was ready to die, and the smile revealed she'd reconciled herself to that fate.

Then Abdul changed his tone. He was angry rather than threatening. He removed his knife from her throat and shoved her down onto the ground. He quickly moved in front of her and thrust the blade toward her eye.

"Child! You find this funny?"

Luke's smiling, loving face passed through her mind. Her smile grew wider. This infuriated Abdul even more. He yanked the gag out of her mouth and shouted at her.

"You will not disrespect me!" He thrust the knife at her face again.

Vida surprised even herself with what came out of her mouth next.

"Praise Allah! You found me, as I knew you would, Abdul. *Allahu akbar!*"

She bent over at her waist, a sign of submission as she bowed before her community's spiritual leader.

He grabbed her by the chin and pulled her face up where he could study it. He turned to his men. "Give me light to see her!"

Seconds later, her smiling face locked eyes with Abdul. His dark, piercing eyes tried to look into her mind. He wasn't sure what to believe.

"You don't fool me, child!" he yelled, once again threatening her face with the knife.

"I know who killed my father," she blurted out without considering the consequences of her actions.

"What? You know the killer of our brother, the father you abandoned?"

Vida sighed and bowed her head out of respect. "I have prayed to Allah for forgiveness for my childish actions. I have shamed myself, my family, and my community. I was returning home when I learned of my father's death and who killed him. He is near."

"Continue!"

"His name is Matthew, and he was at the arsenal when the shooting occurred. I heard him speaking with his family about my father's car speeding toward him. My father was defenseless, driving the car, and this infidel, Matthew, fired into the car to kill him."

Abdul relaxed. He glanced around and looked at each of his men. He took a deep breath.

"Leave us. Outside, everyone."

Vida remained on her knees with her hands tied behind her back as the men shuffled out of the abandoned produce stand where two of their Afghan scouts had run into the pig farmer's papa from hell. She had to play this out, hoping that Abdul would release her so she could warn the Cubbisons.

"You live among them," he said. "Is that correct?"

"Only temporarily until I could escape. I was, um, injured, and they took care of me. They were kind like the wolf who wears a sheep's disguise. Several days ago, they were attacked by a group five or six times their size. They killed all of the attackers, and none of them were hurt. I tried to lure the man, Matthew, into the open so he could be killed, but I was unsuccessful."

"Why didn't you shoot him yourself?" asked Abdul.

"They will not give me a gun," she replied.

Abdul pointed toward Jenna's home. "Why were you at that house?"

"She is a neighbor. Matthew and another member of the family left two days ago. They are supposed to be back the day after tomorrow. I tried to find out from the neighbor where he went. I hoped to surprise him with a knife to the throat."

Abdul's previously tense body noticeably relaxed. He was buying the ploy. "You are certain of this?"

"Yes. I will be ready for him when he—" said Vida before Abdul cut her off.

"No!" he said sternly. "I will administer the punishment that Allah sees as appropriate. You will find out when and from where he will return."

Vida's heart leapt. Her ruse was working. She spoke with confidence. "That is my plan. I must be careful and secretive. This family does not trust me. They have already told me that I must leave soon. I pretend that my injury is more severe than they think."

"Where are you hurt, child?" Abdul asked.

"I am not. I am lying to them to get my chance to avenge my father's death."

Abdul seemed pleased with this response. He placed his knife in the sheath tied to his waist. He reached under her armpits and helped her to her feet. Then he untied her bound wrists. Her arms were shaking from the nervousness she continued to endure.

"Do not be afraid, child. You will help avenge the death of your father, the great Jamal Khan, my brother."

"I will make you and Allah proud. But it is growing darker, and the family will grow suspicious of my absence. I must return."

Abdul slowly nodded. Then he grabbed her firmly by the arm and twisted it slightly. He forced his face directly in front of hers, his hot, garlic-scented breath causing her to become somewhat nauseous.

"At dawn, the day after tomorrow, after morning prayer, I will return with Allah's army. You will meet me here to reveal the location of this Matthew, the murderer of my brother Jamal. Do you understand me?"

"Yes."

"Do not fail me, child. If you do, you will beg for a merciful death."

Vida nodded and mumbled her response. "I will not fail."

CHAPTER THIRTY-SEVEN

Wednesday
Cubbison's Farm
Harford, Pennsylvania

Vida did not speak as the two men who forcibly escorted her back toward Cubbison's Farm hissed vile comments and threats in her ear. She remembered that Abdul was certainly their leader, but these men were vicious killers and thugs if they were part of his inner circle. She was keenly aware that they might attack her and swear on Allah that they'd done nothing to defile her.

Just as they came into view of Jenna's house, the men gave her one final push, knocking her face-first into the tall grasses. Not sure if they were done with her, Vida scrambled on her hands and knees to get as far away from them as possible. The men cackled with delight at her frightened state.

Eventually, she found her footing and began running toward the front gate. She spotted Asher, who was making his way on horseback from the west where he'd been patrolling the perimeter. Relieved at being free from the clutches of Abdul and his men, Vida's emotions poured out of her.

Asher encouraged his horse to pick up the pace to ride to Vida's aid. He dismounted before the horse came to a complete stop, stumbling slightly as he rushed to Vida's side.

"Are you okay?" he asked with his hand on his pistol grip and his eyes searching the fields beyond the highway.

Unable to speak, Vida was trying to slow her breathing to avoid hyperventilating. Asher's calm voice and protective nature hastened her recovery. It also allowed her to consider what she planned on doing. Vida needed time to think, so she thought up a plausible lie.

"I was returning from Jenna's," she began. Her words came out slowly, separated by deep, heavy breaths. "I stumbled in a hole and fell near a fallen tree."

While she continued to steady her breathing, Asher asked, "Are you hurt? Your ankle? Or wrists?" He noticed her soiled clothing and scratched hands.

Vida shook her head violently and withdrew her hands from Asher. She didn't want him to notice the ligature marks caused by Abdul's men tying her up.

"A snake. A snake. It was near my face."

Asher began to inspect her face and neck in search of blood from a puncture wound. "Did it bite you?"

Vida's heart was still racing from apprehension as her lies continued. She was able to speak more clearly now.

"It missed me when I rolled away from it. I was so scared. I fell twice more running back to the farm."

Asher, relieved that she wasn't severely injured, helped her to her feet. He allowed her a moment to steady herself.

"Are you okay? Can you walk?"

Vida nodded. "Facing that snake was horrible. I was afraid no one would come looking for me. I didn't want to die alone in the field." She'd begun to use the term snake as a metaphor for Abdul and his men.

Asher gave her a reassuring smile and gently placed his hand on her back. She recoiled slightly from his touch, not because she disliked him. The thought of the men touching her just moments ago was very fresh in her mind.

"Let me get my horse, and we'll walk together," said Asher.

Moments later, they were walking toward the main house. Asher relayed everything he knew about snakes. How to identify a venomous snake from those whose bite will hurt but not likely kill you. He relayed the likely places snakes can be found and what he understood to be the blind season, during which snakes shed their skin, resulting in poor eyesight. They were more likely to strike out at movement than normal.

He continued to talk, but Vida didn't hear him. She was conflicted as to what action to take. All she wanted to do was lock herself away where she could replay everything that had been said between Abdul and herself. She knew she couldn't face Matthew, whom she'd likely sentenced to death. Or his parents, who had taken her in as one of their own. They would lose a son, or more.

And what about Luke, Matthew's twin? Abdul wouldn't differentiate between her father's killer and the young man she'd fallen for. He'd kill them both.

In fact, he'd kill them all.

Vida dropped to her knees and vomited.

CHAPTER THIRTY-EIGHT

Wednesday
Cubbison's Farm
Harford, Pennsylvania

Asher ran inside to fetch Emma and Lauren. They rushed along his side, quizzing him about what had happened. He was puzzled by her sudden reaction to their conversation. Then he cursed himself for going on and on about snakes without realizing Vida was so traumatized by the event. Lauren sent him back into the house to grab a bottle of water and a wet washcloth. Lauren felt she and Emma would be better able to calm the distraught young woman down.

Vida wiped her mouth off on her sleeve and stood, tears streaming down her face. She had to get ahold of herself. Or she simply needed to make a decision, come what may. It shouldn't be hard, she thought to herself as Emma and Lauren approached. *These people love me. My old family and community do not.* Yet the conflict raged within her.

Emma arrived first and immediately tried to comfort her. "Honey, it's okay. You're safe now."

A valid point, Vida thought to herself. Despite the attacks on Cubbison's Farm, she felt safer here than within the clutches of Abdul and the other Afghan men. They'd just not-so-subtly reminded her of that.

"You promise you weren't bit?" asked Lauren. "If you were, we need to act quickly to protect you."

She shook her head side to side. *No, they didn't bite me. Not yet, anyway.*

"I'm sorry," she muttered as she wiped the tears from her face with dirt-stained hands. The soil mixed with her tears to create brown smudges on her face. She held her hands out to look at the mess she'd created. "I must look like, um. I'm so weak."

Asher arrived with the wet cloth and the bottle of water. Emma turned to him and asked, "Would you mind turning on the generator? Then go inside and tell everyone to avoid the use of hot water. I wanna draw Vida a bath."

Asher dutifully hustled off as Emma turned her attention back to Vida. She gently wiped her face clean with the wet cloth and then opened the bottle of water. Vida swished some around in her mouth and turned her head before spitting it out. Then she gulped some down. Her mouth and throat had become very dry as a result of the entire ordeal.

"Thank you," she whispered as she fought back sniffles. "I really don't know what's come over me. It's all, you know, there's been so much."

Lauren adopted her best Jersey girl accent. "Honey, you have no idea. I curl up in a ball twice a day in that barn over there, crying my eyes out because of everything we've been through. Even the horses are tired of my whining to myself."

Emma laughed. "That's nothing. John threatened to sleep on the couch if I didn't stop sniveling about the holes in our house. Now that everything's fixed, I think I might take him up on it so he won't snore in my ear."

Lauren added, "Yeah, about that snoring. Lately, the boys have been sharing a bourbon or two before bed. Asher snores like a freight train after two drinks. I'm ready to railroad him out to the chicken coop to sleep!"

Vida's nerves relaxed as Emma and Lauren ragged on their husbands. Nothing bonds a group of women more than playfully trashing their spouses without their knowledge. It's a right inherent in girl code.

"You are very fortunate to have loving husbands," said Vida. "My mother deserved better than my father."

Emma immediately felt bad. She should've considered Vida's recent discovery that her own father was dead, at the hand of Matthew, no less.

Emma profusely apologized. "Oh, honey. I'm so sorry. That was very insensitive of me."

Vida managed a smile. "It's okay. Nobody should have to walk on eggshells around me. You have made me feel better. Would you mind if I go to bed early? I'm supposed to be on early patrol tonight."

Emma reached out and took Vida by the hand. She gave it a gentle squeeze and gave Vida a loving smile. "Let me run you a bath. Lauren will stand guard and make sure you're not interrupted."

"I sure will. But, um, do you wanna speak to Luke?"

Vida thought for a moment. "I do, but I think I'd like to wait until morning. I don't want him to see me in such a state. He deserves a strong woman as his, um ..." She didn't finish her sentence; however, she imagined Emma and Lauren did in their minds. If they doubted her feelings for Luke, they could confirm them now.

"Okay. While you take your bath, I'll bring up a plate of some bland foods to calm your stomach along with a mug of peppermint tea. That always soothes my upset tummy."

The two women doted over Vida until she was tucked into bed. The rest of the family respected Vida's wishes to be left alone, although Luke's concern resulted in his quietly pacing the floor outside her room in case she called out for him.

Between the warm bath and hot tea, Vida was able to find sleep quickly. She'd slept a few hours when a nightmare stirred her awake. She could see herself in bed, staring up at the ceiling. Suddenly, a black cloud burst into the room, rolling across the bed until it engulfed her. She began thrashing under the covers, fighting to break through the feeling of being smothered. She groaned and repeated the words—no, no, no.

It was Luke who rescued her from the powers of darkness that took advantage of her sadness and despair. He gently shook her awake, causing the black clouds to disappear and the soft moonlight to find its way into her room.

His voice was soft. Comforting. Settling.

"Vida, wake up. It's me. Luke. You're having a bad dream."

She jolted herself awake and immediately sat upright in bed. She was sweating profusely. She reached behind her to feel her pillow, which was sopping wet. In her half-sleepy state, she wondered if she'd fallen asleep as she sipped her tea.

"Oh, boy," she began. "That wasn't a sweet dream at all."

For some odd reason, the way she said it reminded Luke of *Alice in Wonderland*. "Well, you're back and safe with me. Do you want some water?" Luke reached over to the nightstand for the bottle. She took a few sips and handed it back to him.

She was fully awake and had regained her wits. "You'd think I came across a giant bear in that field."

Luke nodded. "Hey, no judgment here. I had nightmares for several days after you rescued me from that fire. In my dreams, I was burned up in more ways than you can imagine."

Vida nodded. She recalled Luke's nightmares. They'd passed within a few days. Her nightmare was continuing. In two mornings, it'd be everyone else's as well.

"Thank you for waking me up," she said softly.

She leaned forward and kissed Luke on the cheek. She stayed close to his face for what seemed like an eternity, hoping he'd return the kiss with more passion. Luke did, but it was not the passion she'd hoped for. He was still holding back. But why?

"You're welcome," he said. "Vida, there's so much I want to say to you. About us. You know, everything. But, um, you've been through a lot today, and you need your rest."

She reached up to touch his face. "Luke, it's okay. I think we can talk now."

Suddenly, Emma entered the room. "Is everything okay? I heard noises."

Luke jumped off the bed. "Yeah, Mom. I think she's fine. She had a bad dream."

Vida pushed herself up in bed against the headboard and tugged the covers up to her neck. "Yes, I'm fine. I guess my brain won't let go of the snake."

After Emma and Luke wished her good night, closing the door behind them, Vida lay awake for hours, debating what to do.

Should she warn the Cubbisons? Or at least Matthew?

Should she sneak out of the house and return to her community to face certain punishment? Would that suffice to save Matthew and the rest of his family?

Should she simply run away like she did to begin with, putting all of this behind her, knowing that eventually, it would be a distant memory?

The debate raged on until she finally passed out, weary of thinking, but fearful that the snake would return to take her in her nightmares.

PART 4

Thursday
Welcome, my friends.

CHAPTER THIRTY-NINE

Thursday
Gibson, Pennsylvania

Unbeknownst to Fred, he was the last to arrive on the highways leading through Gibson, just a few miles east of Cubbison's Farm. His men hid their Humvees and the M35 cargo trucks throughout the small town, which was nothing more than a crossroads between county roads heading in multiple directions. If he'd searched, he would've found an M35 tucked behind the chapel at the Methodist Church or a Humvee pulled into the quarter car wash. Their other operating vehicles, obtained through his barter operation in Harford, blended in with the abandoned cars and trucks stranded at the post office or the antique store.

The early arrivals saw the rest of their comrades arrive periodically throughout the night. Each of the men had a genuine concern about garnering the attention of the local residents or, worse, running into a convoy of Pennsylvania National Guardsmen who were searching for them. Neither concern materialized, and the men got some much-needed rest as they readied for dawn to come.

Fred slowly drove through town, unaware that his men who stood watch that night noticed his arrival. Disciplined, they resisted the urge to wave him down or otherwise get his attention. Instead, the vintage Ford Econoline van continued through town and turned down the county road leading to Cubbison's Farm. After a short drive, he pulled the van onto the side of the road near a pig farming operation and decided to catch a little sleep before dawn.

By design, the men assigned to the Pontiac GTO who'd participated in the defense of the farm days ago would be the first to arrive. The familiarity of the car would ensure they'd have an opportunity to announce their presence without being shot at. Despite this prearranged arrival, Fred hoped to arrive shortly thereafter in case he needed to remind the Cubbisons' patrols that they were friendlies.

Fred and his fellow ex-Marine were asleep in the front seat of the van when a rapping on the hood of the van startled them. Their bodies were jolted awake by the sudden noise. Fred, who had his rifle lying in his lap, awkwardly pulled it up and pointed it toward the windshield.

After a moment, he was fully awake and aware of his surroundings. The GTO was parked ahead of them on the shoulder of the road, patiently idling.

"Hey! Do you wanna follow us in?" asked the driver. The sun was just beginning to peek over the horizon behind them, barely illuminating his bearded face.

Fred glanced to the left and saw a faint glow emanating from a barn at the farmhouse. Solar lighting illuminated a sign at the entrance to the farm. It read Hogs & Hens.

"Have you checked that out?" he asked.

"Nah," his man replied. "Seems to be some kind of pig farm. Chickens, too, I guess. Main house burned down, it appears. Do you want us to go in alone, or do you wanna follow us?" He repeated his question.

Fred glanced at the charred remains of the house before turning to his driver. "Follow them." He started the Econoline, prompting the Pontiac's driver to hustle back behind the wheel.

Seconds later, they eased back onto the road and began rolling toward the Cubbisons'. Fred turned slightly in his seat to observe an older man in overalls who stood in the middle of the gravel driveway. He'd hitched a trailer to an old four-door sedan and was in the process of loading an old tractor onto it.

He stepped down off the back of the trailer and wandered toward the road. His hands were shoved in his pockets, nonchalantly watching as the two cars pulled away. Fred shrugged at the oddity of a sedan towing a tractor. Then again, everything was out of the ordinary nowadays.

He returned his attention to the GTO, which led the way slowly toward the farm. It was a little brighter now, and he had to assume that the Cubbisons' patrols would recognize the car. Nonetheless, as soon as the two vehicles approached the farm's front gate, Fred exited the passenger side of the van and marched up to the gate, with his arms spread wide beside him. The whinny of a horse gave away the fact they were being watched from the many barricades leading up the gravel driveway.

Fred shouted toward whoever was watching, "Hello! It's Fred. I've brought the Marines!"

"Fred?" It was Grandpa Sam's voice. He and John, the earliest risers on the farm, routinely took the first morning shift. They were able to patrol the grounds while also tending to the livestock, including their newborn calf. "What are you doin' here?" A logical question that came out a little ruder than Sam intended. Fred wasn't sure how to take it.

"Well, can I explain?"

Sam picked up on the hesitation in Fred's voice. He realized he had been a little brusque in his greeting. He waved over to John, who broke cover at the same time. They shouldered their rifles and approached the front gate.

"Of course, Fred. It's good to see you. Um, all of you," said Sam as he noticed the other men approaching the gate. They all carried rifles over their shoulders.

John unlatched the gate and immediately shook hands with Fred and the three familiar faces who accompanied him. It was the same contingent who'd defended the farm against the bikers. John and his family would always be grateful to these men for saving his family's lives.

He shook Fred's hand. "Welcome, my friends." He turned to the other men and shook their hands as they passed through the gate. They exchanged pleasantries for a moment. Sam looked at the vehicles.

"Do y'all wanna pull your cars in before we lock up?" he asked.

"Well, about that," said Fred. "We need your help."

Both Sam and John stopped and immediately became quiet.

Fred continued, "We ran into some trouble in Harford."

"Oh no," said Sam, assuming the worst, namely that he and his men had upset the locals.

Fred uncharacteristically fidgeted as he spoke. "The National Guard arrived with a couple of FBI agents who were investigating the bombing in Scranton. We had information to provide them, but the guardsmen were there for other purposes."

"Like what?" asked John.

"Looting," replied Fred. He took a deep breath. "Long story short. I made a deal to give them the information if they'd leave us alone. I got nervous about them keeping up their end of the bargain, so while the agents and the squad's sergeant headed back to Scranton to get a letter confirming our arrangement, I kinda, um, did a thing."

Sam was confused. "Did a thing? What kind of thing?"

Suddenly, off in the distance, the low rumble of trucks approached, grabbing Sam and John's attention. They pulled their rifles off their shoulders and nervously began looking to the east and west to determine which direction the vehicles were approaching from. John became dumbfounded when he noticed neither Fred nor his men were moving.

"Am I missing something here?" asked John as he lowered his rifle.

Fred exhaled. "Yeah, sort of."

The first of the Humvees appeared over a rise to the east of the farm. Soon the M35 transports came into view as well as several more cars and pickup trucks.

Fred explained, "They're with us."

"The National Guard?" asked Sam.

"No, just their trucks and weapons. The guardsmen were left half-naked near the state line."

"And in the woods," added one of Fred's men.

"Yeah, and tied up near the fairgrounds, too," said another with a laugh.

Sam looked to John and shook his head in dismay. "Is this the thing you were talking about?"

Fred grinned. Oddly, for the first time since he'd left Harford with his vanload of prisoners, he was enjoying himself.

"Yep. This is the thing. Now I need your help."

CHAPTER FORTY

Thursday
Cubbison's Farm
Harford, Pennsylvania

Vida was awakened by the sudden commotion that filled the house. While most everyone typically was awake just after dawn, excited voices and shuffling feet was a clear indication that something extraordinary was happening. She sat upright in bed and tried to make sense of it all, briefly putting out of her mind the decision she needed to make regarding Abdul and the fate of the Cubbison family.

It was Lauren who knocked on her door and opened it. "Vida, wake up. There are vehicles at the front gate. Get dressed and bring your guns."

Vida's eyes grew wide, and her body began to convulse. Abdul had lied to her. He'd outsmarted her after all. They were ready to attack the family, and her. She'd been duped, and innocent people would pay the price for her indecisiveness.

She quickly dressed and rushed down the stairs, trying not to slip on the slick oak treads. The front door was wide open, and the house had been emptied of its occupants. She was the last to exit.

Vida had to find Luke. She needed to apologize or try to explain.

No, she told herself. It was Matthew who needed to know what she'd done. The deal she'd made with Abdul to save herself while putting his life in jeopardy.

Or should she explain herself to John and Emma? Or maybe just Emma? She was a woman and might be more understanding. But it was her son whom Vida had exposed to the brutal men from her community.

She was out of breath as she ran around the side of the market, her chest heaving in the damp morning air. She glanced to the east and saw several large trucks approaching with other kinds of vehicles. They looked like military vehicles, yet the cars were ordinary, kind of like the Pontiac her father drove.

As she raced up the driveway, Luke was running back toward her. He was the last person she wanted to see first, but fate had other ideas. As he approached her, she began talking, the words rapidly spewing out of her mouth.

"Luke, I'm sorry. I really am. I had no idea that this would—"

Luke cut her off. "Vida, big news. Fred and his men are coming to the farm. It may just be temporary while we figure some things out. But, wow. Look at all those trucks. Humvees, too!"

Luke's youthful exuberance caught her off guard. She had been prepared to spill her secrets to him. However, he was so excited at the turn of events that he hadn't heard a word she'd said as they greeted one another.

He lifted her up in the air and gave her a kiss on the mouth. It was spontaneous and wonderful at the same time. Vida appeared surprised and then appreciative as she kissed him back. It was the breakthrough moment their relationship needed. The two had danced around their feelings for weeks. Now it was out in the open, and they were both thrilled.

"I love you, Vida!"

She shyly responded, and then the tears began to pour down her face. "I love you, too." Her excitement was subdued by her expectations. Their romance was likely to be one of the shortest in history once she revealed the truth to the Cubbisons. If anything came of the first kiss, it was the decision she'd mentally toiled over. She would stand with Luke and his family.

"Come on, let's join the others," Luke said, pulling her by the hand toward the gate.

"Luke, what does this mean? What's happening?" she asked.

"It means we have our own army," he replied gleefully.

Vida's mind raced. An army. Trained ex-Marines who were more than capable of repelling any attacks by Abdul and the other men in the community. But there were so many Afghans. She tried to recall how many. With older teens, maybe forty? The women would fight, too. They were as indoctrinated in their radical religious beliefs as the men.

Luke and Vida stood aside as the convoy entered the farm. If the Cubbison contingent had had small American stick flags, they'd be waving them high over their heads as if they were welcoming home a conquering army.

The three Humvees and M35 transports led the way, followed by eight vintage vehicles carrying supplies and more men. Twenty hardened fighters who'd spent their careers fighting in Afghanistan and Iraq. They brought with them food, supplies, and weapons. More importantly, they brought experience to fight all types of enemies, including Abdul and his men.

As they made their way past the market and began parking in the fields on both sides of the house, the Cubbisons together with Lauren and Asher walked behind the last truck. The sense of relief and cheerfulness was obvious on their faces. Only Vida appeared to be uncertain about the turn of events, a fact that was quickly picked up on by Emma.

She peeled away from her husband and walked directly over to Vida. Luke traded high fives with Matthew and exchanged a glance with Vida as if to ask her permission to celebrate with the others. She smiled and nodded, waving her arm slightly. The twins hustled to catch up with the others, leaving Emma and Vida alone.

"How are you feeling? I'm sorry about the commotion. None of us expected them to show up."

Vida managed a smile. "I'm feeling better. Thank you. Um, why are they here?"

"Apparently, there was some trouble in town. Or, well, some potential trouble, so Fred and his men needed to find another place to live."

Vida looked at the military vehicles. "Did they always have those?"

Emma laughed. "No, apparently that's part of the reason they're in a pickle."

"A pickle?" asked a confused Vida.

"It means they're in a mess. A little bit of trouble. Well, or maybe a lot of trouble. In any event, they came to us for help."

"What kind of help?" Vida was looking for confirmation of what Luke had told her.

"They need a place to stay or hide out. It depends on how you look at it."

Vida continued to quiz Emma, who became suspicious. "For how long?"

Emma scowled. "We don't know, Vida. If they stay, will you be okay with it?"

It was the moment of truth. Vida had to pick a lane.

CHAPTER FORTY-ONE

Thursday
Haleakala Observatory
Maui, Hawaii

Neil Burgoyne started his day fresh, internally trying to convince himself his observations of the gunmen at the park administration complex a couple of days ago was much ado about nothing. Yet he couldn't let go of that nagging sensation, a feeling of trouble on the horizon, that sent adrenaline coursing through his body. Yesterday, they'd taken additional measures to make access to the observatory difficult for anyone on a motorized vehicle, including the scooters the gang supposedly utilized. At the risk of blocking their ability to leave, he had more measures to implement that day.

The challenge he faced was blocking the road without making it look like he blocked the road. Growing up, he used to tell his friends that large homes with walls and gates either had something to hide or something worth stealing.

Although Hawaii had not suffered the same issues of downed power grids as the mainland had suffered following the perfect storm, the islands certainly were falling into the throes of societal collapse. The gangs that were forming and taking root on Maui were astute enough to see through his countermeasures. For that reason, Burgoyne wanted to think through every road blockage and supervise its construction.

The inhabitants at the observatory would never survive the storming of the facility by the Yakuza. They would all be assaulted or killed. Their escape options would be to race down the trails leading to the base of Haleakala on foot or in the two Jeeps and one Ford Bronco. They didn't seat enough to carry everyone.

The night before, he'd sat down with Baxter and two of his more mature graduate assistants to discuss their plight. The prospect of evacuating the observatory to avoid a possible attack by the vicious gang was discussed. Everyone agreed that they had no place to go. Their scouts had reported chaos, and looting was the norm across the island. There was no place of refuge.

Certainly, nobody would be willing to take in such a large group. Besides, they had little to offer a group with the benevolence to give them protection. Climbing down Haleakala meant they'd have to leave practically everything behind except a weapon and a pack on their back.

They didn't possess the skills to grow food, and they weren't excellent marksmen. In fact, they hadn't practiced using the weapons they'd managed to gather the first day the solar storm swept across the mainland because ammunition was too scarce to practice.

After a lengthy discussion, the small group that constituted the leadership team of the observatory began to recognize their fate was sealed unless the government came to the rescue. Setting aside the immediate threat they faced from the Yakuza, at some point in the near future, they would run out of food and supplies.

They would either have to become the scavengers and looters that others on the island resorted to being or find their way to Kahului, hoping FEMA or the Maui Emergency Management Agency had sufficient food supplies to support them, too.

The group of four voted and decided to continue their planned road blockades. Burgoyne and Baxter would lead a team down the mountain to the narrowest part of the highway. Two others would ride the trails to the point where the highway was visible. Using one of their operating vehicles and some boulders from above the road, they'd try to create a landslide or two. Slightly more than that might be suspect but enough to thwart intruders in cars or trucks.

As they set out for the day, Burgoyne chuckled as he thought to himself, *Too bad we can't conjure up a volcanic eruption.*

Goto couldn't let it go. The accident scene, what had appeared to be a multi-car pileup, was so out of the ordinary that it didn't make sense. He wanted to take another look, but he and his fellow Yakuza spent the day in the coastal communities of Maalaea Bay. Law enforcement was nonexistent, and because of the limited number of guns available to the islanders, there was virtually no armed resistance.

His raids on a community took several steps. After identifying a target, he'd embed a team to conduct surveillance. He had them determine if there was any type of organized security force. Second, he tried to identify any competition in the form of groups of looters rather than the occasional desperate refugee breaking into a property. Third, he'd analyze whether the spoils of victory were worth the risk and effort.

If all the boxes were checked, and they had been in the other communities his men attacked, then a plan of action was undertaken. The first order of business was to instill fear in the residents. As they swooped into the community, if anyone raised a hand or even hurled expletives at his men, they were killed. Certainly, this was unreasonable and unnecessary. However, it was a lawless society, and the rules had changed. Brutality won the day in most cases.

Once the local residents understood their fate if they resisted his men, the process of stripping them of their assets became easier. Logistics was a factor. His men had to be divided up between perimeter security and those who searched properties to gather items of value.

As always, guns and ammunition were the first priority. Sure, you can't eat a bullet, not in a nutritional sense, anyway. However, you can prevent others from using a weapon against you. More guns and ammunition made it possible to recruit more soldiers into the Yakuza. The larger his gang, the better able he was to attack the real prize on Maui—the midsize city of Kahului.

Kahului, according to his scouts, had not been ravaged by looters because the police presence was concentrated there. However, by his scouts' estimates, his gang's numbers might be on a parity with the city's police department. He believed that nearly half the force quit to protect their own families rather than guard the residents and businesses of the city.

The Hawaii Army National Guard had concentrated its efforts on Oahu, where its main base was located, and on the Big Island. Maui and the other six of the major Hawaiian Islands were left to be protected by local law enforcement.

With this overall game plan in mind, Goto decided to move on Kihei, where the bulk of the businesses and hotels were located. They would take control and establish a perimeter. Then they'd confiscate guns, seize food, and search for life-saving medications that could be used for barter.

The bulk of his gang would be busy along the coast for several days, enriching themselves through force and instilling fear in the residents. His top lieutenants were more than capable of overseeing the operation, and Goto rarely participated in the actual raids.

Today, he'd undertake another mission. Finding another, more secure location for the Yakuza's headquarters.

CHAPTER FORTY-TWO

Thursday
Haleakala Observatory
Maui, Hawaii

Burgoyne and the group spent more than an hour locating the two ideal spots to park the least useful cars within their fleet. Both were students' vehicles that were low on gas, making them expendable.

One member of their group, known as Sy, revealed a talent none of the others had—siphoning gas. Raised on a farm in Iowa, Sy, which was short for his nickname of *SyFy* after the television channel of that name, was adept at extracting fuel out of all makes of vehicles. The irony of the young man's nickname being Sy, coupled with his valuable talent of si-phoning fuel, was not lost on Burgoyne.

He and the young man parked the vehicles that would become part of the blockade, siphoned out the remaining fuel, and then drove down the mountain to just uphill from the park administration building to retrieve the Ford Bronco that was low on gas.

By the time they returned to the trailhead halfway up the mountain from the observatory, Baxter was waiting at the trail entrance with both Jeeps at the ready. One of the Wranglers, a four-door, had a powerful winch mounted to the front bumper. The other, a two-door, was equipped with oversize all-terrain tires and tubular steel bumpers, both front and rear.

The Bronco, which did not have the rugged nature and the suspension of the Wranglers, was nonetheless capable of driving up and down the rough, mountainous trail. Burgoyne sent Sy to the part of the trail that afforded him an unobstructed view of the park administration complex and a half mile of the road leading up the mountain. Should anyone approach, he could return to warn the others.

Once everyone was in place, Burgoyne assessed the terrain at the top of the hill overlooking the second parked vehicle. He and Baxter stood there with their hands on their hips, looking at the loose rock surrounding them and then across the ravine that had been created when the road was built.

"This side is going to be more difficult," began Burgoyne. "Well, by that, I mean time-consuming. Look across the way." He pointed to the steep, almost cliff-like slope that rose thirty feet above the parked vehicle.

Baxter turned to study the two-door Jeep. "It's almost too perfect for this one. They're lined up, just begging to be pushed over the ledge."

"I know that trail," said Burgoyne. "My guess is the boulders were put there to either keep hikers from walking over the edge, you know, like a guardrail, or they could sit there and take selfies with the observatory in the background."

"That's what I did when I first came to DKIST," added Baxter.

Burgoyne laughed. "Well, that sounds to me like you volunteered for the job. Can you handle it alone?"

"Sure," she replied.

"Good. I'm gonna need them both. There's gonna be a lot of cable work to pull these rocks to the edge before pushing them down the hill. I can't be jumping in and out of the Jeep. It'll take too long."

Baxter provided Burgoyne a thumbs-up and hopped into the Jeep. She was a natural driving the older model with a manual transmission. Most of the students at the observatory had never driven a stick.

With Sy easing down the mountain to get to his surveillance position and Baxter hustling around the other side, Burgoyne began the arduous process of wrangling lava rock. As he worked, he admired the incredible beauty of the rough landscape that had been likened to the surface of Mars. The clouds were low that day, obstructing their view of the rest of the island. He'd never tire of spending his days above the clouds as if they were on another planet. If only the inhabitants of the world below the cloud cover would leave them alone.

Goto met with his men before their second day of raids on the Kihei community. There were several small grocery stores in the area. Safeway was the largest, and Foodland was slightly smaller. They'd already been looted, an opportunity missed for Goto and the Yakuza.

However, that food had to go somewhere, and his men spent part of their day interrogating the locals to determine who'd done the bulk of the looting. It turned out an organized group of well-to-do residents of the Maui Nui Golf Club had arrived in the early days of the collapse. The group of lawyers, accountants, and business owners had been well armed. They'd moved quickly to take everything they could haul in a single day. Then they'd blocked the entrance to Lipoa Parkway with vehicles and guarded the entrance to the golf club twenty-four hours a day.

After his men determined much of the community had been picked over by the golf club residents, Goto ordered an attack. They planned to swarm the entrance with such swiftness and use of force that the white-collar looters would run for their lives.

Confident that his men would not only be successful but enjoy their day, he kept back a driver to accompany him to the summit of Haleakala. He instructed him to load two of the Hooligan scooters into the back of a pickup. They grabbed their rifles and began the slow drive up the mountain.

The diesel pickup groaned under the strain of the rising elevation as it pulled its way up the winding road. Goto was in no particular hurry as they drove along in near silence. He wanted to take in the view and imagined his gang defending this one-of-a-kind volcanic mountain complete with a solar observatory.

His mind wandered as they drove, chugging along up the dormant volcano. He hoped the telescopes came with some kind of instruction manual. He'd always been interested in the stars and planets. That was, before he became a gangster.

"Not much farther, Boa," his driver said, interrupting Goto's thoughts.

He simply nodded in response, his eyes looking upward through the windshield, wondering when the clouds would open up so he could see.

Baxter made such quick work of pushing the boulders over the side of the cliff that Burgoyne was able to be selective in the rocks he chose to dislodge. They only needed to drop enough of the mountainous debris around the car to prevent any vehicle, both four wheel and two wheel, from getting around the blockage.

Naturally, from this point, anyone interested in walking the final eight miles could do so. However, at this altitude, unless they were in incredible physical condition, their trek would likely require many long stops to rest and catch their breath. Burgoyne suspected even the most determined looter would give up the notion of climbing to the summit on foot.

After they completed this barricade, Burgoyne and Baxter waved to one another. Burgoyne pointed down the hill to where they'd parked the next vehicle about midway between this one and the park administration complex. Baxter waved back and provided him two thumbs-up before loading herself into the driver's side of the Jeep.

The two made their way down their respective trails. For a long stretch, Baxter's trail took a series of winding turns toward the base of the mountain. She was so confident in her ability to handle the Jeep on the rocky terrain that she continued to follow the paved road below unless she had to circumvent a crevasse.

When Burgoyne arrived on the ridge overlooking the next parked car, he was better able to assess the task he faced. The two Jeeps, each of which had its own strengths and weaknesses, were on the wrong side of the road. Based on the terrain and the rockslides from years past, he needed the Wrangler that was better capable of pushing the boulders on his side of the road. He, on the other hand, would be able to pull and tug boulders in place on the other side, setting them up to tumble down the slope.

He was frustrated by the additional time it would take to move the Jeeps around. The learning curve associated with the first blockade took a little longer than he expected. He studied the sun and its relation to the horizon. It was around noon. Even with redeploying the Jeeps, they should be able to finish before dark.

While he waited for Baxter to appear on the other side of the road, he studied the rock formation and the options they afforded him. He walked along the ledge overlooking the parked car. A slight V-shaped cut in the terrain formed a chute that led to the road just above the location of the car. He stood in the center of it and looked upwards toward a pile of rubble that had accumulated near the top of the small ravine.

He jutted his chin out and nodded. If he could dislodge the right boulders using the winch, the whole thing could break loose and be funneled down the cut in the terrain directly toward the car. To pull it off, he and Baxter would need to work together on this side of the road. He would secure the winch cable around the boulders at the base of the rubble pile. Baxter would position her Jeep above the rubble and push it like a bulldozer once the stability of the pile was compromised.

Burgoyne would have to be careful to get out of the way of the sudden avalanche, and Baxter would need to extricate herself from the pile to prevent the Jeep from riding it down the ridge. It was risky, but it would do the job quickly.

Just as he internally signed off on his plan, Baxter appeared on the other side of the mountain, separated by the road. She held her hands apart and shrugged, indicating she saw the issue they faced. Burgoyne waved his arms to confirm his directive. She needed to go back and join him on this side. Once again, with two thumbs up, the dutiful assistant was back in her Jeep and making the trip around the highway to join him.

SyFy was bored with his assignment although it was something different than the humdrum of lazing around the observatory, listening to the others complain about how much weight they'd lost. He moseyed around the Bronco, occasionally picking up rocks and throwing them down the hill toward a small tour bus.

His attention perked up when he heard the rumble of a diesel engine in the distance. There weren't any diesel trucks at the observatory, so he assumed it was coming from the bottom of the volcano.

Sy walked to the edge and hid behind a grouping of large rocks. He waited for what seemed an eternity as the sound of the engine grew louder. Eventually, a dark pickup truck eased toward the parking lot and pulled into a space. The passenger and his driver exited with guns drawn, waving them around the parking area. A moment later, they cautiously made their way across the park administration grounds, quickly searching the buildings and remaining vehicles.

Sy wasn't sure if he needed to raise the alarm with his professor and the others or not. Maybe these men were simply looking to steal something. He tried to get a closer look at their truck. When the men suddenly emerged from the largest of the buildings down the slope from the parking area, Sy stumbled and fell to avoid being seen.

He lay prone on the ground, his heart pounding in his chest, as he tried to focus his hearing on the men below. He heard the sound of the pickup tailgate opening and then a loud-pitched screeching sound of metal on metal. It caused him to shudder.

Sy took a risk and poked his head up above the rocks. He was able to see the scooters.

"Shit! Shit! Shit!" he whispered loudly to himself.

He scrambled backwards on his hands and knees, keeping a wary eye on the two men to determine if he'd been discovered. They continued to unload the scooters, so Sy stood and ran toward the Bronco. He quietly slid into the driver's seat and slowly shut the door.

He took a deep breath and exhaled. If the men heard the truck start, they'd pick up their pace and soon would be racing up the mountain directly toward his friends.

While they waited for Baxter to make her way around the highway to join them, Burgoyne worked with the two other students to wrap the steel cable around the boulders that stood in the way of the larger pile of rubble.

The powerful winch pulled one of the five-hundred-pound rocks loose. Burgoyne placed the Jeep in reverse until he could drag the boulder out of the way. Then they repeated the process with another. One by one, the boulders at the bottom of the pile were pulled away, allowing those above them on the short ridge to be exposed. Burgoyne would've continued except he became concerned about the stability of the pile. He and his students could be crushed if the avalanche occurred prematurely.

They had just pulled the last boulder when he heard a vehicle rapidly approaching on the trail. The motor sounded different from the Jeep, causing Burgoyne to become concerned.

His helpers walked away from the boulders and climbed up the ravine toward the sound of the approaching truck. Once they reached the top, they shielded their eyes to block out the sun, which was lowering itself on the horizon.

One of them shouted to Burgoyne, "Professor, it sounds like Sy is on his way up the hill. I caught a reflection of the sun off his windshield."

Burgoyne scowled. Why would he be returning? Unless ... His eyes grew wide. He ran several steps toward the trail where Sy would appear. He turned back toward his Jeep, unsure of what to do.

Sy was driving erratically up the trail, clearly panicked by something. He was waving his arm through the driver's window, yelling at them.

"They're coming! Somebody's coming!"

Burgoyne was frozen. Behind him, the sound of Baxter's Jeep lumbering along the rocky trail could be heard. He looked down to the parked car. They'd done nothing to block the road other than put the car in place. He silently cursed himself for not doing this location first.

By the time the entire scenario ran through his mind, Sy had arrived and was frantically warning them of the scooters driven by armed men approaching. Baxter had driven into position, parked up the ravine, and was waving at Burgoyne to get his attention.

She shouted her question. "What do you want me to do?"

Burgoyne was still in the ravine at the base of the cliff of boulders. He could hear their voices but was unable to discern what they were asking.

They stumbled down the slope to make eye contact with him.

"Professor!" yelled one.

"Should we go?" asked Sy.

A million thoughts swirled through his mind as he tried to make a decision. Then he noticed the winch cable was still wrapped around the boulder they'd just pulled away from the pile.

Then Burgoyne heard the high-pitched whine of the scooters as the men who drove them raced up the mountain. The small engines struggled under the drivers' attempt to push them to their limits.

Sy's panicked voice could be heard easily. "Professor! They're coming."

Burgoyne turned to Baxter and yelled while waving his arms, "Push! Push the pile toward the road."

"Okay!" She rushed into her Jeep.

Then he shouted at the students, "Go back to DKIST. Warn the others to be ready. Hurry!"

"But, sir, the cable!" One of the students pointed toward the steel cable wrapped around the boulder. Burgoyne had already seen the problem. Once Baxter started the avalanche, the other boulders could grab the cable and drag the Jeep, and him, down the ravine with it.

Burgoyne started toward the bottom of the rubble pile. He needed to unhook the winch cable or their Jeep would be destroyed. He could hear the scooters driving up the hill in one ear and Baxter's idling Jeep in the other. She wasn't moving.

He began to frantically wave at his group of students hovered around the Bronco. "Tell her to push!"

"You're in the way!" they hollered back.

"Push, dammit!" he shouted much louder.

Baxter revved the engine and began pushing the top of the boulder pile. Burgoyne pulled and tugged at the load hook that was firmly wrapped around the boulder and attached to the cable. It wouldn't budge.

He needed some slack. He tried to dislodge the heavy rock, but it wouldn't move. He panicked. He attempted to scramble back to his Jeep to pull the vehicle forward slightly. This would provide the slack he needed to disconnect the hook. Instead, he slipped and fell, tumbling backwards until he landed hard against the stubborn rock.

Baxter revved the engine again, spinning the tires in loose stones as she shoved the steel bumper against the larger boulders. A few broke loose and came tumbling down the rubble, bouncing past Burgoyne toward the road.

He regained his footing and tried to climb up the incline again to get out of the way. This time a boulder sailed past him, bounding by en route to the bottom of the cliff. Another one rolled behind him, striking the stubborn boulder tied up by the cable. The two rocks slid together down the ravine, tumbling slightly as they started their descent.

Burgoyne caught a break. The boulders bounced off each other, which released the winch cable's death grip on the massive rock. Now that it was loose, Burgoyne was able to pull himself up the ravine with the assistance of the cable.

"They're coming around the corner!" shouted Sy.

Burgoyne shouted as he hoisted himself up the ravine, "Push, Baxter. Give it everything you've got!"

She did. The final thrust of the Jeep shoved several boulders on top of the rubble, causing the weight to shift suddenly. Just as Burgoyne pulled himself out of the ravine, the entire pile of rocks, weighing many thousands of pounds, broke loose. The resulting avalanche was unstoppable.

Gasping for oxygen in the thin, high-altitude air, Burgoyne tried to avoid passing out as he watched his plan come to fruition. What happened next was totally unexpected.

Bounding down the ravine and knocking into each other like the running of the bulls in Pamplona, Spain, the boulders were drawn downward by gravity. The massive pile of rubble arrived at the parked car at the same time as the men on the scooters did.

Screams of agony and unimaginable pain filled the air as the massive rocks, which had bounded down the hill, bounced into the air in leaps and bounds before crashing into the car and scooters. The riders never had a chance, as they were caught completely by surprise. Goto, who was the farthest away from the oncoming rubble, nearly escaped until two large boulders tackled him. One crushed his lower left leg while the other slammed into the middle of his back, knocking the wind out of him.

The rest of the rocks that followed, none of which were large enough to cause death, did pack a powerful punch to the men's already battered bodies. The driver passed out from the excruciating pain. Goto, stunned, tried to maintain consciousness.

Burgoyne rallied his troops. He ordered Baxter to stand by until he could assess the damage below. He led the Bronco up the trail back to the road. Once they arrived, he ordered Sy to take the others back to the observatory. Under an abundance of precaution, he told them to be ready in case there were more men on the way.

He turned down the highway and raced to the bottom. He slowed as he pulled up to the landslide. The results of his plan were greater than he'd imagined. In fact, Burgoyne was very pleased with himself as he nonchalantly exited his Jeep.

His attitude changed when bullets skipped along the ground near his feet. Frightened, he jumped back into the Jeep and search for his gun. He found the pistol lying on the floorboard, dislodged from its holster by all the activity. He reached for it just as more gunshots rang out.

One or both of them was alive, he surmised. They were either ready for a gun battle or desperately trying to fight back. He'd thought it was over. He wasn't emotionally or physically prepared for a gun battle with gangbangers.

He fired wildly in the direction of the car. He struck a tire, causing it to blow out. The loud explosion echoed up and down the canyon. The gunman fired back, still skipping bullets along the pavement.

"He must be under the rocks," said Burgoyne to himself. He had an idea. He began blaring on his horn in an attempt to get Baxter's attention. He yelled so loud he almost lost his voice. "Push! Push!"

Somehow, Baxter heard him. Seconds later, more boulders began rushing down the side of the ridge, bounding haphazardly until they struck the road. The second boulder found its mark, hitting the trunk of the car before rolling over the side on top of one of the men. He screamed with anguish as the boulder landed on top of him. The man began to cough violently until Burgoyne thought he'd heard the last of the air in his lungs expire.

Baxter, however, continued to force rocks down the ravine. Several more hit the car and the scooters. Burgoyne grimaced at the thought of the men's mangled bodies underneath the pile of rubble. He pushed on his horn several times and then stood on the nerf bar of the Jeep.

"That's enough!" he yelled. "Wait there!"

Baxter waved back and stood atop the hill, looking down. Burgoyne cautiously walked around the rubble with his handgun pointed to where the men were partially buried. The first man he came across was clearly dead, as evidenced by what remained of his skull. The other man's body was twitching uncontrollably. His almost dead brain desperately reached for his rifle, which had been destroyed by one of the boulders landing on it. Blood poured out of the man's body across the pavement.

Even the decaying bodies he'd discovered at the park administration building were not as grotesque as the men's mangled torsos. When the second man stopped twitching and his bowels released, Burgoyne knew it was over.

He would never know that the man he killed was Tatsuki Goto, the head of the Yakuza gang. Those who remained at the Sandalwoods resort located at the base of Haleakala didn't share the same curiosity as their now-dead leader. They didn't venture up the road to explore the observatory. They simply did what they did best. Loot and kill to better themselves. Until they eventually met a larger, more powerful force that eliminated them from the island—the Company.

He stood over the gruesome scene for a moment. He confirmed that the road was sufficiently blocked. He told himself the dead men didn't deserve a burial, that their rotting corpses would eventually disappear. *Besides*, he thought, *let their remains be a warning to anyone who dares travel beyond that they may not live if they try.*

With a quiet determination, Professor Neal Burgoyne waved to Kelly Baxter and provided her a thumbs-up. He couldn't see the smile on her face, but her thumbs-up response spoke volumes. It was time for them, and the others holed up in the observatory, to do what they did best.

Study the universe and try to survive the apocalypse.

CHAPTER FORTY-THREE

Thursday
Cubbison's Farm
Harford, Pennsylvania

Emma was beside herself as she stomped through Cubbison's Market, which was growing darker by the minute, reflecting her angry mood. Vida had just revealed the truth about Abdul's presence near the farm and her abduction. She'd tried to explain to Emma what her motivation was in lying about her ties to the Cubbisons. However, once Vida confessed she'd thrown Matthew's name out as the killer of her father, Emma lost it.

"Okay. Okay," she hissed. Emma's anger was revealed further through the use of salty language, something totally out of character for her. "I get why you concocted the damn lie. You were trying to save your own ass. Why did you have to implicate Matthew? I mean, you couldn't just make somebody up?"

"I, I, um, I was afraid he'd know I was lying," Vida stammered as she spoke. Then she began crying. "I didn't want them to rape me! I didn't want to die like that!" She spoke through fits of sobs and wails.

"What's going on?" asked John, who'd suddenly appeared in the doorway. Sam was close behind. "Why's it so dark in here? Why is she crying?"

Sam moved past John to the checkout counter and lit a couple of candles. The dim light revealed Emma's angry, distraught face. Vida stood on the other side of the building, her shoulders slumped and her face buried in her hands.

"We need to talk," began Emma. "All of us. Maybe even Fred."

John moved to comfort his wife. "Honey, what has happened?"

Sam, who was now standing near the doorway, leaned back to see Luke walking toward the market. "Luke is coming."

"Get rid of him," ordered Emma. "The adults need to deal with this."

"Honey—" began John before Emma cut him off.

"Sam, please. Give Luke something to do. We need to talk before, um, well ..." Her voice failed her as the tears began to flow down her face.

Sam shot John a glance and then hustled to intercept Luke. Confused, John paced the floor, his eyes darting between the two women, who were both very emotional. He tried to imagine the worst, not sure of what *the worst* looked like. He would soon find out.

"Okay, he tried to argue, but I've got him checking on the calf. Again," said Sam. "Now, what's going on?"

Emma waved her arm at Vida. "Tell them. Everything!" The last word startled the young woman, who jumped and began crying in earnest.

Sam moved by her side and wrapped one arm around her. "Calm down. Clearly, this is important. We need you to get ahold of yourself so you can explain it to John and me so we can help."

Emma was snarky as her anger consumed her. "Go ahead, Vida. Please, do tell."

John immediately hugged her and whispered in her ear, "Whatever she's done, we can deal with it. I promise. Please calm down."

"You have no idea," she whispered as she buried her face on his shoulder and closed her eyes. As he comforted her, she nodded slightly and let go of her wrath.

John pulled away. Emma immediately wrapped her arms around her waist, hugging herself. He turned to Vida.

"Go ahead, please." His voice was unemotional. He hadn't seen Emma this distraught in many years. Even when they'd discovered Luke in the burning field, she'd led the charge to get him help.

"I was coming home, um, back from Jenna's when two men grabbed me. They covered my head so I couldn't see, and covered my mouth so I couldn't yell."

"Wait," interrupted Sam. "When was this?"

Vida hesitated and began to kick nervously at the dusty floor. "Yesterday afternoon."

"So you didn't fall near a snake?" asked John.

"No. I'm sorry," she replied. "I lied."

John took a deep breath to maintain his composure. "Why, Vida? We've trusted you. We've made you a part of our family. Why would you lie to us?"

"Abdul. He is our, um, my old community's spiritual leader. He is also the man who leads the men when they, um, plot against America."

John glanced at Sam. "I bet he was at the arsenal that night."

"Yes," said Vida. She began to cry. "You have to understand. You must know how they treat women. Plus, I defied them and left without permission. What they do to girls like me is beyond your imagination."

Sam said, "Why did you lie to us? We would've supported you."

"Grandpa Sam, they were going to kill me. I'm sure of it. But first, they would've raped me. All of them. And beat me. Only when they tired of their brutality would they kill me."

"Tell them the rest," said Emma, who'd recovered somewhat.

"So I could get away, I thanked Abdul for rescuing me. I told them I'd learned of my father's death and had discovered who his killer was."

"My god," said John as he began to pace the floor. He walked toward Vida. "Did you tell them about Matthew?"

Vida covered her mouth and began crying again. She didn't have to respond to his question. The answer was obvious.

Sam tried to remain calm despite his anger. "John, there isn't much time. These people will be coming for us."

"Not until tomorrow," interjected Vida. "I told them Matthew was gone and not expected back until Friday. I am supposed to meet Abdul in the morning at dawn."

"Why?" asked John.

"He thinks I will tell him all about your family. How many men there are. Number of guns. Your routine. Everything."

John shook his head in disbelief. "Where are you supposed to meet him?"

She pointed toward Gibson. "I'm not completely sure where I was. After they grabbed me in the field across the road, they dragged me up a hill into a small building. They forced me onto the floor before removing my blindfold. It was a simple building with some counters like this one and some empty vegetable crates."

Sam addressed John. "The empty produce stand where you thought you saw a vehicle of some kind parked nearby."

John nodded and added, "Asher checked it out. He said there was no vehicle and no sign of anyone having been there."

"Yeah, that's true. But that doesn't mean they haven't been watching us. They may know more than we realize, son."

John turned to Vida. "Is there anything else?"

She shook her head.

"Is that all she told you?" he asked his wife.

"Pretty much. John, what are we gonna do?"

"First, I'm gonna thank God for Fred and his Marines," he replied. "Then I'm gonna ask them if they're willing to fight for us again."

"What about her?" asked Sam.

"Yeah, the others are gonna want to know what's going on," added Emma.

John looked from Sam to Emma and then stopped at Vida. "Can everyone here keep their shit together?"

The group all nodded.

"No drama during breakfast. Sam and I will pull Fred aside and work out a plan."

"Do we let her back in the house?" asked Emma in a scornful tone of voice.

John walked up to Vida. He placed his hands on her shoulders and studied her eyes. Then he replied.

"I trust her. I think we all should. That said, we've got trouble ahead, and we may need her help."

CHAPTER FORTY-FOUR

Thursday
Cubbison's Farm
Harford, Pennsylvania

Fortunately, with the addition of nearly two dozen ex-Marines to feed, that morning's breakfast was more potluck than it was a sit-down meal. One by one, everyone on the farm made their way through the kitchen to make themselves a plate of leftovers. Some sat in the family room, while Fred and his men took their plates to the picnic tables under the trees.

To minimize Luke's contact with Vida, John pulled Lauren and Asher aside to fill them in on what had happened. They kept their time apart from the others to avoid raising suspicion. Emma fixed Asher and Luke a plate wrapped in aluminum foil. Asher headed out to the calving barn to bring Luke something to eat, and then the two were assigned patrols along the east and front perimeter of the farm, including Jenna's property across the road. Lauren and Matthew patrolled the rest. This would keep both boys away from Vida.

John ate quickly and nodded to Sam, who'd been the first through the line. They quietly left the house to join Fred and his men under the tree canopy that covered the picnic tables. The leaves had begun to change color, revealing the dark green string lights that wrapped around their branches. The scene had been so beautiful the night Cubbison's had hosted the soiree of local dignitaries. It was amazing how things had changed in less than a couple of months.

Fred had finished his meal and was walking around engaging in conversation with his men when the Cubbison men arrived. He noticed their arrival and immediately introduced them to the rest of his crew.

"Guys, you know I've talked about these gentlemen before. Now you can put a name with a face. Sam and John Cubbison, this is our bunch of misfit Marines who found a home in your fair community. Until it was time to go, I guess."

John managed a laugh although he didn't feel the least bit humorous. "First of all, welcome to all of you. As you know, we met Fred and a few of you guys under some pretty dire circumstances. In fact, I'll readily admit we might have lost everything if not for your help."

"Including our lives," added Sam.

"That's what we do, sir," said one of the men.

"The few. The proud," said another in a deep voice.

"Semper fi!"

"Oorah!"

Fred stepped in. "It was our pleasure, John and Sam. Hell, if anything, the rest of these boys were damn pissed they missed the action."

"Damn straight!" said one of the men before several of them exchanged high fives and fist bumps.

John took a deep breath and motioned for Sam to take a seat. Fred frowned as he picked up on John's serious mood.

"John, is everything cool? I mean, I'm sorry I couldn't call first. If we need to leave, please say so, and we'll roll out."

John shook his head and held his hands palms down by his sides. "No, Fred. It's nothing like that. In fact, it's just the opposite. Listen, I've already thanked God for delivering you to our farm. Now I'm gonna thank you for being here. We've got a problem. Maybe a pretty big one."

Fred motioned for John to speak. "Let not your heart be troubled, my friend. What's going on?"

John explained how Vida had come to be a part of their family. He explained that although there were trust issues, they'd given her the benefit of the doubt because she'd helped save Luke's life. Which, in turn, had led the Cubbisons to Fred at the Harbor House.

Then John relayed more details of their encounter with the Afghans at the arsenal. He reminded Fred that the GTO had been driven by the man Matthew had shot and killed. And that man, they'd now learned, was Vida's father.

As John spoke, Fred interjected his experience with the men who closely resembled the Taliban fighters they were all intimately familiar with from their days in the Middle Eastern theater.

After additional conversation back and forth involving all of Fred's men, it became obvious there was a connection between these men, led by this Abdul person, and the arsenal encounter. Further, he was likely responsible for the bombing of the Viewmont Mall.

"All right," began Fred. "It seems we're all in agreement these connections, while coincidental, have led us to the point in which we might be fighting toe-to-toe with these Taliban bastards. Am I right?"

Everyone agreed by responding in one form or another.

Fred addressed John. "This is a battle we'd love to fight. Not just for you and your family, but for us as well. We had unfinished business in Afghanistan. We were wrongfully pulled out with our tails tucked between our legs, something no Marine will ever forgive or forget. In a small way, this will be some form of vindication for us and those who died at the Scranton mall that day."

"Oorah!"

"Thank you," said John. "In return, we would like to offer you a home here. With us. On Cubbison's Farm. We can feed you. We'll find a way to provide you a place to sleep even if it means we give up our own beds."

"That won't be necessary, John. We've slept under the stars. Heck, a barn would be deluxe accommodations compared to some of the places we've laid our heads, right, guys?"

"Sir, there is one thing," interjected one of his top lieutenants. "We've got to stash these National Guard vehicles. They could come around or even send drones looking for them, you know, if they have any that still work."

"I might be able to help you with that," said Sam. "We've got some heavily wooded forest at the back of the farm made up of evergreens. With a little camouflage added, I suspect we can keep them out of sight. Plus, there are the barns."

Fred turned to John. "What about this girl Vida? Can you trust her?"

"I want to," he replied. "I really do. Her story makes sense, but that doesn't mean crap. I think we have to assume Abdul will bring his men fully armed if they had a good haul at the arsenal. Now, whether it's tonight or tomorrow is hard to tell."

Fred thought as he strolled through the picnic tables. All eyes were on him as the men awaited his instructions.

"Here's what we're gonna do. We'll test her while conducting some surveillance at the same time. I'll take some of the guys and Vida to their community. We'll determine if they're preparing to attack the farm, while testing her truthfulness at the same time."

"If there's room, let me go, too," said Sam. "I believe she's most comfortable around me."

"Dad, it could be dangerous," said John.

"No more so than not knowing what they're planning or having a spy among us," Sam argued.

Fred shrugged. "I can't argue with that." He turned and selected three of his men. They got a vehicle ready while the rest followed Sam's direction on moving their convoy to the back of the farm. Afterwards, they'd set up defensive positions around the perimeter.

If Abdul attacked earlier than expected, they'd have something for him.

CHAPTER FORTY-FIVE

Thursday
Lake Wallenpaupack
Wayne County, Pennsylvania

Abdul Rahimi was reflective as he prepared to do battle. It had been many years since he wore his uniform as a member of the Taliban Badri 313, a feared division of the Red Unit. The Afghan Taliban had formed the special forces unit in response to an unprecedented challenge to its insurgent dominance in the region.

The Red Unit was subjected to rigorous military training utilizing combat gear and techniques similar to their Western counterparts. Divided into several battalion-sized teams of three hundred men handpicked by their commanders based on their discipline, commitment, and performance in battle, the men fought with honor and were revered by their peers.

Abdul and Jamal Khan were members of the Badri 313, a rapid response force under the Red Unit's most famous leader, Pir Agha, from Kandahar. Their battalion was named after the Battle of Badr when the Prophet Muhammad vanquished his enemies with only three hundred and thirteen soldiers.

Their insurgency strategy was second to none. They operated in the shadows. Unseen. Stealthy. Deadly. An invisible army enveloping their target before it strikes.

Within the Badri 313, Abdul had been looked upon as their military strategist. Pir Agha often included Abdul in strategic planning sessions prior to launching an offensive. Abdul was honored to play a part in his superior's decision-making, so he studied insurgent strategies from the past, including those in America.

He would never admit this verbally, but Abdul had been most impressed with the engagements during the American Revolution where guerilla warfare was used against the larger, more powerful British Army with great success. The colonists had formed an insurgent arm known as the Mechanics that launched raids, ambushes, and surprise attacks against the British detachments.

Led by ordinary men who overcame extraordinary challenges, they'd wrested the New World away from the British to form the United States. In Abdul's mind, it wasn't much different than what the Taliban did in 2020 when it regained control of Afghanistan.

The Taliban were patient, fully aware the American government would grow tired of its military occupying Afghanistan. They used insurgency tactics to annoy American forces. They were able to manipulate the media into making the American people weary of the longest war in the nation's history.

When the Americans suddenly pulled out, leaving a void, the Taliban were poised to seize power. And Abdul and his best friend, Jamal Khan, had been given the opportunity to continue the fight against the infidels.

This afternoon, he stood on the precipice of another battle. The assault on the Picatinny Arsenal was necessary to arm his fighters. The bombing of the Viewmont Mall was a message to America that the war was not over. However, the attack he was preparing for against this family of infidels who were responsible for the death of his spiritual brother was purely and simply for revenge.

Abdul, who'd been crouching in front of Lake Wallenpaupack, marveled at the stillness of his surroundings. The water was like glass with the lone exception of a flock of waterfowl circling about, periodically dipping their bills beneath the surface, sifting through it to devour any small creatures that would satisfy their hunger.

It was beautiful. Serene. Perhaps the most beautiful place he'd ever lived. Yet it was not his home. He'd willingly displaced his family and the families of his men in order to pursue a battle against an enemy that he couldn't quite remember why he hated. For the entirety of his adult life, the American military had occupied Afghan soil. They claimed to be there as a force of good. The Taliban didn't see it that way. When their family, friends and neighbors got caught up in military actions, the young men of Afghanistan flocked to the Taliban to join their cause.

It was all Abdul had known since he was a teen. He couldn't imagine doing anything else except killing Americans. The reason did not matter, although this one was different. He managed a smile as he summoned his top lieutenants to join him in the barn, where they laid out the strategies for their attacks. Revenge would be sweet.

Once everyone had gathered around, he addressed them with words of encouragement. "My brothers, this is a day we've looked forward to since the day Jamal Khan was taken from us. We all loved him like a brother, and when he died, part of us died as well. Today, we exact revenge on the infidels responsible for his death."

"*Allahu Akbar!*"

Earlier, he and his men had made a crude sketch of the Cubbisons' farm and surrounding areas. He believed in attacking a target from all points of ingress and egress. Using his vehicles, he could approach quickly, catching their enemy off guard. Their pickups could be used to breach the three farm gates they'd identified along the front and east side of the farm. Their other vehicles would carry gunmen on country roads south of Gibson to approach the farm from the west.

It was a forty-mile drive to the farm through a number of small towns. Ordinarily, Abdul would avoid bringing a convoy of several vehicles. However, contrary to what he'd told Vida, he had no intention of waiting until she met him at the abandoned produce stand.

After reflection, he was angry with himself for not bringing her back to the compound to administer the most severe forms of punishment imaginable in front of the entire community as a deterrent to future betrayals.

Besides, she'd given him all the information he needed to administer justice. It didn't matter how many members of this farming family held a rifle. They were no match for the entirety of the men in his community, who were hungry for vengeance.

One of his most trusted men was placed in charge of their armory. Between the raid on the Picatinny Arsenal and the weapons found at the Viewmont Mall, they were well equipped for a bunch of farmers with hunting rifles or pistols.

Not to mention, Abdul had one weapon that he referred to as the Great Satan Killer—the Precision Shoulder-fired Rocket Launcher-1, or PSRL-1. The Americans had created their own, more advanced version of the Russian RPG-7, shoulder-fired rocket-propelled grenade launcher.

He hoped to save its use for another attack he planned against the U.S. regional headquarters in Philadelphia. However, if he deemed it necessary, he'd use the PSRL-1 to reduce the family's farmhouse to cinders.

He would send two vehicles on the southern route to attack the west side. They would have the Great Satan Killer at their disposal. His plan was to begin the assault from the east with the largest portion of his new Taliban army. He expected the farmers to pull all of their fighters to that side of the farm in response, perhaps leaving a couple of shooters to defend their western boundary. They'd be no match for Abdul's seasoned warriors.

They continued to discuss their plan of attack and possible unforeseen contingencies. The more they rehashed the scenarios, the more confident they became. The men dispersed to review their role in the assault with their respective squads and to load their vehicles. Abdul remained behind, staring at the map to determine if there was any aspect of his mission that he hadn't contemplated.

Satisfied they were ready, he confidently left the solitude of the barn to a compound bustling with activity. He stopped for a moment, proud of his people and the warriors who would accompany him as they exacted their revenge.

Abdul had been a student of modern history regarding the subject of guerilla warfare and insurgencies. He had not studied one of the most ancient military strategists known to man, Sun Tzu, who wrote *to not prepare is the greatest of crimes as to be prepared beforehand for any contingency is the greatest of virtues.*

CHAPTER FORTY-SIX

Thursday
Lake Wallenpaupack
Wayne County, Pennsylvania

After John made one last-ditch effort to prevent Sam from accompanying Fred and his men to the Afghan community, during which his father pulled the patriarch-of-the-family card, the Ford Econoline van pulled out of Cubbison's Farm and headed southeast toward Lake Wallenpaupack.

Sam, who'd been a lifelong resident of the area, was a vital asset to Fred as they made their way along the dark county roads toward Vida's old home. She was only marginally useful in finding the fastest route to cover the forty-mile trip. Her usefulness would come as they reached the outskirts of the community located on the lake.

Fred brought three of his men, who were equipped in their tactical gear with night-vision capability on their rifles. Lack of communication devices was their biggest regret. However, they'd been trained in the use of hand signals. Even in the darkest of conditions, with the benefit of the night-vision scopes, they could spread themselves out around the perimeter of the community and signal to one another.

They hid the van at the entrance to the Goose Pond Scout Reservation, the fifth-oldest Boy Scout camp in America, having been founded in 1920. The yellow swing gate that once blocked the entry between the stone columns had been rammed repeatedly by a vehicle until it had been knocked off its hinges. Fred was unconcerned that there might be refugees inhabiting the camp, as he didn't intend to stay there very long. Sam agreed to stay with the van in case anyone did come upon it. The last thing they needed was to be stranded an hour away from the farm.

Fred led them down the wooded, two-lane road for a mile until he deferred to Vida's directions. Then she directed them off the road through a trail that cut through the dense forest.

She explained in a loud whisper, "This trail goes around the entire community. The kids use it to play during the daytime, and sometimes the men patrol it at night."

Once they were into the woods a hundred yards or so, Fred asked, "Is there a place where we can view the center of the community? You know, where they might store their weapons or hide their vehicles?"

"Yes. This way." She pointed deeper into the woods and began walking briskly in the darkness. It was apparent to Fred that she was familiar with the trail because she had no concern of tripping over fallen trees or protruding roots.

Within minutes, Vida slowed down and then stopped as lights began to shine through the foliage. She knelt down and motioned for the others to follow suit.

"We are almost there. The trail surrounds our community before it opens up near the lake. In the center are many small homes and a couple of barns. The men gather in the center of the compound, where they light a fire and sit on rocks to talk. Abdul and my father used to hold secretive meetings in the largest barn. A man always stood guard at its entrance. Also, the cars were usually parked near it."

Fred turned to his men and gave them instructions. They were to fan out along the trail. If they encountered a roving patrol, take him out with their knives and hide the body, then quickly double back to report the kill. The death of a patrol started the clock ticking on when they needed to leave and return to the farm.

Each of his men hustled off, leaving him alone with Vida. They crouched behind a log while Fred began his surveillance using binoculars. Just as he instructed his men, he was making mental notes as to the number of hostiles, their weapons, and vehicles.

As he continued to study the compound with his binoculars, he asked, "I think I've got eyes on Abdul, but to confirm, can you describe him for me?"

Vida did, and Fred nodded. Abdul stood in the middle of the compound, looking in all directions and summoning people to him. Others came to him, spoke for a brief moment, and then hustled off to perform one task or another.

Vida whispered, "We can get closer if you want. It will give you a better view of the barn and the cars. We must be very quiet, however."

Fred put the binoculars back into his tactical vest, took a deep breath and exhaled to let out some tension. He turned toward Vida to see as much of her face as the low light would allow.

"I am trusting you with my life, the life of my men, and those innocent people at Cubbison's Farm. You understand that, right?"

"Yes, of course."

"That man is a murderer. He killed soldiers at the arsenal. He orchestrated the murderer of hundreds of hungry civilians at the mall. He plans on killing the people who took you in and protected you."

"Yes, I know these things." Vida tried to show her sincerity.

"If you expose us, that makes you a murderer, too."

"I know," she said sheepishly.

"And if you do, no matter what happens next, you will be the first to die. Am I clear?"

Vida gulped and nodded. Then she whispered, "You can trust me."

Fred raised his glasses one last time to get his bearings, stowed them away, and then motioned for Vida to get them closer. To her credit, she moved like a deer in familiar territory. Slowly. Sure-footed. Unafraid of her surroundings, which prevented her from making a mistake.

They were just at the clearing, providing Fred an unobstructed view of the residences, the storage building, and all the activity associated with Abdul's preparations. With a trained eye, he quickly counted the number of fighters and the weaponry they carried. It didn't take him long to realize they had the numbers. Even with the Cubbisons joining the fight, the Afghan fighters outnumbered them by at least six men, maybe more.

He also noted that they appeared determined and disciplined. This was not a ragtag bunch of wannabes. He and his men would have their hands full.

As they loaded their vehicles with supplies and cans of ammunition, he noted the number of fighters in comparison to the vehicles in the compound. He wondered how they'd cram everyone into the pickups and sedans. Then the unmistakable rumble of an M35 deuce-and-a-half rumbled around the barn into the center of the compound. They'd commandeered a National Guard truck like the three Fred had.

"Troop transport," he muttered to himself. He was so intently focused on the activity that he lost sight of Vida, who had been crouched behind him. He turned to look for her and noticed she was gone.

"Shit!" he whispered loudly as he stood, risking breaking cover.

He turned in all directions, and then he caught a glimpse of her fifteen feet to his left, hiding behind a fallen tree. He rushed to her side, careful not to step on a broken twig or rustle low-lying branches. He brusquely grabbed her by the arm and pulled her toward him.

"What the hell are you doing?" That was when he noticed she was crying.

She'd covered her mouth with her right hand and pointed toward one of the homes with her left. Through a window, in a candlelit room, sat a woman eating alone at a table. Her face was forlorn. Miserable. Her body revealed someone who dreaded their life. Hopeless with no chance of happiness.

"My mother," she managed to whisper as the tears streamed down her face. "I want so badly to go to her, but I cannot."

Then, in an emotional moment that caught Fred by surprise, she turned and buried her face in his chest. She began to sob, somehow controlling her sorrow by forcing her face into Fred's body.

He became filled with compassion as the raw emotions poured out of Vida. The young woman was grief-stricken as her mother, whom she loved, was barely fifty feet away yet so far. Fred consoled her and whispered hollow promises into her ear. He doubted that she could ever come back here, and most likely, the Cubbisons weren't interested in opening their home to more refugees. None-theless, Fred, who hadn't had to show compassion to another human in a long time, managed to console her.

After she calmed down, they retreated to the trail, where he gathered his men. As the Afghans appeared ready to move out, Fred and his team needed to hurry in order to return to the farm. They needed to formulate an unconventional plan for the defense of the farm or risk being overrun.

PART 5

———

Friday
Peekaboo!

CHAPTER FORTY-SEVEN

Friday
Wayne County, Pennsylvania

The passengers in the Econoline were full of chatter as Sam drove at a high rate of speed back to the farm. It was approaching midnight, and there were no other vehicles on the road, not that he expected any in a powerless world. As he drove, Fred and his men compared notes and shared their observations of the Afghan fighters.

Fred led the discussion. "So we all agree. They've got the numbers."

"No doubt about it," replied one of the men. "And I studied their faces through my scope. I felt like I was back in Kandahar or Parwan Province. I don't know if all of these guys were Taliban, but they sure look like them now."

"Formidable," said another man.

"Roger that," said a third.

"Did anybody else catch the AirTronic rocket launcher?" asked the fourth man, referring to the PSRL-1.

"I did," replied Fred. "Only one, though."

"It would be nice to take that puppy out of the game," said one of the jarheads. "If not, this shit'll be over before it starts."

Sam had to know what they were referring to. "What are you guys talking about?"

Fred replied, "Basically, it's a shoulder-fired rocket launcher. These Taliban types love them. The Russians left them behind decades ago. But the one I saw was the American-made version. Am I right, guys?"

"Yeah," one of the men replied. "Did you notice which vehicle it was loaded into?"

"I did," said Fred. "A black pickup."

"How many of those were lining up to haul their fighters?" asked Sam.

"Three."

"Swell," mumbled Sam.

Fred's man continued his thought. "Maybe we can take out the truck before it gets to the farm?"

Fred turned in his seat to address Sam. "How far out are we?"

"Fifteen minutes."

Fred thought for a moment, and his men respectfully remained quiet as their leader concentrated. After a minute, he turned in his seat to address his guys.

"Okay, listen up," he began. "They're not going to come at us from just one direction. Do you agree?"

"No doubt," replied one. "I mean, I don't know much about the north side of the farm and any possible ingress or egress. They can approach from the Harford side. I can't imagine this guy abandoning a prong of attack. That said, he'd have to drive right past the front gate of the farm to get his people in position. We'd cut them to shreds."

"With pleasure," said one of the ex-Marines, slapping his rifle.

"He ain't stupid, either," added another. "He's not gonna drive vehicles right past the front gate to position his troops."

Fred looked at Sam. "Is there a way to the other side, um, the west side of the farm from here? We have to assume that he's gonna split his forces to hit us from both sides."

Sam explained the zigzag route along the back roads that came out near the Yoder place two miles west of the farm.

Fred raised his chin and nodded. "We'll send a two-man team in a Humvee to wait on their arrival. At the very least, take out their vehicles. I'm pretty sure we can stage the perfect ambush to eliminate a sizable part of their force."

"Maybe throw in a sniper, sir. You know, if the terrain lends that opportunity."

"Agreed," said Fred.

"Is that where you expect them to have the rocket launcher?" asked Sam.

Fred grimaced. "I don't know. I doubt it. If they had more than one, Abdul would've brought them all. Just in case. I suspect that was his only one, which means, if I were him, I'd keep it close by to pick the appropriate time to use it. I believe he is most likely to put the bulk of his people on the east side that he's most familiar with. They have the high ground there."

"Speaking of troops, most of his fighters will be in the M35," began one of the ex-Marines.

"Yeah," agreed another. "What if we take the deuce-and-a-half out of the game before it gets to the farm?"

His buddy leaned forward in his seat and nodded. "That's exactly what I was thinking. The two of us patrolled Gibson while we were waiting for the rest of y'all to arrive. There are plenty of ambush points to pin down the caravan."

Once again, Fred fell deep in thought. All of a sudden, his limited personnel were being spread even thinner. That said, the ambush assault plans were viable and could reduce the Afghans' numbers considerably.

He looked to Sam. "I need someone with local knowledge of the farms surrounding your place. If we place a couple of guys outside our defensive perimeter, they'll be cut off from the rest of us."

Ironically, Sam was pulling into Gibson as they spoke. He glanced all around, as did the passengers, assessing the best locations for an ambush. After a moment, he replied.

"Luke would be best. Of course, John and I are very familiar with the properties around us. However, we're too old to keep up with your guys. Luke wouldn't have a problem, and he's pretty good with a weapon, especially from a long range."

Vida, who'd sat in silence throughout, just realized her beloved Luke was going to be placed in one of the riskiest aspects of Fred's defensive plan. Had it not been dark, the occupants of the van would've noticed her turn pale and watched as she repeatedly wiped her sweaty palms off on her jeans.

This is getting real, the teen thought to herself.

CHAPTER FORTY-EIGHT

Friday
Cubbison's Farm
Harford, Pennsylvania

John and Emma anxiously awaited the return of Sam, Fred and the others by strolling along the gravel driveway leading to the market building. Both of them were tense and fearful for the safety of their family. Undoubtedly, the gun battle they'd endured with the criminal bikers paled in comparison to fighting men who'd seen real battle during a time of war. Although neither said it, they internally wondered if they should abandon the farm for no other reason than to save their lives.

"I'm not being stubborn or stupid," said John unexpectedly. It was if he verbalized the raging debate in his mind.

"What?" asked Emma, confused, suddenly stopping to study her husband. "Nobody said you were."

"Wait. Did I say that out loud?"

"Yes, honey," she replied as she reached out for his hand. She wasn't surprised to find it as clammy as hers. "I know what you're thinking. I've been arguing with myself about the same thing since Sam and Fred left earlier. I mean, this is our home. However, is it worth dying for? We can find another home."

"Can we?" asked John rhetorically. "I mean, wouldn't that make us no different from the rest of these thugs, thieves, and terrorists who want to take the farm from us?"

"I suppose you're right," she replied sullenly. "There are no good options other than to defend what is ours. At least we have help."

"Thank God. If we come through this, I don't know how we'll ever be able to repay them."

Emma motioned toward the gate. She and John needed to remain vigilant despite the fact the ex-Marines were somewhere nearby, not that they made themselves visible to anyone. It was comforting yet disconcerting at the same time.

"All they want is a home," she explained. "They thought they had something in Harford at the motel. Although, I think Fred knew that wasn't sustainable. It was fate that brought us together. They have something we desperately need in the form of protection. We can ramp up our farming activities to feed us all."

"Can we?" asked John. "This will be a lot of mouths to feed."

Emma laughed. "Well, they're gonna have to learn how to multi-task. For example, they're gonna have to put down their rifles and pick up a hoe. Some will have to park their machine guns and carry a hunting rifle. We can't eat deer that have been riddled with a dozen bullet holes."

John laughed heartily and stopped to hug his wife. "You have a way of making me feel better, especially when I'm all stressed out."

"That's why I'm the best wife in history, right?"

"Yes, ma'am." John bent over to kiss her, when he heard a car in the distance.

"Are they coming back?" Emma asked.

"It's certainly not a truck. Let's see." John raised his rifle and squinted his eyes as he concentrated on the point in the road where it sloped down toward the property. He instantly recognized the light configuration of the Econoline's grille.

"Well?" she asked.

"Yep. That's them. I'll get the gate; go tell the others to meet in the market. I rearranged things so we can all discuss what's next."

Emma began jogging back toward the house, where she was greeted by Luke and Matthew. Asher and Lauren followed closely behind.

"They're returning," she said, slightly out of breath. "John wants us to meet in the marketplace."

"Jenna and the kids, too?" asked Lauren with a hint of doubt in her voice.

Emma looked back toward the gate and then to the house. "No, you're right. They don't need to be involved. Would you mind—?" She began to ask Lauren to stay with them before she was cut off.

"Absolutely. Asher can fill me in later."

Emma led the way to the market. She instructed the boys to light the candles and illuminate the Coleman lantern over the folding banquet tables she'd retrieved earlier at John's request. He'd also laid out the plat maps of the farm and surrounding areas that Sam had utilized once before.

A minute later, John arrived at the market's porch just after the van arrived and its occupants spilled out. Fred was the first to speak.

"Where are the trucks?"

"For now, we pulled them behind the house so they're hidden from the road," replied John.

"Okay, good. We need to stash the cargo trucks as far away from the road as possible. I need two of the Humvees up here ASAP."

"Luke, Matthew, you heard the man. Bring us two Humvees."

"Leave the third where it is for now," said Fred. He turned to the men who rode along with him to the Afghan community. "You two set Matthew up with ballistic protection and a full auto rifle. You'll have to teach him how to use it on the way. Luke, I'll need you to carry the best rifle at your disposal for long-range, night-time shooting."

"Like a sniper?" asked Luke.

Fred nodded.

Emma stepped in with a frown on her face. "Wait a minute. On the way to where?"

Sam explained, "Emma, they're coming. We have to set up two ambushes. One in Gibson and the other past the Yoder place on Upper Podunk Road. Matthew will be going with the Gibson team because he has experience from the New York trip."

"To do what?" asked Emma, full of apprehension.

Fred answered her. "We expect the Afghans to split their forces so they can attack us from both sides. My men, along with your sons, will take as many of them out as possible before they get here."

Sam added, "Emma, the boys know the surrounding farms. If their vehicles get disabled, they'll be able to guide Fred's men back to the farm without getting shot by the Afghans."

"Or friendly fire," added Fred. "My guys are disciplined, but it will still be dark."

"Makes sense," said John, who supported his wife by taking her hand. "I've set us up inside so you can get a feel for the topography of the farm and the places where we're vulnerable."

Fred led the way just as the boys returned with the two Humvees. The Cubbisons and Asher followed the military man into their version of a war room. Fred gave his men additional instructions on how to effectuate the ambush and admonished them both to remember the boys were teen civilians. "Utilize them," he said. "However, don't put them in harm's way unless absolutely necessary."

Minutes later, they were gone, following one another up the driveway to the road before peeling off in opposite directions. Emma stood on the front porch of the market building with tears in her eyes as her teenage boys went off to war.

CHAPTER FORTY-NINE

Friday
Gibson, Pennsylvania

Matthew sat quietly in the back of the Humvee, listening to the two Marines explain the difference between the rifles he'd shot in the past and the automatic weapon he now possessed. Matthew didn't have the heart to tell them that the bulk of his experience firing a weapon prior to the collapse was playing video games. Granted, he was very good at it. However, it was far different from firing a live round into another human being, as he'd done to protect his father that day on the streets of Weehawken, New Jersey.

Fully understanding that he couldn't hold the trigger down the whole time, otherwise he'd spray bullets into the sky, Matthew then was schooled on the ballistic armor that threatened to choke him by the neck. It was ill-fitting and heavy. It impeded his range of motion. He wanted to take it off. However, he didn't, for he knew if the Afghans didn't kill him, his mother would if she found out.

It didn't take long to arrive in Gibson or for the ex-Marines to realize that Matthew might not be much help during their mission. They whispered to one another in the front seat. Matthew heard them over the roar of the oversized, off-road tires. They intended to keep him out of harm's way because they didn't have confidence in his capabilities.

This raised the hackles of Matthew, who felt he was more than qualified to play a role. He'd killed people. Without regret. He wanted to yell out that fact but kept his cool. Now was not the time to prove points. His family's lives were at risk.

As they approached Gibson, the two men discussed the importance of their mission. Moments prior, as they'd driven past Hogs & Hens, the men had revealed a shoulder-launched missile weapon might be in play. They presumed it would be within the control of the Afghans' leader named Abdul. Both men agreed they'd feel better once they eliminated the threat, as it had the ability to level all the Cubbisons' home and surrounding buildings. Matthew's focus changed as he contemplated their words.

They turned the Humvee into Church Road, which exited onto the highway leading to Cubbison's. The other end of the road was perfectly located in a bend, allowing the Marines to ambush the M35 transport as it came into view.

The hastily concocted plan by Fred was forced to allow most of the anticipated convoy through the kill zone. Eliminating the hostiles in the troop transport could take out half of Abdul's fighters, if not more.

If Abdul turned and counterattacked, Fred's men would retreat through the streets and rejoin Matthew at the Humvee. They could race back to the defensive positions at the farm. If the other vehicles continued on, those defending the farm would have advance notice of their arrival. The sound of automatic gunfire in the dead of night would carry for miles.

"All right, Matt," the driver began. "This Humvee is our lifeline back to the farm. If these scumbags circle around the church and cut us off, we'll be caught in a crossfire. We need you to guard the truck and, just as important, run 'em off if they come down the road from our six. Got it?"

Matthew knew what the military man meant by the word *six*. The characters on *Call of Duty* used the term often when referring to their back.

Matthew's response was simple and sincere. "Hey. You can count on me."

The two men slipped off into the darkness, leaving Matthew standing alone, staring at the simple, white clapboard Methodist Church. Its steeple rose above the roofline, but not nearly as tall as the trees surrounding the church. A smattering of tombstones filled the cemetery although there was certainly room for more. Matthew shivered, but not because he was cold. It was getting real, he thought to himself.

He paced the gravel road around the Humvee, occasionally wandering back toward the stop sign at the highway leading to the farm. Other times, out of curiosity and an intense desire to know what the ex-Marines would be facing, he eased up toward the highway, glancing at the old houses on both sides of the road. The gravel crunched under his feet. It was a noise deemed ordinary under normal conditions, but a sound that might draw the attention of a local insomniac.

He stopped well short of the highway leading through town for fear of drawing the ire of the two men on his team. Bored, he wandered back, walking through the dewy grass to avoid being detected. He aimlessly kicked at a soccer ball that had been abandoned by the road when he suddenly froze.

Matthew turned slightly and closed his eyes. *They're coming. Grandpa Sam and Dad were right. They really are coming.* Matthew nervously ran his fingers through his hair with one hand and gripped the handle of his automatic rifle with the other. He tried to remember the instructions the driver had given him.

He pulled his rifle close to his face to find the select switch for semiautomatic or full auto. Was it already set to full auto? Where was the safety? It was probably on, right?

Suddenly, Matthew's confidence was crushed. He felt vulnerable and very afraid. He desperately wanted to fire off a couple of rounds to make sure everything was ready for when the real battle came his way.

The roar of the vehicles was louder. They were getting closer. He imagined the ex-Marines. Calm and collected. Lying in wait, focusing on their targets. Prepared to send bullets into the bodies of their attackers.

He stared at the intersection where the church road circled into the highway. He noticed the headlights washing the houses. They were about to pass a hundred yards in front of him.

Shit!

He ducked behind a late-model Chevy to avoid being seen. At a low crouch, he ran through the front yards toward their Humvee.

The first vehicle passed the intersection, then another. And another. Within seconds, they'd be making a hard left turn and start toward the farm. Their forward progress would take them past the entry to the gravel road where the Humvee had been parked. He felt exposed and out of position.

Matthew raised his rifle and rested his finger on the trigger guard. For a few seconds, with his eyes closed, he was transformed into *Call of Duty: Modern Warfare*, his favorite video game. In that moment, one similar to the split second he'd needed to kill his father's attacker that day, Matthew's confidence returned. Any doubt about his ability to kill their enemy was vanquished. Any questions he had about where to be and what to do were answered. Even the most rudimentary hesitation regarding the weapon's settings was discarded.

When the duo of hardened leathernecks opened fire on the M35 transport, Matthew steeled his nerves and prepared to kill or be killed.

He took up a position on the gravel road where he could easily observe both intersections on the highway. The gunfire that had erupted to his right was deafening. The screams of agony would've been heartbreaking had the men who died not been intent on killing Matthew's family and their new friends.

The lead vehicle that had passed to his right moments ago sped past the other entrance to the church road. The second vehicle slowed and then continued on. As did the third.

"Was that it?" Matthew asked aloud. Had there only been three vehicles pass the other entrance previously? It was a crucial detail the untrained rookie combatant was expected to mistake.

The effect of his lack of attention to that detail locked Matthew in place even though the other two men in his squad were now engaging in an unexpected firefight. They truly expected the ambush to go quickly because the men in the transport would've been unable to defend themselves.

"There must've been another truck at the back of the convoy," said Matthew aloud as his eyes darted back and forth between the two entrances to the road.

He paced back and forth, trying to focus his hearing on the road noise emanating from the farm. Had the trucks stopped? Had they continued on, leaving their comrades to fight the battle alone? Could the two ex-Marines hold their own?

This time, Matthew shouted at himself, not that it mattered at that point, as the entire neighborhood, as they say, was awake.

"Don't abandon your post, dumbass!" he shouted at himself.

Yet he did. First, he raced back toward the highway where they'd first turned off to determine the whereabouts of the three vehicles that had just driven by. He needed to confirm they'd continued on and not stopped or doubled back.

He eased into the middle of several shrubs at the intersection. It was devoid of activity. Matthew quickly broke cover and began rushing down the gravel road, past the church and their hidden

Humvee, and back toward the highway where the gun battle was taking place.

His unit needed him.

CHAPTER FIFTY

Friday
Near the Yoder Place
Harford, Pennsylvania

Luke settled into the tall grasses on a knoll overlooking the desolate country road. He and his two companions had searched for an area that gave him a clear line of sight to any vehicles approaching the intersection. They readied their automatic weapons and made their way down the hill to ambush the Afghans when they exited their vehicle.

Luke's instructions were simple. Shoot out the tires or otherwise disable the vehicle. It was not his job to eliminate the hostiles. The ex-Marines would take care of that. At that hour, anyone driving along Upper Podunk Road would be in for a helluva shock if they were unrelated to the former Taliban fighters.

Luke searched through the night-vision scope attached to his favorite deer rifle, finding the road to be completely still. He took his eye away from the scope and observed the road to the south. Although the trees lining both sides of the asphalt pavement were still full of leaves, he would be able to identify headlights headed in their direction.

The seven anxious minutes he'd spent in the stuffy backseat of the Humvee would come down to a quick, one-minute gun battle during which Abdul's western approach to the farm would hopefully be thwarted.

As Luke waited, he thought of Vida. Something had happened in the last twenty-four hours. He was sure of it. Not only had she avoided him, she'd been hidden away to an extent. This evening, when he'd learned of a secretive mission to conduct surveillance at her old community, he became even more suspicious.

It was the attitude and demeanor of his parents, and Fred, that added more fuel to the conspiratorial fire. His mom was almost hostile toward Vida, who appeared to be sullen and withdrawn. Why would they treat her that way if she was willing to assist Fred in surveilling her home? And why did they know to do it now? Tonight? With the results leading to their preparation for another battle at Cubbison's Farm.

Luke had a lot of questions, and his speculation ran rampant. However, as he glanced down the road again, he noticed two sets of headlights creating a strobe effect along the tree line. It was time.

Once again, he focused all of his senses on the target zone below him. If the vehicles were moving quickly, he'd have to react with equal speed and accuracy. Now, with two vehicles approaching, it would be vital that he take out the lead vehicle first. Then he needed to lay down cover fire for the other two members of his team. They'd most certainly be outnumbered, although the element of surprise was on their side.

Luke took several deep breaths to relax and steady his nerves. He wasn't shooting people, he reminded himself, although he was prepared to do so.

The cars were moving steadily but not at a high rate of speed. Luke knew Upper Podunk Road well. It was full of potholes, which accounted for the headlights swerving back and forth at times.

The lights grew brighter. He could hear the low rumble of their engines. He eased his finger onto the trigger, mentally gauging the timing of their arrival in the kill window. He took a deep breath and held it, exhaling just as he gently squeezed the trigger.

The powerful Springfield Armory .308-caliber rifle recoiled against his shoulder, blasting the heavy-grain bullet toward its target in the blink of an eye. The rifle's report was loud, piercing the still of the night. The bullet destroying the left front tire of the pickup truck was even louder.

Surprised, the driver jerked the steering wheel back and forth in an attempt to gain control of the now three-wheel pickup. He jammed on the brakes as the truck veered left toward the embankment. The second pickup narrowly missed the first, also screeching to a halt near its companion's tailgate.

As the first doors of the vehicles were flung open, all hell broke loose. At first, it was a one-sided battle. Even from his perch high above the road, Luke could hear the sound of brass pounding the pavement near the front of the parked trucks.

Remarkably, the occupants began to return fire. Luke had to join the fray. He concentrated on the movement below as he studied the monochromatic shapes crouched behind the trucks, firing upon the ex-Marines.

He homed in on a target and fired without hesitation. The man was struck in the side and slammed against the wheel well of the pickup. The bullet's impact in his body was no different than what it did to a one-hundred-fifty-pound buck.

One down.

Suddenly, two of the men turned their ire toward him. Bullets flew all around him, mostly embedding in the soil in front of him. A couple flew past and tore into the bark of the tall pines atop the knoll.

Instinctively, Luke gathered his courage and moved to another location slightly to his right and closer to the road. He had a better shot at the lead pickup at that point.

A barrage of gunshots from both sides caught his attention, giving him a renewed sense of urgency. He fell hard onto the ground, bruising his ribs on a softball-sized rock. Slightly winded, he fought to regain his composure to take another shot.

Groans of pain filled the air. Luke was unable to discern which side was taking on the casualties. More gunshots prompted him to ready his rifle.

He didn't have a clear shot at a human target. He was able to focus on the left front tire of the second pickup. "Maybe?" he muttered to himself as he returned his eye to the scope and squeezed the trigger. The result was the same as his first shot.

The tire exploded as if it were a bomb. Clearly, it startled the Afghans, as they excitedly began shouting to one another. The gunfire stopped momentarily as they barked orders at the top of their lungs. Then there were bloodcurdling screams.

Fred's men advanced on the pickups, catching the Afghans off guard. Luke was able to discern the difference between their automatic weapons and those utilized by the Afghans, who began to fire back.

"I'm hit!" An American's voice.

"Shit!" shouted Luke. He lifted his body off the ground and began running down the slope toward the battle. *One of ours. One left.*

The other ex-Marine continued to advance on the Afghans. His anger enhanced his capabilities. He began to dispatch one hostile after another until he hollered, "We've got two runners!"

"I've got 'em!"

The words were out of Luke's mouth before he thought about the ramifications of what he'd said. Without hesitation, he shifted direction and began running toward the road through the trees, hoping to intercept the men as they attempted their escape.

The hunt was on.

CHAPTER FIFTY-ONE

Friday
Gibson, Pennsylvania

Matthew ran close to the ground, keeping a steel guardrail between him and the road, which undoubtedly was covered with the blood of the Afghans in the transport. Despite the dark conditions, he was able to make out the details of the battle scene.

The tan canopy covering the back of the M35 transport had been ripped to shreds; the blood-covered canvas dripped sticky goo as a slight breeze blew it back and forth. The Afghans had taken a large number of casualties if the bodies draped over the edges of the large truck were any indication. They were riddled with bullets, with their organs hanging out through gaping holes in their torsos.

What puzzled Matthew was the fact that the rapid gunfire he'd heard earlier had dissipated to the occasional gunshot several hundred feet down the highway. He thought he could make out the silhouette of a stalled vehicle in the middle of the highway turned sideways in front of a two-story building that looked familiar.

He jumped over the guardrail and ran along the concrete railing of a short bridge crossing a creek. His heart pounded, as he was fully exposed to anyone who saw him as a target, both friends and foes.

He knew he was taking a risk by abandoning the Humvee at the church. However, his gut told him the other vehicles had continued on to attack the farm. Based on the sporadic gunfire replacing the barrage of bullets early on, he sensed Fred's men needed help. As it turned out, he was right.

He stayed in a low crouch until he arrived behind a mailbox in front of a small residence that had been converted into a post office. Just beyond the post office was a deteriorating old house with a stone wall lining the front yard. As he approached, he saw two men leaning against the wall. Matthew ran onto the porch of the house and dropped to his hands and knees. He crawled behind several pieces of furniture until he could confirm the two men were part of his team.

"Hey! Are you guys all right?"

"Why aren't you with the truck?" came the response in a loud whisper. It was the driver, whom Fred had put in charge of the operation.

"The others continued on to the farm," Matthew replied. "I confirmed—"

His sentence was muted by automatic gunfire emanating from the second floor of the antique shop across the street. The shooter mistakenly thought the new arrival, Matthew, was hiding behind the disabled Chevy pickup in the driveway. The bullets struck the windshield, creating a series of spiderweb cracks before exploding into the front seat.

Matthew used the shooter's inaccuracy to rush to the side of the ex-Marines. Another shooter fired from the antique store, the bullets snapping inches over his head until they embedded in the clapboard siding of the old house.

As he ran, Matthew raised his rifle with one hand and let out a burst that blasted the mansard roofline over the store's front façade.

He missed any targets. However, he did back off the other shooters long enough to join the others.

He dropped to a knee and lowered his body beneath the top of the stone wall. He slowly moved the barrel of his rifle from one upper window to the other. The glass had been blown, and the frames had splintered. He checked for movement.

A shooter suddenly appeared, swinging his arm and pistol into view before poking his head around the edge of the window casement. Matthew fired off a burst, striking the man center mass. He pitched forward and slammed onto the mansard roof face-first. With the pistol still clutched in his hand, he slowly slid down the shingles until he landed headfirst in an open, rollaway dumpster.

Matthew turned his body and slid down behind the wall to rest against it. Before he could speak, the driver told him of the problem they faced.

"He's been hit," he whispered. Matthew leaned over to get a better look. *More than hit*, he thought to himself. A thick stream of blood pumped rhythmically from a mangled stump just below his knee. His entire lower leg had been shattered. The makeshift tourniquet he'd created for his partner was not working very well. All Matthew could do was watch as the man slowly bled out and died.

The driver checked his vitals and shook his head in disbelief. He grumbled, "It wasn't supposed to go this way." As if to put an exclamation point on his comment, bullets ricocheted off the asphalt and embedded in the stone wall's mortar joints.

Matthew resisted the urge to poke his head over the wall again. Instead, he asked, "Any idea how many are left?"

"Five. Maybe four if you just took one out."

"I did. Do you think they're all in the antique store?" Matthew asked.

"Hard to tell," he replied. "We've been pinned down. This one thought it would be a piece of cake. I told him not to underestimate these assholes." He gently mussed the hair of the younger man, who'd seen limited service in Afghanistan before the botched extraction.

Matthew sighed, as he could sense the emotional pain of the driver. He felt responsible for the safety and survival of his small, three-man squad.

"Whadya wanna do?" Matthew asked. Then he foolishly suggested, "We can go in after them."

"Not a chance. Neither of us would walk out alive. We're in a bad spot. We've got to retreat to the Humvee and help them at the farm."

"What about that missile launcher thing?"

The Marine paused before responding. He chastised himself for questioning Matthew's commitment.

"We cleared the cargo truck. Most likely, it was with the lead vehicles."

Matthew thought they should double-check, but they were running out of time. He quickly glanced at the storefront across the street. He ducked quickly after seeing nothing.

"What about these guys?" asked Matthew. "And him?" He pointed at the now dead Marine.

"With their vehicles disabled, it'll take them half an hour or more to catch up to the rest of their group," he replied. "We'll have to come back for him."

"You could get the truck so we can load him up. I can hold my own 'til you get here."

"Too risky," said the driver. He turned to his comrade and began removing his body armor as well as his utility belt full of magazines. He handed Matthew the man's rifle, which was covered in blood. "Here's what we're gonna do. When we break cover, you haul ass back to the truck. I'll lay down cover fire until you round the bend. Do not stop until you've retrieved the truck and fired that sucker up. Got it?"

"Keys?" asked Matthew.

"Yeah, shit," the driver replied. He rummaged through his

fatigues and handed them to Matthew. He shoved them in his pocket and stretched his arm to the driver again. "What?"

"Let me carry all the gear," Matthew replied. "You need to focus on covering our asses."

Matthew couldn't see the jarhead's smile. "Get ready. On my first volleys, run like hell."

"That, I can do."

Seconds later the Marine poked his head above the wall and stitched the siding of the store between the windows, hoping the old walls wouldn't provide any ballistic protection for the men hiding inside. He was right.

One of the Afghans began screaming in pain while another exposed his arm to fire his sidearm wildly in the general direction of the stone wall. That was all the seasoned veteran needed. The powerful rounds from his automatic weapon severed the Afghan's arm at the elbow. Forearm, hand, and pistol crashed off the canopy roof before landing with a thud on the pavement.

At the top of the hill, Matthew once again disobeyed his superior's orders. He hid in a thicket of pines where he could have a clear field of vision toward the disabled M35 cargo truck. As soon as the driver appeared, Matthew confirmed that he was not being pursued. By the time the former Marine reached the top of the hill, he was winded.

"Here, you drive," said Matthew as he handed back the keys.

"You don't listen so well," the man chastised Matthew.

"You sound like my mother," said Matthew with a laugh.

The two of them started down the gravel road to join the Cubbisons' defense of their farm.

CHAPTER FIFTY-TWO

Friday
Near the Yoder Place
Harford, Pennsylvania

Despite feeling obligated to do so, Luke did not join the two-man team of Marines who'd taken the fight to the truckloads of Afghan fighters. One of the men was injured. However, neither had called for his help or stopped him from pursuing the two Afghans who'd fled the small battleground.

Luke was apprehensive as he hugged the tree line along the side of the road. He didn't know if the men intended to retreat to their community or if they intended to ambush any pursuers. Luke wished he had a different rifle. The automatic weapons used by the Marines seemed to make more sense than the bulky deer rifle he carried. Its primary benefit, other than the fact it was familiar to Luke, was the night-vision scope he'd attached to it before they left the farm. It was illegal to hunt with it. However, it had been in the family for years until the day it might come in handy hunting coyotes. Or, now, wayward Taliban fighters.

Hunting prey was far different than cozying up in a hide, waiting for a buck to wander into your killing field. Luke used to laugh about how casual hunters would put on their warmest gear, pack a flask of whiskey in their camo jacket, and maybe a Thermos of coffee in their backpack just to bag a buck or some doe that happened to go prancing by. He'd seen them in action on the State Game Lands nearby.

They'd rest the muzzle of the rifle they'd bought at the local Walmart and pull-jerk the trigger, hoping to catch any part of the animal they'd spotted. To them, if they blew a leg off, allowing the hapless deer to writhe in pain until the great hunter climbed out of the hide, took a piss, and wandered upon it, that constituted hunting. Luke had been taught by his dad and Grandpa Sam that there was much more to hunting than that.

He continued moving away from the occasional gunfire behind him and then had a thought. From what he'd heard on the news about the Taliban, they were dedicated, almost rabid religious zealots who never shied away from a fight. They'd never retreat to their villages in shame. Their attitudes hadn't changed merely because they lived in Northeastern Pennsylvania. They were going to join the battle even if it meant getting there on foot.

Luke began to look for trails or fields where it was logical to head east toward the farm. He was familiar with the large swaths of real estate that lay across the street from his home. He rarely ventured onto the back pastures of his across-the-street neighbors. As a result, he was in unchartered territory to an extent.

Yet he was still a hunter. He just had to modify his thinking. He understood the habits of deer and feral hogs. He knew how they moved. Where they grazed or rooted for food. The men who fled the scene were trying to find their way to his home using logical means of travel. Fields. Four-wheeler trails. And eventually the highway.

Luke began running through the pines and saplings that stood between the large swaths of pasture to his right and the wood areas that ran parallel to the highway. He tried to keep his cover while using his familiarity with the woods to gain ground on the men who had a head start on him.

He'd never hunted men. In a way, he'd presumed it would be easier. Animals in the wild had eons of DNA passed along teaching them how to remain alive. Man, when taken out of his element, was clumsy, sloppy, and prone to making mistakes.

Such as chattering too loud.

The Middle Eastern accents were unmistakable. The tone and tenor of their voices were obvious to Luke despite the language barrier. They were lost and very frustrated.

He continued to move forward, closer to his prey, who'd stopped and wandered into an open field, staring at the heavens as if the stars or the location of the moon was a neon sign pointing the way to Cubbison's Farm.

Luke moved surreptitiously past the two men, positioning his body between them and the farm. He would take the shot. He wanted to. However, if he missed, he wanted them running the other way, not directly into the protective arms of their brethren.

Finally, Luke reached an elevated point where he had a clear field of vision to his targets, whether they stood and took their medicine or if they bolted away. To be sure, a standing target was much easier. However, Luke was an accomplished hunter. A moving target was no match for his skills.

He raised his rifle in a smooth, almost imperceptible motion. He'd practiced for years since Grandpa Sam first put a rifle in his hand. He was equally comfortable shooting from a prone position, as he had earlier, or standing, which made sense now. He nestled the butt of his rifle in his shoulder. His grip was firm so that no sudden twitch of his muscles or elevated pulse of his heart threw off his aim.

He closed his left eye and allowed his right eye to slide behind the scope. The two men were waving their arms in all directions. Animated. Arguing. Unaware.

He slowly flipped off the safety and eased his finger onto the trigger. He chose the smaller of the two men. The one who faced him and provided a nice target.

Despite the fact that the recoil of his rifle blurred his vision slightly as the scope wandered off his eye a bit, Luke knew that he'd found his target. The speed of a rifle's bullet wasn't something most people could comprehend. Even to experienced hunters, the time between trigger pull and impact was miniscule. Luke's position and aim were solid. His first target flew backwards as the two-hundred-thirty-grain bullet blew a gaping hole in the man's chest.

He still had work to do.

Without lowering his rifle, Luke flicked the bolt, ejecting the spent brass onto the pine straw floor of the woods while ramming another deadly round into the gun. It took him only a second to reacquire his second target, who was now running in the opposite direction of Luke down a hill, seeking safety in a pond.

He never made it.

Luke fired again, striking the man in the back, sending him tumbling forward until he rolled to a stop. His body never twitched or moved. Lifeless as it bled. However, unlike the first kill, which no man's body could've withstood, Luke had to make sure with target number two. With a calm demeanor his mother would've bawled her eyes out over, Luke fired another shot into the man's body. If he wasn't dead before, he certainly was now.

With his rifle held at low ready, Luke walked down the hill, his eyes staring at the two corpses. In the darkness, he could've been easily fooled by the men. He arrived at the first kill. As he suspected, the man's chest was obliterated.

He started toward the second man. Just as he approached the body lying facedown in the grass, Luke stumbled in the dark, falling forward slightly until he landed on his hands and knees. The dead man's eyes were open and stared at his killer. Luke stared back, unfazed by the proximity to the death he'd caused.

He took a deep breath and gathered himself. After shouldering his rifle, he turned around and studied the ground much like a city dweller might do after tripping over an unholy crack in the sidewalk. He had to know what had knocked him to his knees.

He shuffled his feet through the tall grasses until his foot struck something heavy and metallic. He bent over and fumbled through the grass until he found the item that had caused him to stumble.

"What the hell is this thing?" he asked as he held the shoulder-fired rocket launcher dubbed by Abdul as the Great Satan Killer.

CHAPTER FIFTY-THREE

Friday
Hogs & Hens
Gibson, Pennsylvania

Abdul was deep in thought as his vehicle led the way toward their war of revenge. His mind had wandered to his days in Afghanistan when he and Jamal had fought side by side against the Americans. The victories they won as insurgents might have seemed small by American standards. However, to the Taliban, they were celebrated with great fanfare and pride. Tonight, he would achieve another great victory in the forever war against the Great Satan. Certainly, it was small compared to his achievements at the Viewmont Mall. The level of pride he'd feel standing over their bloody corpses would be like no other.

When the automatic gunfire disrupted his thoughts and pierced the quiet early morning they'd enjoyed since leaving their community, Abdul instructed his driver to slow the vehicle to a near stop. He'd anticipated the possibility of an ambush along the way. Not by the enemy he would soon be engaging. But, rather, by desperate opportunists along the way. Local farmers, small-town residents, or even law enforcement prepared to lose their lives to feed their families.

For that reason, he'd placed his troop transport next to last in line in the convoy. They'd have the protection of the last vehicle while allowing the rest of his fighters to proceed to the farm. Upon arrival, he'd simply reassign the men traveling with him to attack from the east and north sides of the property.

Within a minute of instructing his driver to continue on to their staging area, something gnawed at him. The first rounds fired were from automatic weapons. That meant his men had been forced to fire first. Had he missed something as his vehicle passed through town? Had his recollection of his days in Afghanistan caused him to lose sight of the potential ambush threat?

They'd gone too far now to help his brothers. They were more than capable of defending themselves. So Abdul continued toward Cubbison's Farm, comforted in knowing that the Great Satan Killer, the equalizer he was sure these farmers could not match, was safely in the hands of his men approaching from the west.

By prearrangement, he was to meet with Vida at the abandoned produce stand east of the farm. He'd assumed she could find her way back there by dawn, not that it mattered. He would never expose himself to the enemy by telegraphing his movements. Rather, he decided to use it as a form of entrapment.

There was a pig farm about a mile before the produce stand. The house appeared to be burned out and therefore uninhabited. There were barns and outbuildings where they could park their vehicles before moving forward on foot. This had been designated as their staging area.

He led the two vehicles onto the gravel drive, where he noticed the signage—Hogs & Hens. He shook his head in disgust. Pork was explicitly declared *haram*, which means forbidden, in the Holy Quran. He managed a slight laugh as he saw the pile of burnt timbers that once was the main house of the farm. He considered it to be a form of karma for the pig farmers.

After the vehicles parked out of view of the road, Abdul gathered his men and gave them instructions. His driver, a top lieutenant vying to replace Jamal as Abdul's number one, was designated to remain at the staging area to assign the rest of the men their positions.

He and two others would immediately conduct surveillance around the produce stand, hoping to catch the farmers unaware if they attempted a surprise attack. The other men would move through the back of the fields toward the house across the street from Cubbison's where Vida had been snatched. Once they'd killed anyone they came across, they were to take up positions across from the front, gated entrance to the farm.

His men would attack through the woods west of the farm, with one maneuvering into position at the top of the hill to take a clear shot at the farmhouse with the rocket launcher. Abdul had a flare gun in his tactical vest, both items procured from the raid on the Picatinny Arsenal. Instructions were simple. If the gunner sees the flare, he destroys the house. It was that simple.

After a brief prayer, every man hustled off to their assigned posts while Abdul's number one stayed behind, waiting on the bulk of their American Taliban fighting force.

Farmer Joe had finished his to-do list the day before, with plans of pulling out just before dawn. He was anxious to get home although he expected the three-hour drive pulling his old International Harvester tractor would slow him down somewhat. On his way, his first stop would be at the large farm down the road owned by the Cubbisons. It would've been a shame to leave his son's pigs and poultry to die from lack of care. He had no way to take them with him, although he did manage to cage a couple of laying hens to put in the backseat of the sedan.

The rig, which he'd kept hidden in the trees behind the charred remains of his son's house, was ready to go and full of gasoline. He'd been sleeping in the barn near the road, fully dressed, with a shotgun by his side and the pistols of his son's killers next to it.

He rarely slept through the entire night, as any sound out of the ordinary would stir him awake. So when in the middle of the night, three vehicles pulled onto the gravel driveway, tires loudly crunching on the gravel, he jumped to attention. With his shotgun shaking nervously in his hands, he rushed to the front of the barn and peeked through the hayloft doors.

Using only the light of a third quarter moon, he studied several armed men talking in the driveway. One man, the tallest of the group, was more animated and seemed to be the one the others were intent on listening to. He led them away, except for one, who wandered toward the road for a moment, staring toward Gibson with his hands on his hips.

Farmer Joe quietly moved through the barn and eased down the creaky wooden ladder leading to the ground. He rushed through a maze of hay bales that he'd positioned in case he needed to hide or escape. This led to a door with a small opening to look out onto the driveway. He saw the three pickup trucks parked in random positions closest to where the house once stood.

Farmer Joe eyed a full-size Ford Bronco like the one O. J. Simpson drove. It was a real beauty, he thought to himself. Better than the Olds sedan he'd retrofitted to tow a trailer. He wasn't even positive it would make it home without abandoning his beloved International Harvester. Depending on where the rig broke down, Farmer Joe would have a tough decision to make on which means of transportation he would keep.

Now, by a fortuitous stroke of luck, for him anyway, three good-lucking trucks were left at his doorstep, belonging to a group of well-armed mean-looking hombres who were clearly up to no good. He assumed they'd left the lone gunman, who wandered around the front of the property, to stand watch or something.

Regardless, the man stood in the way of Farmer Joe trading up to a nicer, more practical vehicle. Namely, the Ford Bronco.

He made his way back to the front of the barn to locate the man again. He'd wandered to a bench right outside the door, barely ten feet away. Farmer Joe raised the shotgun and reached for the door's handle. In a matter of seconds, he could swing the door open, kill the man, and trade cars.

Then he stopped himself. Not because he was feeling remorseful at taking the man's life. He probably had it coming, Farmer Joe surmised. No, the shotgun blast would bring all of this friends back to Hogs & Hens, and that wouldn't end well for Farmer Joe.

He eased back into the barn where the tools were kept. He pulled one of the long, serrated knives off the tool wall, used in the butchering process. He'd seen it done hundreds of times. Only this time, it was on a different kind of pig.

With a firm grip on the knife and a look of determination on his face, Farmer Joe stealthily strode through the barn door with a purpose. He raised the knife high and brought it down hard at the base of the man's skull near the first vertebra of his spine. With a loud crunch, the man's skull separated from his backbone, and he fell forward in a heap. Dead.

Abdul had dispatched his men and focused his senses on any movement coming toward the produce stand from the farm. It had been an hour since he'd left his vehicles at Hogs & Hens. He'd expected the rest of his fighters to arrive within half an hour.

"There is something wrong," he muttered to himself. He had no way of communicating with the two men he'd assigned to place themselves in a hidden position with a clear line of sight to the produce stand. They'd been instructed to hold their fire until any possible attackers were close to the building. Thus far, there'd been no movement from any direction.

Puzzled, he walked into the middle of the highway and looked both east and to the west. He thought he'd detected the faint report of gunfire off to the west, but the northerly wind that had picked up might have distorted the sounds.

Abdul was frustrated as he paced back and forth behind the produce stand. Nobody from the farm was coming toward him in the form of an ambush. The fighters riding in the M35 transport had not arrived. He was unable to call out to his two men for fear of giving away his presence to any perimeter patrols.

With a huff, he returned to the road and began marching angrily toward the pig farm. He was almost halfway there when a group of nine men greeted him. Two were limping, and one was bandaged around his head.

"Where have you been? What has happened?" Abdul fired off the questions before the men could answer them. "Where is Ali?" He was referring to his new top lieutenant, who was to direct the remaining men to their posts.

"He was not there, Abdul," replied one of the men. "We were ambushed by men with automatic weapons in the town."

"What? How many?"

"Two," one of the men answered sheepishly.

"No, many more," lied another in order to save face and avoid the wrath of Abdul.

Abdul looked beyond the ragtag contingent. "Where are the others?"

"Dead."

A single word that carried a heavy weight. The silence was deafening as Abdul processed its meaning. More than half his fighters had been killed. How could this be?

"Ali?" he asked, wondering if the man he'd left at the pig farm was also dead.

His fighters seemed to shrug in unison. "We did not see him. Nobody was there. Just the trucks."

Abdul didn't think to ask about how many trucks. If he had, he would've learned that one was missing.

He counted the heads of his remaining fighters. He contemplated sending the wounded back to the pig farm to locate Ali and protect their vehicles. Then he cursed under his breath. He needed them to fight.

The attack on his convoy and the disappearance of Ali were not coincidental. These farmers were waiting for him.

He had been betrayed by Vida again.

CHAPTER FIFTY-FOUR

Friday
Cubbison's Farm
Harford, Pennsylvania

"Do you think they're ready?" asked Grandpa Sam as he guided his horse down a well-worn cattle path. As they got deeper into fall, the once green and lush pastures were becoming brown and stunted. The grasses were getting shorter as the cattle were shifted about. Throughout Cubbison's Farm, meandering dirt paths leading cattle from one pasture or feeding location to another had been made by their heavy hooves over the years. Each cow had done their part, following the exact same path, ultimately wearing it down to dirt, then a rut barely wide enough for a human to walk along.

"You know, Sam, despite the fact we've all been away from battle for years, we're always ready," replied Fred. "For many of us, myself included, that's a blessing and a curse. We can't put the wars behind us. Many of us became mercenaries, paid soldiers for any nation who'd hire us. We weren't in it for ideological reasons. We just wanted to shoot people and blow up things."

Grandpa Sam shook his head. "And here we are again, preparing to fight an enemy who wants to kill my entire family. The other bunch of criminals simply wanted what we have. This group hates us for who we are, Americans. Or they want revenge, which is more likely."

"A little of both," added Fred. "I've seen them fight. I've gotten in their heads. They are obsessed with our way of life. It's almost a jealousy thing. I was never quite able to figure it out."

"Regardless, they're coming," said Grandpa Sam seconds before the sounds of gunfire could be heard in the distance.

The two men turned their horses to the left and stopped in the middle of a pasture. Fred cupped his hand over his right ear and focused his mind.

"We're engaging. That's our boys."

Before Grandpa Sam could speak, more gunshots rang out from the east. "It's started. You ready?"

Grandpa Sam nodded and urged his horse down the trail. Fred was the group's field general, positioning his men to defend their new home. Grandpa Sam would act as his aide-de-camp. He'd carry messages to the men posted on the far ends of the farm or retrieve ammunition for the men who were running low.

"Let's head to the house," said Fred. "My people know what's coming. Let's make sure your family is in position."

Despite a heated discussion, it was agreed that Jenna would take the children to her place and hide while the battle was fought. Fred assigned two of the former Marines to help guard them while also serving as a recon team for an attempted assault on the front gate.

Unlike the men who'd been spread out along the tree line at the Cubbisons' perimeter, the two men's primary function was to take up a defensive position to protect the most vulnerable members of the family.

It had been quiet the entire evening, and the men had expanded their watch perimeter in preparation for the attack. When the gunfire to their west was heard, they immediately were drawn to it. Then the battle at Gibson raged, drawing their attention to the east.

In the end, they split up and moved farther away from the house. Each crouched in grasses with their backs to the house. They focused their attention and the barrels of their rifles toward the sound of the shooting. They both died near simultaneously from a knife slash across their throats.

Fred and his men had spent the early evening hours studying the defensive position most advantageous for mounting a defense. Each post was instructed on their fallback positions and full retreat options. At the time, Fred would be unaware of his men's successes at Gibson in reducing the number of fighters at Abdul's disposal. He had to assume the numbers favored the enemy.

He stopped at the corner of the fence closest to the road and studied the fields beyond through his night-vision optics. He caught a glimpse of the tall grasses in an ungrazed field moving in a steady, rhythmic motion toward them. He spied a power tower beyond that location in order to remember the potential hostile's location.

He scanned the field on both sides of that mark. More grasses were moving. He whispered to the two men who hid behind hay bales reinforced with medium-sized river rocks.

"They're coming. Crawling directly towards us. The field grasses get shorter as they approach the fence. Give them time to reveal themselves, and then cut them down."

"Yes, sir."

"Don't forget. You may immediately take on fire. Remember how they operate. They'll sacrifice their advance team to flush out our positions."

"Roger that, sir."

Fred gave the horizon one last look and slowly retreated to his horse. It would be his last time riding that night.

CHAPTER FIFTY-FIVE

Friday
Cubbison's Farm
Harford, Pennsylvania

On the rare occasions the ex-Marines had the time to joke around while stationed in the Middle Eastern theater, one of their favorite topics was the difference between actual combat and Hollywood's rendition of a gun battle. Certainly, they all had their favorites scenes from movies old and new. Dirty Harry pointing his beloved .44 Magnum at a criminal, unable to recall whether he'd taken six shots or only five. Or the classic James Bond flicks where the silenced Walther PPK coughed out bullets, putting another evildoer out of his misery.

Every Marine's opinion of Hollywood's efforts to portray battle came down to a simple review—bullshit. Unless they fired live rounds on a movie set, something that should never happen, the sheer sensory overload of letting loose a burst of high-caliber rounds from an automatic weapon, including the recoil, the flash, and the deafening noise, would bring any actor to their knees in a bundle of nerves.

One of the benefits these ex-Marines had over the Taliban fighters was extensive weapons training. In particular, there was what was known as the Mozambique Drill—two to the chest, one to the head. With the increased use of terrorists and fanatical soldiers of Allah strapping explosives to their chests, the Marines were taught to take head shots.

Fred's men were well trained. As the shadows of the Taliban fighters emerged from the tall grasses, standing upright as they advanced toward the farm, the farm's defenders took their aim. Within seconds, several gunshots rang out, obliterating heads and necks in unison. And as expected, the muzzle flash gave away the men's positions, and they immediately took on fire.

Within seconds, bullets were flying in all directions around the eastern and southern fence lines of Cubbison's Farm. Screams of agony could be heard in the darkness amidst the gunfire, somehow indiscernible by native accent. The pain and suffering of being shot crossed all ethnic boundaries.

The battle raged as Abdul sent his attackers on the offensive. He considered it to be Allah's will that the Cubbison family and those unknown infidels who were protecting them should die. His confidence in his fighters was great. He never considered that a more powerful, seasoned group of veterans had waited for this moment for many years.

He tried to study the advance of his men through the night-vision binoculars he'd taken from the armory. The muzzle flashes blinded him at times, and he soon lost his bearings. It was near impossible for him to discern whether his fighters were winning or getting beaten badly. He had to believe in their skills. He refused to let down Allah.

CHAPTER FIFTY-SIX

Friday
Cubbison's Farm
Harford, Pennsylvania

Luke trudged across the field with his rifle shouldered and carrying the PSRL-1. The rocket launcher was not heavy, weighing about fourteen pounds. Nor was it bulky, since it was barely three feet long. However, he treated it gingerly so he didn't accidentally fire the projectile protruding from the tube.

As he walked along through the fields, he alternated between studying his surroundings and the operations of the weapon. It resembled the AR-15 the family came across in many respects. The handle and trigger guard were the same. There was a foregrip attached to a rail and an advanced sight attached to the top of the rail near the foregrip.

It differed in that there wasn't a buttstock that was pressed into the shooter's shoulder. Rather, it rested on top. The primary difference was the large, fluted barrel with an approximately twelve-inch warhead inserted in the end. Luke could only imagine what kind of punch it packed. He didn't want to find out by accident.

Just as he approached the Ledbetter property, he heard a woman's muffled screams. Luke broke out into a run, cradling the rocket launcher in his arms. His eyes darted from the garage to the house in an attempt to discern where the cries were coming from. They'd stopped, which instantly shot apprehension through his body. Jenna was there with the kids, including his little sister.

He stopped just short of the gravel driveway and laid the rocket launcher down in the tall grasses near a horse trailer. He readied his weapon and began to move closer to the house, allowing the night-vision scope to give him a better view of his surroundings.

Then he saw movement. Near the center garage bay, two men stood over a woman on her knees. It was Jenna. The other man was opening the center bay as she plead with him to stop.

Luke raised his rifle and placed the man's back squarely in his sights. He fired. The rifle shot was deafening. His aim was accurate. The man trying to open the garage door was immediately killed. However, the other man did not panic. He wrapped his left arm around Jenna's neck and yanked her onto her feet. He used her as a human shield, keeping her under control with a knife to her throat.

Luke slowly walked forward with his rifle pointed directly at the man's head. He didn't dare risk taking the shot as he moved. His aim was good, but a mistake could get Jenna killed.

"Stay back!" the man shouted, his accent heavy and similar to Vida's.

"Let her go, and I'll let you live," Luke lied.

"Same to you, boy," the man yelled in return. "Drop the gun!"

Luke bristled. He no longer considered himself a boy. He did, however, heed the man's warning. Only because he could then steady his aim.

"Last chance," he hissed at the man, who was barely fifty feet away. Even under these nerve-racking circumstances, Luke could send a bullet through a keyhole.

"I will kill her!" came the man's response, who, in order to prove his point, squeezed Jenna a little harder and lifted her feet off the ground before swaying her back and forth.

Big mistake. Luke quickly changed his aim for the meaty part of the attacker's thigh and squeezed the trigger. The bullet blasted into the Afghan fighter's leg and shattered his femur. He fell hard to the gravel driveway, screaming in pain.

Jenna shrieked and began to run toward Luke. Then she abruptly turned around and rushed into the garage. She shouted into the dark space, "We're okay! It's Luke!"

In a flash, the three young girls came pouring out of the garage. Kay and Jewel stopped to hug their mother while they watched the Afghan writhe in pain. Cat rushed into the arms of Luke, who hugged his sister while he pointed his rifle at the Afghan with his right hand.

"Jenna, where are the men guarding the house?" asked Luke.

"I don't know. Just before the fighting started, they moved farther away from the house. I got nervous, so I took the girls into the garage. We hid out behind boxes and buckets of stuff. I came out the side door to look for our guys, and that's where these two found me."

Luke broke his sister's embrace and walked closer to the man. Without looking at them, he issued instructions to Jenna and Cat.

"Go over to the horse trailer and look in the tall grass near the tongue. There's a weapon there. Like a gun. Bring it to me, but be very careful."

Jenna pointed for her children to return to their hiding places, and she chased after Cat, who was already on the move. Luke got closer to the Afghan fighter, periodically glancing toward the farm where the gun battle was raging.

They carried the rocket launcher carefully back to Luke. Even in the darkness, Luke could see that the man was bleeding out. The dark, sticky substance changed the gray, rocky drive to a dark shade of crimson.

"Do you wanna live?" Luke snarled at the man.

"Allah will take me and reward me!" he replied defiantly before breaking out into a cough. Blood flew out of his mouth, and his eyes rolled into the back of his head.

"Fine. I can make your trip to Allah's place happen much quicker without any more suffering. Just tell me what they planned on doing with this."

The man spit at Luke.

Luke stepped forward and jammed his boot onto the man's thigh, causing him to let loose a painful groan.

"Jenna, take Cat in the garage and pull the door down. Will it lock?"

"Yes," she replied as she hugged Cat.

"Do it," said Luke brusquely.

The second she and Cat turned toward the garage, Luke stomped on the man's thigh again. Blood squirted out onto Luke's boot and pants.

"No more! No more! I will tell you." The man was begging to die. Then he began coughing again. It was more violent this time. His spittle was mixed with blood. After the episode, he managed to whisper the word *please*.

"Talk!" Luke hissed in response.

The Afghan was barely speaking above an audible whisper. Luke pulled his sidearm and pointed it at the man's head as he knelt over his body.

The fighter's voice was now garbled. The air he exuded when he spoke was mixed with blood.

"Our leader. Abdul. He will fire a flare when he wants the rocket fired at the farmer's house."

"Geez," said Luke to himself. Then he turned back to the Afghan. "Where is Abdul?"

"That way. A produce stand." He barely got the words out before he started to cough profusely. More blood spilled out of his leg, and he would soon die. However, Luke told himself he was a man of his word. He aimed and shot the man in the head.

Then he turned his attention toward the fighting.

CHAPTER FIFTY-SEVEN

Friday
Cubbison's Farm
Harford, Pennsylvania

The first rays of sunlight swept across Northeastern Pennsylvania. The hues of dark blue turned lighter, giving way to orange and yellow. It was no different than every other sunrise that took place around the globe for billions of years. Yet, like the day the perfect storm had brought the world to its knees, this one would have a special meaning for the Cubbison family.

Fred and his men had held off the attackers. The night before, as they planned their defenses, he'd told Sam and John that the light of day was their friend. It would take the Afghans' element of surprise away. It would expose their cover. Make them vulnerable to counterattack.

He'd returned to the center of the farm between the family's home and the market building. Emma and Lauren had set up a triage on the picnic table to care for the wounded. Fred needed to monitor his troop strength to ensure there were no gaps in their defensive perimeter.

Sam arrived on horseback, completely spent and utterly exhausted from a night traversing the farm, carrying messages from their field general, Fred, as well as requested ammunition or supplies. It was not as efficient as the ex-Marines were used to. However, it had been successful in its implementation.

John had just returned from the western front, as he called it, although fighting there never materialized. He was accompanied by the ex-Marines who'd successfully eliminated the bulk of the Afghan fighters who intended to attack from that direction. He and his comrade who was injured during the battle had to walk back to the farm, as their Humvee's tire had been shot out.

Emma immediately noticed Luke's absence. "Where's my son?" she asked in a panic. "Luke! Where is he?"

"Ma'am, we were outnumbered. Just before the two of us got overrun, I saw two of their fighters run away from the battle. I believe your son chased after them."

"But where is he?" she began to cry.

John moved in to comfort her. "Honey, please don't worry. If he is tracking them down, it might take some time for him to return. It's a long way from where we are. It took these men over an hour to walk back."

Emma wasn't sure she was entirely comfortable with the explanation. However, she had to hold on to hope, so it would have to do. Then her spirits were brightened.

Matthew and the surviving ex-Marine from the battle at Gibson came around the house near the barn. They were moving quickly, so it was obvious they weren't injured. Emma ran to greet him. She hugged her son, sobbing on his shoulder before pushing him away at arm's length to assess his physical condition.

Matthew's voice was unemotional. "Mom, I'm fine. I swear."

"Sir, we lost one of our own," said the ex-Marine who accompanied Matthew back. His voice was sullen but clear. "We can talk about that more later. Where do you need us right now?"

"Come with me," instructed Fred as he walked around the market building. The gunfire had become more sporadic as the sun rose above the horizon. He led the members of the Cubbison family along with his two men to the barricades that lined the driveway. He stopped and pointed as he spoke. "I've had to pull the men off the front gate in order to shore up our eastern defenses. I'll need my two men at the gate and everyone else falling in behind the—"

Without warning, a bright flash of light caught their eye. A flaming projectile had been shot high into the air in the direction of the Cubbisons' home.

Sam, who'd repeatedly expressed his concern about Abdul's use of the rocket launcher, shouted, "Incoming!"

The civilians ducked or dropped to their knees. Fred and his battle-hardened warriors did not.

Fred tried to calm the family. "It's a flare."

Then another sound pierced the air. It was different from the occasional gunfire being exchanged with the Afghan fighters. The thunderous blast was followed by the whooshing sound of air being displaced. Next came a bright light with a near simultaneous explosion. On the hill where the abandoned produce stand had been located, a fire consumed the wooden structure, and smoke mixed with debris billowed into the sky.

"Let's go, men!" Fred shouted as he readied his rifle and ran toward the fence row. The two ex-Marines dutifully followed, leaving the Cubbisons standing alone in the driveway.

Voices filled the air. The Afghan fighters were yelling in their native language of Pashto. The same word, one that Fred knew well, was shouted out. *Retreat! Retreat! Retreat!*

To the men who'd fought the Taliban in Afghanistan, that word meant nothing. They'd learned the hard way that the Taliban fighters could not be allowed to retreat. Otherwise, they'd remain a future threat. This was war, and the enemy must not be allowed to live to fight another day.

A sudden burst of gunshots filled the air. A cacophony of automatic weapons' fire cut down the fighters as they tried to run up the hill toward the highway. Fred's skilled marksmen did their job with a take-no-prisoners attitude.

A spontaneous roar of approval rose above the pastureland surrounding the Cubbisons' home. The gunfire ceased, and Fred's men shouted to one another. Fred voiced his approval of a job well done but cautioned the men they had mop-up duty to perform. He sent a squad up the road toward the produce stand and beyond to confirm all the hostiles were dead.

In front of Cubbison's Market, the tears flowed as John and Emma hugged one another. They were joined by Sam, who heartily slapped his son on the back. As Matthew hugged his mom, he noticed Vida sheepishly appear on the porch of the market. He waved her over, but she stood still, frozen until she'd been given an invitation from his parents.

Then, suddenly, she leapt off the porch and began running toward the front gate. Her actions were only noticed by Matthew at first and then Grandpa Sam. He tugged at Emma's sleeve and pointed.

As dawn turned to day, the silhouette of a man walking down the long driveway turned into Luke. He was followed by Jenna and her children. Cat walked alongside her big brother, carrying the rocket launcher as if she were John Rambo in the movies.

Vida was the first to greet Luke. She crashed into him and immediately kissed him. As she cried tears of joy, she told him how much she loved him.

Seconds later, the entire Cubbison family had been reunited with one another. Their emotions poured out as they embraced. Tears were shed, and nervous laughter seemed to be contagious as they exchanged heartfelt feelings. Even the animosity toward Vida seemed to have disappeared when she was embraced by Emma.

After more than a minute of the loving reunion, Emma finally noticed that her youngest was holding an ominous-looking weapon. Its tube had stopped sizzling long ago as the heat of the detonator blasting the rocket toward its target cooled off.

"Did you ...?" Her voice trailed off as she realized how absurd her question was.

Luke replied, "No, Mom. I fired it. You know, it was kind of a return-to-sender deal."

"Abdul?" asked Grandpa Sam.

Luke nodded. "The flare he fired was the signal to blow up our house. Instead, I sent it to where he was standing."

"Fred just sent his men to locate Abdul."

Luke let out a sadistic laugh. "Yeah. Good luck with that." He and Matthew exchanged high fives.

Fred came jogging back to the family. "My guys are confident that this is over. It's impossible to know how many men Abdul brought with him. I do know it took a lot for them to call a retreat. Just in case, please stay near the house until I can get a report from my guys at the back of the farm and those looking for Abdul."

"What about their weapons and vehicles?" asked Grandpa Sam.

"We'll track them all down and add them to our own. The spoils of victory, right?"

Matthew stepped forward. "Oh, yeah. I forgot to tell you. When the two of us were returning from Gibson, we spotted their cars at Hogs & Hens."

"I know it well," said Grandpa Sam. "The house must've burned down at some point."

Matthew explained what he'd learned. "There was an older man. Joe something, from McVeytown in the middle of the state. He'd come to check on his son and daughter-in-law. He kinda got upset when he told me about them dying. Anyway, he was going home and asked that we take in the pigs and chickens from their operation. He didn't want them to die or go to the wrong people."

"We'll take good care of them and clean up the place," offered Sam. "This fella Joe might wanna come back some time."

As the family continued to talk about the ordeal, Fred's men began to return to the house. They reported to Fred, who immediately relayed the good news to the Cubbisons. Within twenty minutes, he declared the all clear.

It was over.

Sam Cubbison began to casually walk toward the front gate. He reminisced about his years there and the stories that had been told to him by his parents and grandparents. As the memories flooded his mind, Cat rushed to his side and took his hand in hers.

"Grandpa Sam," she began, "what's going to happen next?"

Sam looked at the sun that shone brightly in the eastern sky. It had unintentionally tried to destroy them. It failed.

"I don't know exactly, Cat. Here's what I do know. The strength of our family is like the strength of an army. Our love for one another is like the loyalty these Marines have to each other. It's unbreakable. So no matter what comes our way, we'll show that our strength is more powerful than any test God puts before us."

"Then we can't lose. Right?" the innocent child added.

"That's right, sweet girl."

They both stood and closed their eyes, allowing their faces to soak in the rays of the sun. It was the start of a new day.

THANK YOU FOR READING THE PERFECT STORM SERIES!

If you enjoyed this final installment in the Perfect Storm series, I'd be grateful if you'd take a moment to write a short review (just a few words are needed) and post it on Amazon. Amazon uses complicated algorithms to determine what books are recommended to readers. Sales are, of course, a factor, but so are the quantities of reviews my books get. By taking a few seconds to leave a review, you help me out and also help new readers learn about my work.

VISIT my website to subscribe to my email list to learn about upcoming titles, deals, contests, appearances, and more!

Sign up at BobbyAkart.com

WHAT'S NEXT FROM AUTHOR BOBBY AKART?

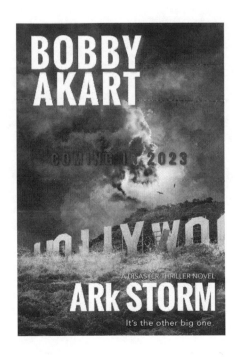

NOVELS BY AUTHOR BOBBY AKART

ARkStorm, The Other Big One (a standalone disaster thriller)

The Perfect Storm Series
Perfect Storm 1
Perfect Storm 2
Perfect Storm 3
Perfect Storm 4

Black Gold (a standalone terrorism thriller)

Nuclear Winter
First Strike
Armageddon
Whiteout
Devil Storm
Desolation

New Madrid (a standalone, disaster thriller)

Odessa (a Gunner Fox trilogy)

Odessa Reborn
Odessa Rising
Odessa Strikes

The Virus Hunters

Virus Hunters I
Virus Hunters II
Virus Hunters III

The Geostorm Series

The Shift
The Pulse
The Collapse
The Flood
The Tempest
The Pioneers

The Asteroid Series (A Gunner Fox trilogy)

Discovery
Diversion
Destruction

The Doomsday Series

Apocalypse
Haven
Anarchy
Minutemen
Civil War

The Yellowstone Series

Hellfire
Inferno

Fallout
Survival

The Lone Star Series
Axis of Evil
Beyond Borders
Lines in the Sand
Texas Strong
Fifth Column
Suicide Six

The Pandemic Series
Beginnings
The Innocents
Level 6
Quietus

The Blackout Series
36 Hours
Zero Hour
Turning Point
Shiloh Ranch
Hornet's Nest
Devil's Homecoming

The Boston Brahmin Series
The Loyal Nine
Cyber Attack
Martial Law
False Flag
The Mechanics
Choose Freedom
Patriot's Farewell (standalone novel)

Black Friday (standalone novel)
Seeds of Liberty (Companion Guide)

The Prepping for Tomorrow Series
Cyber Warfare
EMP: Electromagnetic Pulse
Economic Collapse

Made in the USA
Middletown, DE
29 November 2023

43991354R00194